LEE BROOK

# The New Forest Village Book Club

MIDDLETON
PARK PRESS

*First published by Middleton Park Press 2023*

*Copyright © 2023 by Lee Brook*

*All rights reserved. No part of this publication may be reproduced, stored or transmitted in any form or by any means, electronic, mechanical, photocopying, recording, scanning, or otherwise without written permission from the publisher. It is illegal to copy this book, post it to a website, or distribute it by any other means without permission.*

*This novel is entirely a work of fiction. The names, characters and incidents portrayed in it are the work of the author's imagination. Any resemblance to actual persons, living or dead, events or localities is entirely coincidental.*

*Lee Brook asserts the moral right to be identified as the author of this work.*

*Lee Brook has no responsibility for the persistence or accuracy of URLs for external or third-party Internet Websites referred to in this publication and does not guarantee that any content on such Websites is, or will remain, accurate or appropriate.*

*Designations used by companies to distinguish their products are often claimed as trademarks. All brand names and product names used in this book and on its cover are trade names, service marks, trademarks and registered trademarks of their respective owners. The publishers and the book are not associated with any product or vendor mentioned in this book. None of the companies referenced within the book have endorsed the book.*

*First edition*

*This book was professionally typeset on Reedsy.
Find out more at reedsy.com*

*For Mandy Wilkinson—*
*Thank you for being a shining light in the darkness that is the world at the moment.*
*I appreciate you, and everything you do.*

# Contents

| | |
|---|---|
| *Foreword* | iii |
| Chapter One | 1 |
| Chapter Two | 4 |
| Chapter Three | 9 |
| Chapter Four | 14 |
| Chapter Five | 20 |
| Chapter Six | 30 |
| Chapter Seven | 37 |
| Chapter Eight | 43 |
| Chapter Nine | 46 |
| Chapter Ten | 54 |
| Chapter Eleven | 62 |
| Chapter Twelve | 70 |
| Chapter Thirteen | 79 |
| Chapter Fourteen | 87 |
| Chapter Fifteen | 94 |
| Chapter Sixteen | 101 |
| Chapter Seventeen | 110 |
| Chapter Eighteen | 120 |
| Chapter Nineteen | 128 |
| Chapter Twenty | 134 |
| Chapter Twenty-one | 141 |
| Chapter Twenty-two | 151 |
| Chapter Twenty-three | 159 |

| | |
|---|---|
| Chapter Twenty-four | 168 |
| Chapter Twenty-five | 174 |
| Chapter Twenty-six | 183 |
| Chapter Twenty-seven | 190 |
| Chapter Twenty-eight | 198 |
| Chapter Twenty-nine | 207 |
| Chapter Thirty | 214 |
| Chapter Thirty-one | 222 |
| Chapter Thirty-two | 229 |
| Chapter Thirty-three | 237 |
| Chapter Thirty-four | 250 |
| Chapter Thirty-five | 257 |
| Chapter Thirty-six | 264 |
| Chapter Thirty-seven | 270 |
| Chapter Thirty-eight | 276 |
| Chapter Thirty-nine | 284 |
| Chapter Forty | 288 |
| Chapter Forty-one | 297 |
| Epilogue | 298 |
| Afterword | 301 |
| *Also by Lee Brook* | 303 |

# Foreword

Whilst the New Forest Village Book Club is very much an actual book club with real people who live in Middleton, each character is entirely fictional.

Springfield House is also entirely fictional.

Names, characters, businesses, places, incidents and events portrayed in this book are either the products of my imagination or used fictitiously.

Thank you,

Lee

# Chapter One

The woman's heart hammered from exertion as she climbed up the hilly Middleton Ring Road, past the district centre and towards the sports centre where she regularly played squash with her colleagues from work.

She was in no mood for exercise tonight, something else entirely encompassing her thoughts.

She hefted her handbag over her shoulder and used her other hand to push a stray blonde hair from her face.

A person watched her from the shadows. Not that she knew.

First, they watched her movements from the bus stop opposite the old bus garage and Co-op depot before following her slowly, keeping their hood up and face down.

She'd paid the figure no notice then and paid them no notice now as she neared her final destination. The figure had researched their victim extensively and knew what route she would take. So, they kept a wide berth, staying far enough away that she wouldn't see or hear them.

Despite being March, the weather was still bitterly cold, and the woman had worn several layers to keep the frost at bay. Up above, the ominous clouds threatened to shower the land. The woman didn't know whether that was with hail, rain or snow. The clocks hadn't gone forward yet, so the darkness swooped in with every step she took.

The figure watched her from opposite the road, at the junction of Staithe Avenue and Middleton Park Road, as the woman greedily gulped each breath. They chuckled at the fat, blonde woman. If they didn't laugh, they would cry. She wouldn't be much fun to hunt, but it was necessary.

The figure kept its eyes on the blonde as she shuffled around the corner towards the sports centre. This was the most dangerous part of the plan because the sports centre usually was busy.

And tonight was no exception.

The figure sprinted across the road once the traffic had cleared and took out their mobile phone. To anybody playing football or to people waiting in their cars, they would just be another person walking about.

Her pace quickened once she turned left into the grounds of the rugby club, her purple coat pulled tight around her generous frame, reminding the figure of a child's TV character. Tinky Winky, Dipsy, or Po.

That was when the heavens opened, and the rain began crashing down. She wouldn't search for her umbrella. There'd be no point. She was nearly at the club. That's what the figure was bargaining for, anyway. The path between the sports centre and the rugby club was dark and secluded, especially today, as no rugby training was happening.

The figure could easily have pounced then but knew of the perfect spot.

But they didn't have long before the blonde reached the entrance, and then it was game over, and the opportunity would be lost. And so the figure narrowed the distance between them, breathing evenly and keeping their steps light.

# CHAPTER ONE

She was almost there, where the road met the path, where they could grab her and, with excruciating effort, drag her into the darkness behind the rugby club.

The figure's heart rate sped up, as did their pace. She was right there, close enough that they could smell her perfume, and the occasion nearly got the better of them as they almost sprinted the last few metres. But instead, the figure took a breath and forced itself to keep a slow and steady pace so she wouldn't hear anything.

And that was when she hit the mark.

And the figure sprinted towards its victim from behind, forcing a strong left hand over her mouth and its right arm around her neck.

## Chapter Two

Ellie Addiman, the book club organiser, stood up and began to applaud the author for his reading. She eyed the rest of the club, and one by one, each member began to clap, though not as enthusiastically as usual, Ellie noticed.

She understood, though. The reading had been dark and violent. The murderer had caught up to their victim, and Balthazar had gone into extremely vivid detail. It was too much, even for Ellie, who read extensively. It had also been rather unexpected as they'd only invited him in to provide the book they would be reading next. If Ellie had known how violent Balthazar's novels were, she wouldn't have said yes to the recommendation. They'd only wanted him to drop off the signed books, yet he'd taken it upon himself to read the opening chapter of his latest book, promising no spoilers for any eventual readers.

Ellie looked around the room to find Ginny, the one who had recommended the local author to her, but it seemed she hadn't arrived yet. Instead, she caught Ginny's sister's eye, Gaynor Eastburn, and playfully scowled. Gaynor ran a manicured hand through her blonde hair and grinned as if knowing the reason for the scowl.

The novelist, Balthazar, was a squat, rotund man with long,

greasy black hair. His black, square spectacles magnified his dark eyes. She'd always assumed most novelists were eccentrics, and the way his dark eyes remained firmly clamped upon her during the reading had spooked her.

Earlier, he'd also made her feel like a piece of meat as those magnified eyes had lingered on her curves and the light amount of cleavage she'd had on show. Even the handshake had been awkward, with Balthazar holding on for far too long, his thumb caressing her own.

"Thank you, Balthazar," Ellie said, smiling, "that was... a lot."

"Yes, well, my novels can be quite dark at times, but they mimic life, I assure you." The author grinned, exposing blackened teeth. "Life is full of darkness and despair, and with my new novel set in the very area we are sat in now, I thought it was apt."

"Yes, I'm sure I can speak for the entire group when I say I was shocked that the murder in your book happened just outside this room." She pointed out of the window to where Balthazar had gone into extensive detail about what the figure had done with their knife to the fat, squat blonde woman. "Well, thank you so much for bringing us copies of your debut, The Teacher Terminator."

"You're very welcome. It's based upon a real murderer that was active in this very area." The author grinned once again. "I know the SIO."

Ellie had heard of the Miss Murderer, of course. Everybody who lived in Middleton had heard of that monster. But as for knowing the SIO, Ellie didn't believe him. She'd known George Beaumont for many years. They'd been boyfriend and girlfriend in secondary school; he was probably Ellie's first love, and she'd even lost her virginity to him. Ellie had even been hoping to encounter George, having been a blonde teacher with blue eyes with the initials E and A. However, she was rather grateful for her life, considering she'd worked at Hunslet Park Academy with Mia Alexander and the Miss Murderer.

But she'd still wanted to 'bump' into George, and that desire had only intensified after finding out about his and Mia's split. He was a kind, hard-working man with gentle eyes who wouldn't provide a man like Balthazar Crane with delicate information about the case.

There was just no way.

Which meant he was a charlatan or was receiving information directly from one of George's team. She'd know once she read the stupid book.

"Well, thank you, Balthazar." Ellie headed towards the door and gestured for the author to leave the function room at the Corinthians Rugby Club, where they held their meetings.

But the novelist did not move. "I've never been to book club meeting before. Would you permit me to stay?" He gestured at the women but kept his eyes on Ellie. "All of this is so interesting to me."

"I'm sorry, Balthazar, but this is an all-female book club," a scouser named Sophie with long, dark hair said.

She stood up next to Ellie, and the author took her in. He was sure the scouser must have had a Chinese or Thai parent or somewhere else from Asia. It was her eyes; he thought, perfect almonds with double eyelids. Though the oval face, pointed, narrow chin and plump lips certainly added to her beauty. Though compared to Ellie, Sophie was nothing.

"We appreciate you dropping the signed books off, but we

like to discuss our books in private," Sophie said.

But still, the writer did not attempt to move.

Flora, Ginny's daughter and Gaynor's niece, stood with her two friends, Lesley and Julia. "Sophie's right. Thanks for dropping them off and giving us a fascinating reading, but you need to leave now."

In truth, the group of women spent most of the night drinking alcohol from the bar instead of discussing the book they'd been tasked to read, and whilst they were usually laid back, Balthazar was giving off an aura not one of them liked.

Rebecca stood tall, a slim bobbed brunette whose caramel-coloured skin contrasted Ellie's porcelain complexion and folded her arms across her chest.

Ellie blew a stray strand of blonde hair away from her face. The colour of Ellie's eyes matched a warm summer's sky, and whilst they were friendly, they were at the same time shrewd and distant. The lines around the side of her eyes—which suggested laughter and fun—intensified as she frowned at the author, the light irises, the core, said no nonsense. They missed very little, and she could see the group of women were making the man uncomfortable.

Rebecca said, "We don't normally invite authors to our meetings, so you've been quite lucky." She, too, gestured to the door.

Aurelia smoothed her wavy, hennaed hair and adjusted her bright, flowery scarf, a grunt of disapproval coming from the back of her throat. The elder stateswoman of the club, she wasn't to be trifled with.

But still, the novelist didn't move. In fact, he straightened his back and grinned.

And that's when the landlady, Florence, got involved. "You

need to leave, and now!" she commanded, moving around the bar and pointing towards the exit. "That's now five women that have asked you to leave." She pulled out her mobile. "My rugby player husband is literally in the larger function room across the hallway." Florence raised her brow. "Do I need to get him and his mates in 'ere?"

"Absolutely no need, my dear," Balthazar said and stood up. His eyes were still roaming in places they shouldn't be, and Ellie could feel herself shivering. "I meant no offence; I just was really interested."

He stood up, retrieved his trolley filled with books, and headed towards the door, his swinging right hand glancing Ellie's buttocks as he left. "Thank you for taking a chance on a local, self-published author," Balthazar said as he left the room.

That was when the screaming started.

## Chapter Three

The location would have been perfect for a creepy Hollywood film, not that Detective Constable Jason Scott would ever say that aloud especially as he was perched next to his boss, Detective Inspector George Beaumont.

George was wearing his usual tan trench coat, but Jay had opted for a heavy jacket and was still shivering as the damp air rose from the concrete floor.

The DI's eyes were glued to the window via a pair of night-vision binoculars, scanning the expanse of moonlit yard for even the slightest movement in the ostensibly abandoned warehouse twenty to thirty yards beyond.

Jay accidentally let out a yawn, and George turned to him. "Tired DC Scott?"

"Bored, boss," Jay said. "Reckon anyone will show? We've been here for two hours and seen nothing."

George, too, thought this was a waste of time but said nothing. Instead, he put the binoculars back to his eyes and continued to watch.

"I'm serious, boss. This is a bloody waste of time. Plus, I think my bollocks are frozen to this bloody crate!"

The DI removed the binoculars and gave a weak smile, unperturbed by the young DC's flamboyant language. Nobody could say anything to him that he hadn't heard before. Plus, his own bollocks were starting to freeze off, so he sympathised with the lad.

"And why here, anyway? What's so special about this warehouse?"

They were at Beeston Royds Industrial Estate just off Gelderd Road. "Because this is apparently where Jürgen Schmidt runs his heroin business." George frowned. "I thought you were at the briefing?"

"Dicky tummy, boss. I missed most of it."

"Well, why the hell didn't you say?"

The young DC shrugged and pulled up his binoculars. To his right was a packaging company, and an Italian food import company was to his left. But the warehouse they were spying on was straight ahead. "We've got movement, boss," Jay suddenly whispered.

George pulled up his binoculars and quickly focused on the unit they were tasked to observe.

As a dark transit van drove between the open gates, the unit's metal roller doors started to roll up, exposing the warehouse. A few moments passed before the van reversed, blocking the open door. Then suddenly, the passenger door was flung open, and a tall, black-cladded man with a matching balaclava came out to survey the scene.

After a few moments of checking and evidently satisfied, he moved around to the back of the Transit, where the driver met him and opened the rear doors.

George clicked the broadcast button on the radio pack-set strapped to his chest, adjusted the plastic earpiece, and then spoke softly into the mouthpiece. "This is Bronze Beta Leader. I have a visual. Targets present at the front of the building."

## CHAPTER THREE

"This is Silver Leader. Understood, DI Beaumont," George's new DCI, Alistair Atkinson, muttered. "Stay where you are and report back once they enter the building."

George acknowledged the instruction, feeling the excitement bubbling inside his stomach and started breathing deeply to try to tame the sudden, heavy adrenaline rush.

The moon vanished behind swirling clouds, rendering the night almost wholly black, as two more men, each decked out in full black, came out of the unit. George watched the men survey the area momentarily before seeing one of them, clearly a leader, speak into a radio.

"This is Bronze Beta Leader," George said. "Two more targets have left the unit."

"Keep watching. Bronze Alpha Team, be on alert," the DCI said.

And then everything changed. Through George's binoculars, his eyes met with the leader's. The leader slammed the rear doors shut and got into the Transit before reversing the vehicle into the unit.

"This is Bronze Beta Leader," he exhaled. "They've entered."

Atkinson rapped, "Gold has signed off. Bronze units only. Go! Go! Go!"

Jay sprang to his feet, but George quickly grabbed his arm. "You're a beta, not an alpha," George reminded the DC. "You stay with me until Alpha vacate the building."

"Sorry, boss."

The AFOs—Authorised Firearms Officers—moved silently into position, imposing in their dark Kevlar vests and helmets, weapons at the ready, quickly encircling the warehouses.

"Are we clear to engage, DCI Atkinson?" the Bronze Alpha

leader asked. He possessed the 'big red key' that would allow a quick and noisy entrance.

"Gold approval," the DCI said.

Spurred into action, the boots on the ground thundered on the concrete and converged at the door. George could hear everything happening through the comms. And after three metallic thuds, the AFOs were inside.

"Armed police! Armed police!"

Without a shot being fired, it was over in a little more than twenty minutes when two AFOs emerged from the doorway, dragging what appeared to be the leader outside into the moonlight.

George watched the man violently writhe and yell abuse at his captors as they dragged him into a waiting patrol car.

Then a second man was pulled through the splintered door, though he appeared to have accepted his fate and walked docilely between two additional AFOs to a second patrol car.

Both police cars then reversed in a flurry of gravel, their blue beacons blinking, signalling the end of the operation. They then exited between the gates.

Beaumont and Scott didn't leave the building until the DI had received the 'all clear' word from the DCI on his radio.

* * *

By the time George and Jay arrived at the warehouse's front, the DCI was pulling up in his beamer. The DCI wound down his window.

"Sir," George greeted. Jay did the same.

"Has the super called you yet, George?" DCI Atkinson asked.

"No, sir. Is everything OK?"

"There's been a murder in Middleton. You're SIO. You'll have DS Mason, DC Malik, DC Scott, and DC Blackburn. If you need DS Williams for CCTV, then let me know."

"I'll need her, sir." Then he met eyes with his boss. "What about DS Wood, sir?"

"She's busy working on a different case, George."

# Chapter Four

After showing the uniformed officer his warrant card and pulling into Middleton Leisure Centre, Detective Inspector George Beaumont saw a hive of activity, with blue lights blaring, in the distance.

He parked next to the entrance to the rugby club and walked along the path he assumed the victim had walked, sweeping a torch in front of him. He was wary of holes and debris hidden by shadows and figured he could look for evidence while walking.

George soon reached the common approach path, a designated way all the officers used so they didn't accidentally tread on any evidence. The uniform who was on guard at the tape nodded at George after he showed his warrant card and signed in.

Situated slightly away from the club, half on the path, half on a rugby pitch, a white forensics tent was already draped over the body. The metal fence that extended behind them, which was adjacent to the Middleton Park Academy, made their investigation visible to anyone passing by. However, as it was late, George hoped there would be no additional attention to the crime scene.

Shivering and dressed like a snowman without an orange

nose, Crime Scene Co-ordinator Lindsey Yardley stood before him. She was demonstrating something on her phone to pathologist Dr Christian Ross who acknowledged George by raising his hand.

George greeted the pair with an, "Evening," as he moved closer. "Any ideas yet?"

Lindsey nodded towards the tent. "IC1 female who according to her provisional licence, was forty. Ginny Creaser. She was stabbed—"

"She was stabbed rather a lot," Dr Ross added. "It was a fierce attack. We've measured the entry wounds, and once Lindsey sends the report to the Calder Park lab, they can check the profile against known weapons."

"Time of death?" George asked.

Both Lindsey and Dr Ross shook their heads. "Hard to say, but recent. She was found about half-eight, so I'd say between six and eight."

"Was the attack sexually motivated?"

"I don't think so, no," Dr Ross explained. "I'll check during the post-mortem, but as you'll see, her clothes weren't disturbed."

George nodded. "Any forensics?" He looked at Lindsey.

"There's nothing under the fingernails, which isn't surprising. I've identified a sticky residue around her wrists." She pointed to the tent. "The culprit most likely secured her hands with the tape before she had a chance to defend herself. They also had the foresight to take the tape with them once they'd finished with her." Lindsey grimaced and then pointed up. "And with the amount of rain, this area has had tonight, any fibres on her skin or clothing may have washed off. The rain will have severely reduced the forensic information we might have collected."

George knew that with such a fierce attack, there would have been a lot of blood spattered on the killer's clothes, though rain may have washed it away.

As if reading the detective's mind, Lindsey said, "I've advised a search of the surrounding area. We may find something."

"Just do what you can," George said as he looked around the area for any evidence bags but couldn't find any. "I thought you said we had a licence?"

Lindsey said, "Yeah, it's inside the tent. Her wallet and phone were discovered on her; however, the phone had suffered some damage from her fall. The screen is broken, but it still functions. However, it requires a passcode."

"Is the address on the licence close by?" George asked.

"A flat on Lanshaw Crescent," Lindsey replied. "You know the area, right?"

George nodded. "Just off the Ring Road. Any murder weapon?"

Lindsey frowned. "No, not yet, anyway."

"Thank you both." George inhaled deeply. "We can continue putting together what happened after we take a look. Jay and Tashan are on their way. But first, do we have a timeline?"

"She had not been dead for long when she was discovered. At most a couple of hours ago."

After donning his own whites, George entered. The interior of the tent was oppressively warm. A collapsible table was set up to the right with a few things already on top of it. A forensic photographer stepped aside to allow them to approach while she was taking pictures of the body.

The DI didn't recognise her. She was slight, probably in her forties, with short black hair.

A woman was lying on the wet ground, her hands behind her body. Dizziness overcame him as he walked towards the corpse, and his back felt wet. George's back had sweat running down the centre of it. By the time he returned outside, he would be completely soaked.

Blood soaked the ground. That coppery smell, along with the heat and the cloying atmosphere of the cramped interior, caused George to pause and breathe through his mouth.

She wore a purple coat highlighting the entry wounds, with black jeans and baseball shoes. She had two tattoos, one each on her hand. Despite having her details, at least that would make her easier to identify.

The photographer stepped aside for George, who crouched next to the body for a better view. Pale skin from too much time in the home and hazel eyes were fixed ahead. Her blonde hair was plastered to her face.

Who killed you, and why? George wondered. Had she been there at the wrong time? Or was it pre-meditated? She didn't appear to have been robbed, but then again, he couldn't tell from just looking. He turned to Lindsey and Dr Ross. "Any money in her purse?"

"Five twenties," Lindsey explained.

"A hundred quid." George whistled. "Not a robbery, then."

"Doesn't look that way."

"Although," George said, "this place gets pretty busy. Maybe the attacker was disturbed?" He'd played rugby union for Leeds Corinthians as a teenager but much-preferred rugby league and had ended up playing for Hunslet instead.

Dr Ross pointed towards her mouth. "There's some more money in there."

"Inside her mouth?" George asked.

Christian Ross nodded. "Money talks. Money speaks. I'm thinking something along those lines."

"Maybe she owed somebody money?" George pondered.

The DI then heard an, "Alright, boss?" and turned to find a forensically suited and booted DC Jason Scott. "Tashan's outside."

George nodded.

"What was she doing here, boss?" Jay asked.

"She lives nearby, so there could be many reasons." George indicated behind with his thumb. "There's an event at the rugby club. Uniform's up there, waiting for us."

"What kind of an event, boss?"

"A book club, I think." The DCI hadn't given George much as he'd ordered the DI away from the raid.

Having exited the tent and peeled off his white suit, George looked around. There was only one way in and out of the rugby club, and that was via the leisure centre. There used to be a road that came out at the back of the district centre, but that had been closed off years ago. The DCI had called him on the way over to explain the landlady of the club had already given Sergeant Greenwood copies of the CCTV they had. George only hoped the sports centre had security cameras that would cover the entrance to the club. He also looked up at the school and wondered whether getting any footage from them was worthwhile.

"Maybe she was a member of the book club, boss?"

"Aye, I thought the same."

"Me too, sir," came a deep voice. DC Tashan Blackburn smiled at his senior officer. Behind him, George could see DS Luke Mason making his way down the path towards them.

## CHAPTER FOUR

The DI spent a few moments updating the young DC and then gave out orders. "All the people who were here at the time of discovery are upstairs in the main function room. DC Scott and I will interview them in a separate room upstairs whilst you, DC Blackburn, are to go with DS Mason to the deceased's address."

## Chapter Five

Ellie Addiman was eventually taken into the smaller function room by the young detective, and her knees nearly buckled when he shared with her the news of Gin's murder. She sank onto the sofa, putting her palm to her mouth. "What happened? Is it really her?"

"We don't know yet," said the young DC, "that's why we're questioning you all."

"You couldn't possibly think I had anything to do with it?" Ellie asked. She looked around the room. "We were all in here. Had been for an hour."

"Did you not think it was strange when she didn't arrive?"

"It's not unusual for Gin to turn up late or be found in the larger function room next door. I did wonder where she was, though, because that author coming to do a reading was all her idea."

"And what author would that be?" DC Scott asked, writing notes on a pad. His tongue was stuck out, and she couldn't help but grin. He barely looked old enough to drive, let alone be a detective. In fact, some of the lads she taught looked older than him.

"Balthazar Crane, the short, fat man with long, greasy black hair." The young DC nodded but said nothing. Instead, he stared at her, unblinking. Eventually, she said, "Why?"

"The pathologist suggests Ginny was already dead before the meeting started."

"So we're all suspects?" Ellie asked.

Jay grinned. "Not necessarily, but it's why I'm here. My job is to eliminate you from the investigation, so please answer honestly."

Ellie took a sharp breath, then nodded.

"Thanks. So, when was the last time you saw Ginny Creaser?"

"Last month at the February book club," Ellie said.

"You're sure of that?"

Ellie paused and looked down at her nails. They were flawless, only having been done that afternoon. "I'm sure." She watched the young man scribble more notes and found herself more and more wanting to grab it off him and read what he was writing about her.

"Did you know Ginny well?"

"Not particularly," Ellie explained. "We weren't close friends."

"What do you mean?"

"Her daughter and sister are part of our club, and I know she's been out for meals with Tasha a few times. But I have a close circle of friends I see regularly, and Ginny wasn't one."

"I see, so you wouldn't know whether somebody had a grudge against her or whether somebody would want to hurt her?"

"I'm sorry, I've no clue."

Jay looked at her for a moment, thinking about his next question. She reminded him of Isabella Wood. He couldn't put his finger on it, but it was something about how she presented herself and her confidence. "What time did you arrive at the club today?"

"As the organiser, I like to get here first." Jay watched as she looked down at her watch. "I'd say I got here about seven."

"And you didn't see Ginny's body outside?"

"No. I live in the New Forest Village, which isn't far away, so I always walk."

"But I haven't told you where her body was found," Jay explained.

"Bea found the body. Beatrix Watson. She was late for the meeting and told me where she found Gin."

"Gin?"

"Ginny. That's what she's known as. Gin. Anyway, I walked in front of the rugby club to enter it, so I wouldn't have been near the body. Plus, the floodlights weren't on because rugby training wasn't on. Bea drove, so she walked straight past. I assume some of the others did the same, except Bea told me she could smell copper. Which was why she put her phone torch on."

The young DC was furiously scribbling notes now, trying desperately to keep up. "Can anybody confirm you arrived here around seven?"

"Florence can, as she let me into this room," Ellie explained. "Unfortunately, I'm single, so there's nobody at home who can let you know what time I left."

\* \* \*

After leaving Tashan's vehicle at the scene of the incident, they went to Ginny Creaser's address. It was late Thursday evening, and it would only take a few minutes in the detective sergeant's

## CHAPTER FIVE

car.

Luke turned left at the roundabout, then turned right across the road. Lanshaw Crescent was the next street to the left.

As Luke traversed the narrow crescent, the semi-detached houses gave way to flats on his left, situated behind a large green that, despite the sign, many youths no doubt played ball games on.

"I hate this part the most, sir," Tashan said as Luke pulled up at the kerb.

"Me too, son, me too." Luke tapped a drumbeat on the steering wheel, took a deep breath, and then pushed open the car door.

Luke pulled out his warrant card before rapping on the door.

After a short moment and a muttered, "Where the fuck did she put the bastarding keys?" A tall, thin man opened the door and took in the two detectives.

Luke displayed his ID and began by asking, "Mr Creaser?"

"Yes."

"This is Detective Constable Blackburn, and I'm Detective Sergeant Mason. Could we please have a moment inside?"

The man's expression changed. "What's wrong?"

"Can we talk inside, if you don't mind?" Luke asked.

He opened the door for them and led them to a living room.

The living room was attached to the kitchen, and Mason was sure he could smell the remnants of a doner kebab and chilli sauce. His stomach gurgled. He hadn't eaten anything since dinner, having been on standby at the station during the raid. The room was cosy but cramped, with a large TV on one wall and a three-seater on the other. In the window was a leather chair.

Mr Creaser invited the pair to sit down, and as he did, his

eye caught the couple's wedding photo hanging on the wall. There were six people in a line, the bride and groom flanked by two men and two women. The three men wore matching suits, and the two women wore matching floor-length skirts in a rich purple to match the bride's flowers.

"Are you here by yourself, Mr Creaser?" Mason inquired.

"It's Nick, but yeah, I'm alone; why?" Nick Creaser looked between the two men and frowned.

"I'm afraid we found a body of a woman earlier this evening who we believe to be your wife," Luke informed him.

Nick gave them each a look but said nothing.

"You are Ginny Creaser's husband, right?"

Nick nodded.

"We found her outside Corinthians Rugby Club, and I'm sorry to say that she was declared deceased at the scene."

"What?" His voice wavered slightly. "When was she found?"

"Eight-thirty," Luke advised. "Can you tell us why she was at the rugby club?"

"She has a monthly book club meeting. Every first Thursday at half-seven."

"How long does the meeting usually last?" Tashan cut in.

"I dunno," Nick said. "Hour and 'alf, or two hours. Sometimes she gets in later." He shrugged. "They have a drink in the bar. Our daughter and her sister are both members, too." Then both detectives saw the realisation hit. "Do Gaynor and Flora know?" Mason saw Nick slouch further into the leather chair, his cheeks covered in tears. "Are you sure that it's her?"

"What was she wearing when she left the house?" Luke asked. Poor fella was in denial.

"That stupid purple coat." He shrugged. "Jeans and a T-shirt, I think."

"Does she have any identifying features, such as tattoos or birthmarks?"

"She has a black rose on the side of her left hand and purple butterflies on her right hand. They snake down from the top of her wrist and down her fingers, but you already saw them, right?"

Luke nodded. He texted George with the word, 'identified'. "Were they at the meeting tonight?" Luke asked, and Nick nodded. "The Senior Investigation Officer, my boss, DI Beaumont, is at the rugby club interviewing people as we speak. So if they're at the club, they will already know."

Luke turned to Tashan and nodded. They'd devised a set of questions and a plan on the way over.

"When did you last see Ginny, please?" Tashan gently enquired.

"Gin," he announced. "No one addresses her as Ginny. Since she was a little girl, she has been referred to as Gin."

"Oh, OK," Tashan said, taking notes. "Would you prefer if we called her that as well?"

Nick nodded. "She set off about half six. She's trying to lose weight, so she decided to walk. I did offer to drop her off, but she was insistent."

"Half six?" Tashan enquired, and Nick nodded. "And the meeting usually starts at half seven?" Again, Nick nodded. "Then why did she set off so early?"

"I think she needed to finish the rest of the book they were set, so she decided to leave early to go and have a drink."

Tashan noted that down.

"What happened to her?"

Mason had been waiting for that question and was surprised

it wasn't one of the first out of Nick's mouth.

Tashan eyed his sergeant, who nodded. "She was stabbed multiple times," Tashan explained.

Nick inhaled deeply. "Someone intentionally hurt her?" He paused. "She was murdered?"

"That's correct, Mr Creaser," Tashan said.

Tears began to fall faster. "Did she—did she suffer at all?" Tashan was about to explain there was no way they could know that when Nick said, "Please tell me she died peacefully."

Neither detective said anything. They had no idea whether Ginny had suffered, and neither had seen the body yet, so they couldn't even guess. Still, Luke knew he needed to reassure the man. "I'm sorry to say I wouldn't think she knew much about it."

"So, it'll have been over quickly?" Nick asked. But when neither detective spoke again, he said, "Good. I'm glad."

"We need to ask you a few questions. Is there anyone I can call to come and sit with you whilst we do?" Luke asked.

Nick shook his head. "No."

"OK, so how has Gin been recently?" Luke asked.

"Fine." He shrugged and shook his head. "Same as usual, I guess."

"Same as usual?"

"Yeah, her usual pain in the arse," Nick said, and then the realisation that she was gone hit him again. Luke saw it in Nick's eyes first, then in the shaking of his shoulders. The man tried to wipe the tears away, but Luke saw them. He respected them. It should be OK for men to cry, but the world was against it for some reason.

"Does she have any close friends or family members?"

"There's Gaynor, her sister, and Flora, Gin's daughter. She

also spends quite a lot of time with the women from the book club. Rebecca and Sophie, I think their names are. There's a pregnant woman from the book club, too, but I can't remember her name. They went out last week for a meal."

"Where did they go?"

"The Italian on Leeds Road. I didn't think we could afford it. We argued."

Nick stopped speaking then, realising he'd told them they'd argued. Luke wanted to know how often the couple argued but knew not to press the matter. Spouses were high up on the list of culprits. As were sisters, daughters, and friends.

"Does Gin often go out for meals?"

"Not often, no, but more often than me."

Luke wondered what that meant. "Are you sure we can't get somebody to sit with you?" he asked. "You got a best mate we can call?" He pointed at the Xbox. "Got any gaming mates?"

Nicky shook his head. "I'm fine."

"What does Gin do for work?" Tashan asked.

"She doesn't," Nick said.

They'd find out more about Ginny's background once they were back at the station and checked through the various databases, but it was always a good idea to get the information first-hand. It meant she had no colleagues they could speak with, though.

Luke knew the Italian on Leeds Road was decent, but with prices to match. He wondered how she'd afforded it if she was unemployed, and also wanted to question the argument.

"Is she disabled? Or searching for work?" Luke asked.

"Bit of both.

"How old's your daughter?" The plan was to ask questions that weren't explicitly linked. It would keep Nick on his toes and help Luke determine whether Nick was involved in Ginny's death.

"Twenty-two."

"You don't look old enough," Tashan said, and Nick smiled for the first time since the detectives had been in the flat. "How old are you?"

"Flora is my stepdaughter. Gin was married before." Nick scratched his stubble. "Gin's forty, but I'm only twenty-nine."

"And Flora lives here?"

"Correct, it's a two-bed."

Luke wondered how the dynamic was. He was closer in age to Flora than he was to Ginny. "How long were you together?"

Nick stood up and clutched the wedding photo. "Eight years. I was twenty-one when she seduced me." He tried to grin, but more tears fell from his eyes, and he began coughing.

"Do you need me to make you a hot drink, Mr Creaser?" Tashan asked.

"I'm fine," Nick said. "I need a stiff drink, I think."

"I understand," Luke said, "but I would advise against it. You'll need to keep your head clear for what's to come."

Nick shrugged and then shook his head.

"Did Gin have any enemies? Is there somebody out there who would want to cause her harm?" Luke asked.

Nick shook his head. "Gin was the life and soul of the party."

"What have you been up to this evening?" Tashan asked. It was a planned question, and Luke grinned at the lad. He'd executed it perfectly.

"What, since Gin left?" Nick asked, and Tashan nodded. "Sat' ere watching telly for a bit. Ordered a takeaway from the kebab place in the district centre." He pointed to the kitchen but furrowed his brow. "Leftovers are in there if you want them. As is the receipt. It lists what time I ordered it."

"What did you watch on the telly?" Tashan asked.

It took a long moment for Nick to answer, and Luke wondered what Nick was keeping to himself. When the answer came, it seemed forced. "One of the soaps. I can't remember the name. To be honest, I was watching YouTube videos on my phone."

"Thank you for that," Tashan said. "We'll need you to come to the station to make a formal statement, as well as provide a DNA and fingerprint sample, OK?"

"DNA and fingerprints?" Nick asked. He turned to each detective as he spoke, the look in Nick's eye the same as when he stalled for time earlier. "Is that normal?"

"Perfectly normal," Luke explained. "It's to rule you out of our investigation."

## Chapter Six

Jay took a deep breath and pulled open the door to the smaller function room, wondering who he had next. He was assaulted by the smell of spicy perfume and looked around to find the culprit.

A woman was pacing left to right, backwards and forwards, her dress billowing in the wake. Jay watched as her dress swung around her sun-kissed legs. In the artificial light, the gold of her shoes glittered. His throat tightened as his breath became laboured. She was stunningly attractive. Her tightly curled hair highlighted her beautiful face, delicate lips, and tiny ears that wore enormous silver hoops. She looked at him and immediately caught his attention with her piercing brown eyes.

"Flora Ogram?" he eventually managed to ask.

"That's me."

He extended his hand. Detective Constable Jay Scott. The quick shake felt awkward, her hand clammy and shaky.

"I'm here to talk to you about Ginny Creaser."

At the mention of the dead woman's name, Flora narrowed her eyes and drew a thin line across her mouth.

"Do you know who killed her?"

"Not yet," he said.

"Do you have any leads?"

"Not yet; we're in the very early stages of our investigation Miss Ogram."

"Flora."

"Flora." He paused. "When was the last time you saw her?"

"Who, Gin?" she asked, and Jay nodded. "This afternoon. I went for a coffee with Julia and Lesley."

"And they are?"

"Two of my friends."

"Are they also part of the book club?"

"Do you mind if I take a seat?" she asked.

Jay needed one, too, feeling a little dizzy from the overwhelming perfume.

"Yes, both Julia and Lesley are part of the book club. Why?"

The way Flora spoke was poetic, a delight to Jay's ears. However, her eyes were wide, and her makeup ran like she may have been crying.

He found he was unavoidably struck by the woman. She was a similar age to him, in her early twenties, and something about her made him want to reassure her and lessen her suffering.

They were irrational notions, he reminded himself, yet Flora Ogram struck him deeply. "Did you know Ginny Creaser well?"

"I should think so, considering she is my mum," Flora explained.

The shock on Jay's face must have been evident because Flora offered him a consoling smile.

"I'm so sorry for your loss, Flora," he eventually said.

"Thank you."

"I really need to ask you these questions. Are you gonna be OK?" Jay asked. Flora nodded, so the DC collected himself and said, "Let's begin with the time you last saw your mum."

"As I told you before, I left to go and have a coffee with the girls."

"And what time was that?"

"Two, half two, I think. We met in Leeds separately."

Jay scribbled some notes. "How did she seem?"

"She was fine. Excited, even. She'd picked the novel, 'The Teacher Terminator', and invited the author to attend the meeting tonight to give out signed copies of his book. That book is set in this area, you know? It's about a real murderer." She then whispered. "I think your boss outside was involved in the case."

Jay, of course, knew because he took part in the case, the novel was based on. He wondered whether to share that with Flora but decided against it. It wasn't strictly professional.

"And what time did your coffee finish?"

"We went to see a film after, so all three of us got the bus home from town and went straight to the meeting."

"So, the three of you were together until what time?"

"Half-six."

"But the meeting didn't start until seven-thirty. So where were you between those two times?"

"Between half-six and half-seven?" Flora asked.

"That's right."

"I went to B&M. I wanted some snacks for the meeting."

"With Lesley and Julia?"

"No, they met me there." She blinked her eyes in quick succession. "I'm sorry, Detective, this is difficult for me."

Jay scribbled down some more notes. He'd probably interview the two other women, so he would ask them for the timings. "Do you need to stop? Or have a break?"

"I think I need a glass of water; I'm a little bit drunk."

Jay got up and headed behind the bar. He found a tall glass and filled it with tap water.

"We can do this later once you've sobered up if you like?"

Flora paused. "No, carry on." She took a large gulp, and Jay watched her throat as she swallowed.

"Does your mum have any enemies?"

Flora's mouth fell open, and her eyes grew large. "She was the life of the party, Detective. Everybody loved her." She paused again. "No, I can't think of a single person who would want to harm her, let alone kill her."

"Thank you. How is your mum's relationship with your dad?"

She raised a brow. "My dad?"

Jay nodded. "Are they still together?"

"Oh God, no. They haven't been for years. She remarried, though."

"I see. To Mr Creaser?"

"Nick."

"Makes sense now why you're an Ogram," he said.

"Don't bloody remind me. What an awful surname."

"Try having a first name for a surname," Jay said with a grin.

She mirrored his grin and said, "You're hilarious, Detective."

"Are you single?" Jay asked.

"Why, you interested?" Flora asked with a smile on her face.

His cheeks began to colour in embarrassment. "I'm sorry; I–I didn't mean it like that," he stammered. "I just meant do you have somebody at home so that you won't be alone tonight."

She touched his hand with her free hand. "I knew what you meant; I was only joking." She took another gulp and maintained eye contact with Jay.

Jay was still determining how to get back on track because he felt he had deviated so far from the purpose of the interview. So instead of struggling against the tide, he stood up and extended his hand. "Thank you for your time, Miss Ogram."

She shook it, but when it was time for her to let go, she didn't.

"Do you need anything else?" Jay asked.

"No, do you?" She smirked. "Anything at all?"

\* \* \*

"When did you first meet Gin?" Luke asked Nick.

"I met her in a bar," Nick explained. "We got talking, and despite the obvious age gap, we got on well."

"Is Flora's father in the picture?"

"As in, does he see his daughter?" Nick asked, and Luke nodded. "She's twenty-two. An adult. They see each other when they can, but it's not as if she goes there every other weekend. It's never really been like that, to be honest."

"What's her father's name?" Tashan asked.

"Gary. Gary Something." Nick shrugged. "Sorry."

"What's Flora's surname?"

"She's an Ogram, not that she likes it. She has Gin's maiden name. It's only just worse than Creaser, though."

Luke wondered about the words that Creaser had used. Made. That suggested force, or at least coercion. "How long have you been married?" The wedding photograph appeared to be a recent addition to the house, and Nick didn't look all that different.

"Nearly two years," he said. "Two great years."

"Did you ever think about having kids?" Tashan asked.

"I wanted them, but Gin already had Flora. Plus, she wanted a bigger place, and the fact I lost my job a year ago didn't help."

Luke took another look around. If it wasn't for the TV, the gaming consoles, and the smell of takeaway, it was obvious the family was struggling. "We talked earlier about anybody wanting to hurt Gin," Luke said, and Nick nodded. "Other than her sister and daughter, does she have any other relatives in the area?"

"No. Gin's parents are dead, her mum of cancer last year, and her dad about a decade ago in a car accident."

"And you?" Tashan asked.

"I'm an only child, and my parents died when I was a teenager."

Luke was about to ask a follow-up question when a text came through from George. "My boss wants to know whether you can tell us Gin's passcode to her phone?"

Nick's eyes grew wide. "She had it on her still?

"Correct, and her purse, too. That was how we identified her."

"So she wasn't robbed then?" Nick asked.

"We're not sure, but it doesn't seem like anything was taken from her," Luke explained. "She had a hundred quid in her purse."

Nick's eyes grew even wider. "I don't know her passcode, but I could really do with that cash to pay the bills. When can I get a hold of it?"

"You weren't aware of the cash?" Luke asked, and Nick shook his head. "Forensics will need it for a few days, Nick," Luke explained. "It could be that the assailant took half her money and left evidence behind."

"Call the companies and tell them what's happened,"

Tashan explained. "Actually, we can do that for you. You'll be assigned an FLO, a family liaison officer, who will assist you."

"I can do it," Nick said.

"We also need to tell you that a roll of notes was found inside Gin's mouth."

"As in bank notes?" Nick asked, and Tashan nodded. "Fucking hell."

"Did Gin owe anybody any money?" Luke asked.

Both detectives saw the hesitation. But to his credit, Nick's façade was only down momentarily. "Not that I'm aware of."

Luke didn't believe him. They'd look into the Creaser's financial details. "Do you please have a recent picture of Gin that we could use?" Luke asked.

Nick scrolled through his phone until he found one he liked. "Will this be OK?"

Luke took a quick look. It was a selfie of Gin taken at Bridlington. Luke knew the harbour well. It was one of his favourite places. Gin looked as if she enjoyed the place, too. And now, she'd never walk on that harbour again.

"Thanks, Nick, it's a beautiful picture," Luke said, pulling out a business card. "If you could email that picture here, I'd be grateful."

Nick started tapping and swiping whilst Luke said, "As my colleague explained, a family liaison officer will also be assigned to you." His phone pinged, and Nick raised his thumb. "They'll keep you informed about what's happening, answer any questions you may have, and also let you know about any developments we make while we're not around."

## Chapter Seven

Two hours later, and after everybody from the rugby club was allowed home, George, Luke, and the two detective constables arrived back at Elland Road station.

Detective Constable Reza Malik was already home when the DCI had ordered George to the scene, so with only the four of them, the DCI had housed them in one of the smaller incident rooms, but at least it had a Big Board.

Tashan immediately fired up his laptop and printed out the image of Ginny Creaser that her husband had sent DS Mason. Then, after a nod from DI Beaumont, he tacked it to the board. DS Wood usually managed the board, and it was strange without her. He wondered how his boss felt. DI Beaumont had never been SIO without DS Wood as his deputy. But Tashan guessed now that they were engaged to be married, the higher echelons may start and get them working on separate cases more.

"We need hot drinks, son," DS Mason said, looking at Tashan's colleague, DC Jason Scott. "Be a love and sort us out, will you?"

Despite working on the team longer than Tashan had, Jay always seemed to get the short straw, though tonight, Jay had worked with the DI instead of DS Mason. He was good like that was the boss, Tashan thought. He was always willing to let the younger members crack on and gain valuable experience.

Carrying a tray of hot drinks into the Incident Room, DC Jason Scott looked at the team and then down at the tray. He'd not made enough. There was DI Beaumont, his deputy; DS Luke Mason, the older statesman of the group; DS Yolanda Williams, their CCTV expert; and Jay's competition—DC Tashan Blackburn.

But that wasn't all. A familiar face beamed at Jay.

"There are plenty of cameras on the Ring Road, and we know where she lived," George said, his eyes trained on Yolanda. "Get the footage from every camera you can and trace her route to the rugby club."

"Will do, sir," DS Williams said, jotting down notes.

So shocked was Jay that the young constable nearly dropped the tray. It was PC Candy Nichols, the sexy redhead he had been chatting to, and chatting up, since meeting her last month.

"Everything all right, Detective Constable?" the DI asked.

"Aye, boss, grand," Jay said with a grin.

"Been ages with those drinks, son," Mason said, mirroring the young DC's smile.

"Here, Jay," Candy said, holding out her hands, palms up.

Confused, Jay stepped into the space between Candy's hands, and Luke started pissing himself laughing. "I think she wanted to help you with the tray, son, not give you a bloody cuddle!"

Suddenly, the blood vessels on Jay's face opened wide, flooding his skin crimson.

They drank the drinks whilst DI Beaumont presented from the front.

"Most of you already know this, but I feel it's beneficial to go over the details. Commit them to memory, and if you can't take notes." He was staring at Jay whilst he said this. "DS Mason will oversee orders. DS Williams will be in charge of CCTV. DC Blackburn, you're on exhibits until I can get PC Nichols up to speed, OK?"

Tashan nodded.

"What about me, boss?" DC Scott asked.

"You'll be working with me, Jay," George explained. "Taking statements, interviewing witnesses. I want to see what you're made of." Jay beamed, but George continued. "Once PC Nichols is up to speed, I also want you out in the field, Tashan. You and Jay will work together as a team, OK?"

"Thanks, sir," said Tashan.

"Yeah, cheers, boss," Jay said.

"I'll be here at the station running the case. Allocate all actions to me, and I'll submit them to the receiver to be put on Holmes, OK?"

The team nodded back at him.

George pointed at the victim's photograph behind him, took a deep breath, and composed himself. "The victim is forty-year-old Ginny Creaser, also known as Gin." Tashan had put up a picture the SOC photographer had taken, and the before and after pictures were in stark contrast to each other. "Gin was walking to the monthly New Forest Village Book Club meeting when she was murdered."

DS Mason stood up. "Despite the late hour, the boss wants you in early tomorrow so we can get a decent start on the case. Sergeant Greenwood and his team of Uniforms will be on house-to-house tomorrow, following Gin's route from home to the rugby club. PS Greenwood will liaise with me, and I will then liaise with you, DC Blackburn and DC Scott. OK?"

The two young detectives nodded in unison.

"Good," George said. "If we include PC Nichols, DC Malik, and DS Williams, it's just the seven of us. We will be stretched, but I have faith that we can find Gin Creaser's killer, OK?"

The two young detectives once again nodded in unison.

"DS Williams is on CCTV and will be tracking Gin's route to the club. She's also going to look at previous months to try and establish a pattern, though, from DS Mason's interview with her husband, Nick, she set off earlier than usual." George paused to take a drink. "Gin's phone is with IT as we speak. It may take a little while to get anything useful from it considering her husband couldn't provide the passcode, but the results will be in the shared inbox. The same goes for forensics. If anything comes through in the night, I'll have expected them to have been read before your shifts start tomorrow."

"I want both of you on background checks tomorrow morning once you're in, lads," DS Mason said. "Concentrate on Gin and Nick Creaser and the daughter, Flora Ogram. Then extend it to the book club and rugby club members who were there last night."

George looked at Jay. "Other than Gin, did anybody else not attend the meeting yesterday?"

Jay shook his head. "No, boss. Everybody was there because they'd invited the author. That's what Ellie, the organiser, said."

"What did you think of the author?" George asked. He'd spoken with him briefly and got a bit of a weird feeling from him though that may have been because the guy had written a novel based on the Miss Murderer case.

"Other than being weird as fuck, boss?" Jay asked, and George nodded. "The opening to his new book has a woman murdered very similar to how Gin Creaser was killed. That in my book needs looking into."

"And it was Gin's idea for the author to attend the meeting, right? So she was the one in contact with him?"

"Correct, boss." Jay pulled out his notebook. "Well, Gin and Gaynor," Jay explained. "Gaynor is Gin's sister. She took the news badly and is going to Wales tomorrow to escape."

"Suspicious?"

"No, boss. She had two people who could alibi her, and she them."

George nodded. "And the author?"

"He's coming in tomorrow at ten to give a formal statement. We could ask him for his phone and see the messages between him and Gin."

"Good idea, Jay," George said. "Get a forensics officer to take prints and DNA, too. You never know. He could have killed Gin and then gone upstairs and read what he did aloud."

"Wouldn't surprise me, boss. It takes a bit of a loony person to write novels about murder all the time. I couldn't do it."

George grinned. People like that always got the procedures wrong, too. But, then again, they were writing fiction, not fact. "Anything interesting I need to know about your interviews, Jay?"

"Flora Ogram was a bit suspicious, boss."

"How so?"

"She couldn't give me a concise story and kept leaving parts out. It could be suspicious."

"It could also be because her mother was just killed," DS Mason said.

"Good point, sarge."

"What are we doing about the press, boss?" DS Mason asked

George.

"I'll deal with them tomorrow morning. They no doubt already know that something's happened. I'll have a chat with the DCI in the morning and see how he wants me to handle it." George shrugged. "He may want to take press duties himself; who knows."

The DI checked his watch. It hit midnight. "Get home you lot, and get some rest. I expect you all here bright and early in the morning."

# Chapter Eight

Lesley Ibbetson stumbled out of the pub on Thorpe Lane and turned right, heading for her home in the Heritage Village.

Each step was a stumble, and she had to stop for a moment, despite being barely ten yards away from the pub.

She saw a couple approaching her. After stopping to kiss, Lesley let them enjoy their moment as she drew level with them and lowered her eyes. They moved a short distance from her, heading towards the bottom of the ave, before starting up again.

Lesley soon got to the junction of Redbarn Close she needed to navigate, and once across the road, she had to stabilise herself on the wooden fence.

She needed a fix. And fast. No amount of alcohol could numb her want, and she felt as if everything was crumbling around her.

The pub had been shite.

After leaving the book club, Lesley decided to go for a few vodkas and see if she could score some smack. But she couldn't take her mind off Gin Creaser. What had happened to the fat bitch proved that life was definitely too short.

What was worse was that she'd then argued with Julia, who decided it was a good idea to lecture her on what she should and shouldn't be doing, considering one of her acquaintances had just been murdered.

But in the end, Julia got what she deserved. A slap in the face. A proper slap, too. As Lesley leant against the open metal fence just beyond the junction, where horses usually stood in wait for people with apples, she laughed aloud at the memory of the slap. The whip had been perfect, and she'd cupped her hand just enough for it to hurt.

Fucking stupid silly bitch wouldn't be messing with her again.

Julia had left then, and Lesley had sat alone and drank a few more drinks. Her mood darkened, and anybody who tried to speak to her got told to 'fuck off'. She knew that was one of her issues. One minute she was wonderful, happy Lesley, and the next, she was telling everyone to fuck off.

Lesley thought that ever since COVID, people had lost their desire for a pub night out. It pissed Lesley off. She was only twenty-two years old, so most of her adult life had been spent trapped indoors.

As she took deep breaths to try and fight the rising nausea, she could hear somebody in the estate behind her playing loud music. Lesley turned, though it was more of a slow sway so that her back was to the road, and entered the farmland through the open gate to get a closer look at the house having the party.

It was pitch black behind the estate, so she pulled out her mobile to try and put her flash light on, but despite bringing it near her face, she couldn't see any of the buttons. They were all just a blur.

But she did feel a nice breeze blowing over her as the tree branches rustled. She raised her face to it and enjoyed the sensation on her skin. It was icy, but she was so pissed that she wasn't really feeling it.

The bass from the music pumped along with her heart. She imagined herself in a club, not giving a fuck. COVID had taken her youth from her. She was convinced of that. But life was too short. Gin Creaser had proved that.

Maybe I'll go out clubbing in town tomorrow? She thought.

Lesley continued like that for a few minutes, eyes closed, face against the wind.

And that was when a strong hand gripped her mouth from behind and pulled her to the ground.

She was already unsteady from the alcohol, and the heels she was wearing gave her no grip on the wet ground.

"Who are you?" she mumbled through the gloved hand, but the person said nothing. She tried fighting but couldn't even feel her body. She had no strength. Had somebody spiked her at the pub? And if so, then who?

And then suddenly, she was let go and fell to the ground. Lesley tried to focus her eyes, but they widened at the feel of a sharp scratch. She looked down and saw a syringe in her arm.

"What are you doing?" She craned her neck to see. She blinked but saw nothing.

Her vision started to fail, and her pupils constricted. Then her breathing began to slow.

She felt warm, and momentarily happy.

Lesley Ibbetson started choking and making gurgling noises.

And then she was gone.

## Chapter Nine

George Beaumont leaned across to his bedside cabinet and reached inside, searching for the ringing phone that had rudely disturbed his sleep. He sighed as he lifted his head off the pillow and noted that it was only half-six.

His fiancée, Isabella, yawned and pulled the duvet over her head, "Is everything OK?"

The window was framed in a blazing light as the early sun peaked through the edges of the curtains. It appeared that the day was going to be better than yesterday. Or at least weather-wise.

The fact that his work phone was ringing, however, could only mean one thing.

He uttered, "DI Beaumont," his voice raspy from sleep. Then, from the words that came back at him, he shot up with a start, dragged aside the covers, and sat up in bed. "OK, sir, I'll head that way now."

"What's happened?"

"There's been a murder," George explained.

"But you're already SIO on a murder case, George," argued Wood.

"The DCI thinks the two murders are linked."

"Linked how?"

## CHAPTER NINE

Removing his pants, George said, "Lesley Ibbetson, the dead woman, was part of the New Forest Village Book Club too."

"Fair enough. Don't work too hard," she said.

"It's me who needs to say that to you," George said. "The DCI says you're SIO on a different case?"

Isabella smiled at George. The past few months had been fantastic, especially since they learned about the pregnancy. As a couple, they couldn't have been any stronger. "I can't talk about it, sorry."

After showering and dressing, George headed downstairs to find Isabella in the kitchen, washing up. On the table was a cup of coffee and two slices of toast. George stepped in close behind her, snaked his hands around to cradle her stomach, and kissed her on the neck.

"I love you," he said.

"We love you more," she replied.

\* \* \*

In his Mercedes, George approached the Falconers Rest pub thirty minutes later. The body had been found on some farmland just off Thorpe Lane in Middleton.

Emergency vehicles were already on the scene despite the early hour, so he pulled as close as he could, which was in front of the pub. From what the DCI had told him, traffic cops had blocked off Thorpe Lane and were diverting all traffic from Middleton Lane up Towcester Avenue and onto Throstle Terrace.

It was still pretty early, but George knew it would soon be manic once the school run started.

Turning right out of the pub, George could see people

watching him from their upstairs windows. It irked George how much was available for public viewing nowadays. The main issue was smartphones because it meant anyone could act as a mobile reporter by recording video and quickly posting it to social media. It's certainly what YappApp did, and George wouldn't be surprised if there were already a post on Facebook.

A horn pipped at him, and he turned to find his junior colleague, DC Scott, arriving. He, too, parked at the pub, got out and jogged over.

"Morning, boss," the DC said.

The DC put on his sunglasses, and George smirked. "Not been home yet, Detective Constable?" George asked. Jay wore the same white short-sleeved shirt yesterday, except the top button was undone now. Same navy suit trousers, too and the same striped tie.

Jay said nothing but smirked. Despite the sunglasses, George could see the smirk that met the young man's eyes. "Her name doesn't happen to rhyme with Randy and Tickles, does it?"

Jay laughed aloud, clapped his boss on his shoulder, and walked towards the activity forty yards away.

The two detectives soon arrived at the cordon, and as George was about to pull out his warrant card, the female PC said, "Good morning DI Beaumont."

"Good morning, PC…"

"PC Blackwell," she said.

"Thank you." He pointed to the tape. "How far back is the cordon?"

"To Martingale Drive, sir," PC Blackwell explained.

"I want it extending," George ordered. "Extend it to the roundabout where the road meets Towcester Avenue for now." George knew the area well, having lived in the Heritage Village as a teen. He knew the pub well, too. He'd successfully and unsuccessfully tried to get served there without ID.

PC Blackwell nodded and relayed instructions via her radio.

"CSI here yet?" Jay asked.

The PC nodded. "Pathologist here, too."

"Who found her?" George asked. "Was it the usual? Jogger or dog walker?" Most mysterious deaths or unconscious assault victims discovered the next morning were discovered by dog walkers or joggers.

"A farmer, actually, sir," PC Blackwell explained. "That's his field. Somebody told him his gate was left open, so he came by this morning to shut it." She nibbled her lip. "He did a rough search of the area to see if any kids had been messing about when he found her."

"Where's the farmer right now?"

"Marked vehicle with one of my colleagues giving a statement."

George gave a grateful nod. "Good work. Make sure he doesn't leave before I get a chance to speak with him."

"Of course, sir."

"How was the victim identified?" George asked.

"A lantern device. She's on the PNC." A lantern device was a handheld fingerprint reader they used to ID people, but like DNA, it only worked if their prints were on the database.

"What for?"

"She's a known drug user with a preference for heroin, though we've never been able to charge her."

George nodded. It wasn't unusual. "Do we have her next of kin details?"

"They're coming through, sir," PC Blackwell explained.

George turned to DC Scott. "Call the station and follow it up for me."

"On it, boss," said Jay.

"Good. And let the DCI know, yeah?"

"Sure, boss."

George shivered, the chilling cold stiffening his bones. It was going to be a long and cold morning. The steel-grey clouds above were threatening to burst. He wasn't getting any younger and knew he'd suffer when trying to sleep that night, especially in the back where the Miss Murderer had stabbed him. March was one of those awkward months where you had cold days mixed in with pleasant days. And there were no places open nearby to get a hot drink from.

"They're working on next of kin, boss," Jay explained once he'd hung up his mobile.

George nodded at Jay, then looked at the PC. "Would you sign me and DC Scott in, please?"

PC Blackwell signed them into the log and handed over SOC suits.

Once dressed, they ducked under the tape and headed towards the scene.

\* \* \*

At twenty-two years of age, it wasn't the first time Flora Ogram had woken up disorientated and on the floor. The morning light was streaming in through the windows, so she glanced through her splayed fingers to get her bearings before sitting up. She was in Nick's room. Confusion gripped her brain and squeezed like a vice.

Flora spied the vodka bottle as she pulled herself onto her knees, and the reality of the situation came whirling back at her like a constant whirlwind. Shaking her head, she picked up the bottle and took it into the kitchen.

She'd had a bad dream and recalled wanting her mum. Was it guilt that made her go into their bedroom? Or something else?

And where the fuck was Nick.

She looked at the bottle again. It was nearly empty. How full had it been? Her memory failed her. Flora didn't feel like she needed her stomach pumped. Not like before.

But what she did need was a shower to wash the stale, sweaty smell from her body and brush her teeth.

Flora scrubbed herself red raw under the scalding jet of water. What the hell had happened last night?

Then she remembered. Her mum had been killed.

But what happened after? What had she done?

Unable to dredge up any other significant memory of the night, Flora gave up and got out of the shower. She wrapped a towel around her body and drew a heart on the steamed-up mirror. As she stared at herself, her hair fell into loose curls. They wouldn't dry that way, which was a shame. Apart from the heat blotches from the shower, there were no tell-tale marks that she'd gotten up to anything untoward. It was clear she'd just drunk herself into a stupor last night and then fell asleep.

She wondered whether it was time to go back on her meds. But that meant she couldn't drink, and she needed to drink to dull the pain.

The drinking had worsened. Initially, Flora had only allowed herself a drink on Thursday, Friday and Saturday. And then the Sunday drinking started, and the only days she was sober were Monday to Wednesday. But even then, she was anxious for Thursday to arrive, which meant that for four days out of seven, she functioned in an alcoholic fugue. It was like an itch that was impossible to scratch.

With wet feet, she stomped into her bedroom, dressed in white lace underwear and a short, black dress, and applied her makeup. Then she tied up her hair and slipped her feet into her comfortable ballet pumps. They added no height to her five-foot-two height, but they looked cute with the dress.

Once she was ready, she had an overwhelming desire to have a drink before she left. Not water. Not tea or coffee. She craved a glass filled to the brim with forty per cent proof.

She needed to leave the flat to talk to Gaynor to see how her aunt was coping, but she'd gone to Wales to escape the chaos. The two sisters were close, and Flora had always been jealous of the relationship the two women had, but it was so like Gaynor to just fuck off when they needed her.

Growing up, Flora had wanted a sister of her own. One she could dress up like a Barbie doll, one she could tell secrets to. Or manipulate. Or hurt. Or maybe even kill.

She let that thought linger. Everybody was a suspect, including Gaynor. Especially, Gaynor, Flora thought. She'd caught them arguing earlier that week. What it had been about, Flora didn't know, but she'd seen the sisters coming close to blows.

Flora wondered whether she should have told the police last night about the argument, but she'd been in shock. And that handsome detective had put her off. Maybe she would tell them about the argument, especially if it meant seeing him again.

She pulled out her phone and pressed the camera button. With just enough cleavage and thigh on show, she looked hot. Probably too hot, considering her mother had recently been fucking murdered. But who cared? It's what she did best.

Flora Ogram looked around the flat one more time and thought, where the fuck was Nick?

## Chapter Ten

The sun had only recently risen, its light not warming the air as George gazed into the slight mist suspended above the bushes.

"Body is over here, boss," DC Scott called, walking towards the crime scene.

George followed along the dirt path and through a metal gate. The birds were tweeting, oblivious to the night's horrific events. Soon, the cold drew in, and the sun disappeared as he turned right behind the estate. The foliage was dense here, an opposition to the bare ground he'd just been walking on. George carefully stepped on the tiles that indicated the common approach path towards a white forensic tent erected to protect the victim's body and preserve the crime scene.

Various SOCOs were mulling around the area, searching, but Lindsey Yardley was nowhere to be seen.

The tent's flap dropped behind them as they entered, immediately suffocating George. He fought to regain control and, without speaking, took in the scene before him. The Crime Scene Co-ordinator, Lindsey Yardley, was bent over a slim, black woman with dark braids slumped on the ground.

Other than her being slumped at a weird angle, George couldn't immediately ascertain what was wrong with her.

"What have you got for me, Lindsey?" George asked.

"Dead IC3 female." She picked up three evidence bags. "Phone, bag, and purse. No ID, but there's cash in the purse."

"Not a robbery, then?"

"No. I think you're better off hearing the rest from Dr Ross," she explained. "He's just outside with his tools."

"Is he? I didn't see him on the way in."

"That's because I was behind the tent, son," Dr Christian Ross explained.

"What have we got, Doc?"

"IC3 female," Dr Ross said. "We found her with this in her arm."

Lindsey produced a plastic evidence bag with a tube inside. "It's a syringe. We'll get it tested to see what's inside, but my guess is an illegal drug."

He rubbed his temples and frantically shook his head. "PC Blackwell said she was known to us as a heroin user."

"That would make sense, son," Dr Ross said. "If you come closer, you can see signs of cyanosis. Look here," Dr Ross Instructed and pointed. "In dark-skinned people, cyanosis is easier to see in the mucous membranes. That's lips, gums, around the eyes, and nails."

As soon as the pathologist mentioned it, the discolouration of the skin was prominent. "Cyanosis happens when there's not enough oxygen in your blood or you have poor blood circulation, right?" George asked.

"Correct," the pathologist said, "and is indicative of an overdose."

"Christ," George muttered.

"Was she murdered, or did she just take too much heroin?" George asked.

"It's hard to say, George," Dr Ross said. "I'll need her back at the morgue. I've got your IC1 from yesterday to do first, but I'll try and fit this young lady tonight. I'm not promising anything, though."

"Thanks, Dr Ross." George ground his teeth. "Anything you can tell me now?"

"In the brain, heroin is converted to morphine which causes the rush sensation that users seek. How intense this feeling is depends on how much the person takes and how quickly the drug gets into the brain." Dr Ross paused. "In a situation like this," he said, pointing at the syringe, "an intravenous dose can take as little as 7 seconds to produce a reaction."

"And in terms of an overdose?" George asked.

"A heroin overdose affects heart rate and breathing such that medical intervention is needed to survive. She obviously didn't have that." He pointed at the signs of cyanosis. "The presence of other drugs, chemicals, and substances resulting in an impure mixture can affect survival rates and outcomes. If it were mixed with fentanyl, for example, a strong narcotic, that would explain her death."

"But you can't say whether she injected herself or whether somebody injected her?"

"Not at this stage, son, no."

He turned to Lindsey. "Lindsey?"

She shook her head. "Sorry, DI Beaumont."

"Is there anything else I need to know?" George asked.

Both shook their heads.

As George left the tent, he let his eyes linger over the body one last time.

And then Jay's phone rang.

He watched as the young detective constable answered and listened intently. Then, when he hung up, he said, "I've got

## CHAPTER TEN

Lesley's next of kin details."

\* \* \*

DI Beaumont sped the Mercedes up Towcester Avenue to see Lesley Ibbetson's mum, who lived on the other side of Middleton. George's stomach was a mess. It was like an icy hand had gripped his intestines. He hated this part of the job the most. After all, there was no easy way to tell somebody their loved one had been murdered.

At the Asda roundabout, he went straight across and then across Town Street onto Newhall Road. Mrs Ibbetson lived at an end terrace on Manor Farm Drive. As he slowed to park beside the kerb, he looked at his junior colleague. "Don't just sit there and take notes, Jay. Ask questions. I want to see some initiative, OK?"

"OK, boss."

The first thing George noticed was that the garden was overgrown. It was surrounded by terracotta-coloured fence panels intertwined with chicken wire.

The two detectives risked the uneven paved steps towards the front porch, and George saw movement from the window to his left.

He took a deep breath and knocked on the door.

A short, slim woman in her late forties with an afro blow out pushed the door open.

"Mrs Ibbetson?" George asked, and she nodded. Both detectives held out their warrant cards. "I'm Detective Inspector Beaumont, and this is Detective Constable Scott. We're sorry for visiting unannounced, but we need to talk to you about Lesley. Can we come in, please?" As he spoke, the woman narrowed her eyes.

"That was quick. Have you found our Lesley then?"

"Found her?" George asked. "I really think any conversation we have should be inside."

George smiled at her, and Mrs Ibbetson led them into a humble living room with leather sofas that she invited them to sit in—the faint smell of tobacco in the air.

"That was quick. We only reported Lesley missing half an hour ago. I'm grateful, though, but I would have thought you had better things to do with your time. I heard about Ginny Creaser."

Good, George thought. It would make things easier moving forward. "Please take a seat."

George explained he wasn't here to take the missing person's details. "I'm sorry to bring you such sad news, but your daughter Lesley has died."

There was a stunned silence that lasted for nearly a minute.

Mrs Ibbetson blinked a tear away. "Died?"

George nodded but did not repeat his sentence. Instead, he waited for it to sink in.

Mrs Ibbetson couldn't have looked any shorter as she shrunk into the leather sofa.

"How? When? What happened? Are you even sure it's her?" she asked, her voice hoarse. Then she sat there in stunned silence and looked to have aged a couple of decades, wilting even more as the seconds ticked by. "I heard about the fight last night in the pub, and when she didn't show up this morning, I worried."

As DC Scott spoke, Mrs Ibbetson burst into tears.

"What fight? What pub?" Jay asked.

"Can I see her?" Mrs Ibbetson interrupted.

## CHAPTER TEN

DC Scott looked at George, who briefly nodded his head. Then, Jay said, "Yes, I can arrange for a family liaison officer to take you to the morgue."

"Thank you," Mrs Ibbetson said.

"So, what pub, and what fight?" Jay repeated.

"The Falconers Rest near the top of the ave," Mrs Ibbetson said through tears. "She had a fight with her best mate last night. Slapped her in the face, apparently."

"What's the friend's name?" Jay asked.

"Julia Brown."

"Do you have a contact for her? Or an address?"

"Yeah, she lives on Acre Crescent," Mrs Ibbetson explained. She provided them with a house number but explained they had no contact number. "What happened to my baby?"

"We are still in the early stages of the investigation and can't give you that answer until the post-mortem. What I can tell you is Lesley died from an overdose."

A moan of anguish escaped Mrs Ibbetson's mouth. Grief manifested in many ways. "Overdose? From what?"

DI Beaumont stood up and took in the view of the room. Family photos showing just Mrs Ibbetson and Lesley were dotted around the room. "Do you have any details for Lesley's father so we can notify him?"

She shook her head. "Georges took his life about a decade ago."

George nodded. It was clear then what he suspected earlier was correct. Lesley was her only and most treasured child.

"Do you know whether she was currently using?" Jay asked.

"Is that why you're here?" Mrs Ibbetson asked.

"I don't follow," the DI said.

"You're trying to figure out whether her death was accidental."

"Correct, Mrs Ibbetson," George said. "As you said earlier, Gin Creaser was murdered. Your daughter was part of the same book club. We want to know whether the two deaths are linked or not. Do you know anybody who would have wanted to harm your daughter?"

Mrs Ibbetson stared at the floor and shook her head, tears splattering on the carpet. "There's that boyfriend of hers. He was the one who got her hooked on drugs. We thought she'd managed to get off them, but clearly not."

"What's her boyfriend's name?"

Mrs Ibbetson shuddered, and more tears fell from her wide eyes. "I'm so sorry," she said and smiled sadly, "but she told us it was none of our business, so we have no idea. But when she started seeing him, she changed."

"How so?" Jay asked.

"Well, she became withdrawn. She lost her job. She lost weight. All clear signs, so we took her to see a GP. She was doing great on the methadone."

Jay nodded whilst taking notes. "Other than Julia Brown, did she have any other friends? Any old work colleagues?"

"She loved reading. J K Rowling was a huge influence on her when she was young, and she devoured the Harry Potter novels. She was always reading. It was the one thing that kept her sane," Mrs Ibbetson said. "It's why she joined the book club. She's friends with all the women there, but that's about it. She didn't leave work on good terms."

"OK," George said. "Where did she used to work." It was worth checking the staff out to see if they could potentially have a motive.

"Greggs at the top of the ave."

## CHAPTER TEN

"Finally," George said, "do you know the passcode to her phone."

"To be frank, Detective," Mrs Ibbetson said, "she wouldn't tell us her boyfriend's name. Do you really think we know her passcode?"

"Thank you." George's phone pinged, and he pulled it out to check his messages. It was from the DCI. Nick Creaser had denied the FLO access to the property, saying he didn't want her around. The DCI wanted to know whether to deploy DS Cathy Hoskins to help Mrs Ibbetson instead.

"We'll send a family liaison officer to see you, Mrs Ibbetson. It'll be a woman named Cathy Hoskins, who will be your main point of contact. Think about what we asked you earlier, and if you can expand on your answers or even think of anything else that might help with our inquiries, then you can pass that to us via Cathy. That also works in reverse, so Cathy will keep you informed of any developments. Cathy won't be visiting you to intrude but to offer you any support you need. Don't hesitate to utilise her, Mrs Ibbetson." He met eyes with her to check she understood, and she nodded, her eyes dull and glazed over. He then promised her they would do everything in their power to understand what happened to her daughter, why it happened, and, if necessary, bring the person responsible to justice.

"If you need anything else before Cathy gets here, here are my details." George handed her a card from his inside pocket.

As Mrs Ibbetson clutched it to her chest and sobbed quietly, George felt sick. "I'm—I'm very sorry for your loss," George finally managed.

## Chapter Eleven

Arriving at the station, George rushed up to the second floor, where DCI Alistair Atkinson's office was located. With two murders occurring just a day apart, he knew the DCI wouldn't be thrilled.

George rapped on the door and entered when instructed to do so. Alistair was seated at his desk.

"Good to see you, George, despite the situation, of course." Alistair grinned heartily. "How are you today?"

"I'm fine, sir," George said. Despite being given the job George wanted, the two got along well during the last two weeks. George was sure the super was avoiding him, though.

Alistair gestured for George to take the seat opposite him. "Would you like a drink?"

He desperately needed something warm to drink but said, "I'm good, thanks. I thought I'd brief you first before briefing my team. So I'll get a drink downstairs."

"Suit yourself, George," the DCI said.

George outlined everything he had accomplished yesterday regarding Gin Creaser's death and what they'd found out about Lesley Ibbetson, which, granted, wasn't much. He detailed the individuals he and the team had spoken with, the places he had been, and the data his officers had obtained.

## CHAPTER ELEVEN

"I'll put DS Wood on the Ginny Creaser case for the moment, George, whilst you take the lead on Lesley Ibbetson's death."

DI Beaumont was about to object when the DCI stopped him. "You're waiting on forensics and other lab results to come back. We know Gin Creaser was murdered, and whilst DS Williams can continue working the CCTV, DS Wood can keep an eye out. You must find out whether Ibbetson was murdered or whether it was a fatal accident."

"I'm confident I can handle the two cases concurrently, sir," George said.

"I'm confident you can, too, but concentrate on Lesley's death first. Then, if they're linked, I'll pull DS Wood and put you back in charge, OK?"

He had no choice, so George ground his teeth and nodded.

"Isabella will be your first point of contact, George, OK?" Alistair said. "Think of this as training for when you take the next step. As a DCI, you can't be in the field. You'll have a DI who will take care of that for you. OK?"

"OK."

"Do yourself a favour and put DS Mason in charge of tasks and send out the two lads." The DCI gesticulated in the air for a moment, and George frowned. "DCs Black and Stott will do a good job, I'm sure."

"Blackburn and Scott, sir," George corrected.

The DCI grinned, showing off a filling. "My mistake."

"What are we doing about the press, sir?"

"That's my job, Beaumont. I'll issue a press statement this evening regarding Lesley Ibbetson. We've also received some rather shite CCTV from the council of Middleton Ring Road. Ginny Creaser is easily identified, but there are many people about. So my job this afternoon is to appeal for people to come forward who recognise themselves." Alistair paused. "The TV companies have agreed to play the appeal today and tomorrow. I may need you to attend, so keep your phone on."

"Sir."

* * *

George returned to his desk and started responding to his emails. There was one from Christian stating that the body was available for viewing, so he messaged DS Wood to make sure she knew to contact Nick Creaser.

Another came from the digital forensics team, this time about a couple of messages found on Gin Creaser's phone. It looked as if whoever had killed Ginny had lured her to her death by asking to meet at the club. George replied, asking them to do everything in their power to trace the number and see if they could use the cell towers to triangulate the sender's location.

George steepled his fingers as he considered the implications. Yes, the DCI had asked him to prioritise Lesley Ibbetson's death, but they had a solid lead now. It wasn't that he didn't trust DS Wood. Of course, he did. But it was his case, and he wanted to lead it.

"Right, you three, Incident Room, now!" George said to DS Mason and DCs Blackburn and Scott.

Upon entering, George said, "OK, listen up, I have some news."

The two young detectives pulled out their tablets, and DS Mason pulled out a notepad and pen.

George said, "The digital forensics team's retrieval of Gin Creaser's phone revealed a series of text messages."

## CHAPTER ELEVEN

"What kind of messages, boss?"

"Messages from her killer, Jay," George explained. "He opened them up on the laptop, and they appeared on the whiteboard."

"Holy fuck!" Jay exclaimed.

"My thoughts exactly, Jay," George said.

"The sick fuck lured her there."

"Exactly." George then explained what he'd asked of digital forensics, and each detective nodded. Then he turned to DS Mason. "I want you to look into everybody in Ginny Creaser's contacts and then liaise with DS Wood."

"She back, son?" Luke asked.

George explained the situation to the team and how they should concentrate on Lesley Ibbetson's death.

"What's happening next with Gin Creaser, sir?" Tashan eventually asked.

"Nick Creaser's currently in with DS Wood providing a signed statement, and then he's off to the morgue to identify Gin. He's also giving prints and DNA samples," George explained. "I'd also like to speak to Flora, Gin's daughter, myself. And I think it's beneficial if Gin's sister, Gaynor Eastburn, is interviewed again. All three of them were closest with Gin, so they shouldn't be discounted just yet, OK?"

The three detectives nodded at George.

"DS Wood knows this and has put DC Malik on it," George said. "The DCI will issue a press statement this evening regarding Lesley Ibbetson. DS Williams has managed to procure CCTV from the council of Middleton Ring Road, but apparently, the quality is shit. Ginny Creaser is easily identifiable, but many people were mulling around. The DCI will, this afternoon, appeal to people to come forward who recognise themselves.

The DCI also said the TV companies have agreed to play the appeal today and tomorrow."

George looked at the team. "Is there anything else regarding Gin Creaser that needs our attention?"

At the shaking of heads, George, with Jay's help, detailed what they'd learnt from Mrs Ibbetson and said, "We also need to look into this boyfriend. Digital forensics is trying to open Lesley's phone as we speak, so hopefully, we get some information from there. DS Williams is also securing CCTV from the council. Both should give us an indication as to whether there was foul play regarding Lesley's death." George took a sip of coffee. Then he looked at the two DCs. "Meanwhile, I'd like you two to visit Julia Brown, Lesley Ibbetson's best friend."

"Do you reckon Lesley was murdered, boss?" Jay asked.

"I'm not sure, Jay." George thought for a moment. "It's possible. We just need to know what kind of state she was in last night."

Jay reiterated what they knew about the fight. "The deceased slapped her best friend Julia Brown across the face last night at the Falconers Rest pub in Middleton."

"We don't know why," George explained, "which is why Jay and Tashan are going to visit Julia at home."

The DI's phone rang. "DI Beaumont." He listened intently briefly and then said, "Thanks." He turned to the team. "That was PS Greenwood. One of his Uniforms has taken a statement from a woman claiming to have witnessed Lesley Ibbetson being followed last night."

\* \* \*

## CHAPTER ELEVEN

George parked the car on Goodwood. It was a nice area of the Heritage Village in Middleton, just off Martingale Drive, with a view of the main road where Thorpe Lane met Middleton Lane.

He glanced around as he got out of the Merc. Quite a crowd was gathering on doorsteps, and a few people were sitting on the wall opposite. But it all seemed calm. Word would get out soon, more people would come, and Middleton would hear about another person's life being lost before its time.

He knocked on the door, and after a moment, PC Candy Nichols opened it. After peering over his shoulder and plastering a disappointed look across her face, she eventually said, "Glad you're here, sir."

"Jay's not here," George explained, and Candy turned red.

"Is that the detective?" a hoarse voice asked.

"Yes, Mrs Bruce."

"Hello, Mrs Bruce," George said, entering the living room.

She smiled up at him with false teeth from a lilac-coloured chair. She looked to be in her seventies, with short, silver hair. She wore black trousers, a bright pink top, and pink heel slip-ons.

"I believe you have some information for me?"

"Are you in charge?" she asked.

"I am."

"You look very young to be in charge," the woman went on. "But then again, you all look young compared to me."

George grinned at her remark. "I'm SIO on Lesley Ibbetson's death," he assured as he sat on the sofa.

"What's that blinking mean?"

"Senior Investigating Office, Mrs Bruce. It means I'm the boss."

"Fair enough." She frowned at him. "Better call me Ida,

then."

"Thanks, Ida," George said. "So, you have some information for me?"

"I saw her last night. Lesley. She was off her tree, swaying as she walked down the road from the pub. If you go upstairs and into my room, you can see what I mean."

George smirked. "What time was this?"

"Midnight, I think. How did she die?"

"We'll be giving details out shortly. Mind if I take a look upstairs?" He got up.

"Wait a minute!" Ida cried. "I haven't finished. Somebody was following her."

That stopped George in his tracks. "Who?"

"No bloody clue. They were dressed all in black, wearing one of those bala-thingy-mabobs."

"A balaclava?"

"Aye, son, that's right."

George nodded and went upstairs. He snapped some pictures of Mrs Bruce's vantage and then headed right back down.

There was a lamp post directly outside the property. George hoped it had done its job and illuminated the suspect enough. "How tall would you say they were?"

"No idea, love. They were just dressed in all black. Couldn't even tell you if it were a lad or lassie."

"Seen them before?"

She shook her head slowly.

"No problem. I'll get a uniformed officer to come and take a statement from you; thanks."

As George left and got inside his Mercedes, he wondered whether this was a wasted trip, but then figured it wasn't. If DS Williams could get enough CCTV, they could track the person who was following Lesley Ibbetson.

Then as an afterthought, he got out of the Merc and walked around. Seven houses faced the main road, and if he were lucky, maybe one of them would have CCTV.

## Chapter Twelve

As the two DCs were on their way to visit Julia Brown, and DS Mason was busy at the station doing background checks, DI Beaumont decided to get out of the office and follow up on a lead.

Thorpe Lane was busier than he'd ever seen it before. The road was still blocked off, but that didn't stop people emerging from their houses to find out why there were police present. A couple of men were talking about the tent to each other while washing their cars. A youngster was riding a bike along the path.

George entered the Falconers Rest and immediately found comfort from the heat. It was still the way he remembered it from his teens. The bar had deep-red velvet sitting on dark wooden stools and tables, with beams on the walls that appeared to be supporting the building. After the harsh light of the day, it looked unsettlingly dark.

The landlady had short, bleached hair and large, brown eyes, and she was in her mid-fifties. She grinned as she greeted George. "I'm Angela Hobson; how can I help you?"

He held up a warrant card and introduced himself, then said, "I'm investigating a suspicious death. I have some questions to ask you, but first, would you allow me to view whatever

CCTV you have available?"

The woman gave a hearty nod. "Of course, yes. I'll show you where it is if you come through. Can you tell me what happened?"

"A young woman has died."

The woman briefly covered her mouth with her hand. "Is it somebody I know?"

George knew the woman would know exactly who had died once he started questioning her, so he decided there was no need for secrecy. Next of kin had been informed, and the DCI was prepping back at the station to give a press conference. "Although she hasn't been formally identified yet, we believe it's Lesley Ibbetson. She was here last night, right?"

"Oh, sweet Jesus," the woman said. "I know about the tent in the farmer's field but never once thought it would be Lesley." She paused for a moment then as if working out why George wanted the CCTV. "You think she's dead because of what happened in the pub last night?"

"Correct. What do you know about it?"

"Happened about half-eleven. Something of nowt, to tell you the truth. It was Julia that Lesley slapped, I think. Julia Brown. Anyway, I closed at midnight and kicked Lesley out."

They entered a hallway with stairs leading to the first level through a side door.

"Do you live up here? George inquired.

"No, but I can if I need to." She indicated a door. "It's through here."

Angela led the DI into a small office. She pressed a few keys on a computer, sped up the recording to the desired moment, and then pointed at the screen.

"There you go, Detective. The pub's in Miggy, so I'm used

to fights. But, then again, I wouldn't call one slap a fight." She paused again. "Do you think they took the fight elsewhere? Is that how Lesley died?"

"I can't divulge information relating to the investigation just yet, Angela," George said. "Do you know Julia Brown and Lesley Ibbetson well?"

"Oh yeah, I've known most of them since they were teenagers. On numerous instances when they tried to enter while underage, I caught them and kicked the little shits out. They've been no trouble since reaching eighteen, either."

George nodded towards the PC, and Angela clicked play on the recording.

It was a packed night, by the look of it, which was good because that meant witnesses. They momentarily watched Lesley Ibbetson and Julia Brown engaged in a heated debate. A short moment later, Lesley slapped Julia in the face. Then Julia stormed off, and Lesley sat down.

"Is that it?" George asked.

"That's it, love. I told you it was something of nowt." She closed her eyes and pinched the bridge of her nose. She looked exhausted. "Some of the regulars who were here last night will probably show up later if they need to be talked to," she explained. Then she shrugged. "Just in case they overheard anything that could shed some light on the argument."

"Thanks, Angela," George said. "Got any CCTV outside?"

She shook her head. "It's just for show, love. Too expensive."

"I'll send a pair of detectives out later to interview them. In the meantime, you said you've known both women since they were younger."

Angela nodded.

"Did anything strike you as strange about Lesley last night? Or even other nights when she's been in?"

After giving it some thought, Angela shook her head. "Sorry."

"And Julia Brown?"

"It's been busy recently. I'm grateful, but it means I can't speak to the customers as much as I'd like."

"OK," George said, producing a business card from his inner jacket pocket. "Contact me if you think of anything else."

\* \* \*

Julia Brown and her dad were seated across from each other at the kitchen table when Jay and Tashan arrived. When Jay first saw them both, it was apparent to him that there was some hostility between them, and he immediately wanted to know why.

"Would you like a drink? Tea? Coffee?" Mrs Brown asked.

"It's a bit nippy today, isn't it?" Tashan said. "I'd love a brew, thanks."

Mr Brown had wholly lost his hair and looked older than the background check had revealed, whilst Mrs Brown had aged well. Jay noticed her eyes were a piercing blue when she asked, "What about you, love?"

He was flagging from last night, so he said, "A strong coffee, please, with two sugars if possible."

Jay pulled out his notepad. "We're here to talk to Julia about what happened last night."

"That stupid girl assaulted my daughter is what happened, Detective," Mr Brown said. He probably thought he gave off an air of authority, but instead, all he gave off was overpowering aftershave. This guy had nothing on DI Beaumont.

"We can speak with you after, Mr Brown, but we really need to speak with Julia and get her story," Jay explained. Then he turned to Julia. "Would it be better for you if we did this back at the station, Julia?"

"Absolutely not." She turned to her dad. "Dad, let me speak to the detectives."

"Fine, love," Mr Brown said. He turned to Jay. "But I will be sitting here whilst you chat, OK?"

"Fine with me as long as it's fine with your daughter," Jay said. Julia nodded, so Jay said, "I obviously need to talk to you about last night, Julia."

Tashan tapped him on the shoulder and handed him a Dictaphone. "May we record this conversation?" DC Blackburn asked. It was better to be safe than sorry.

"It's fine, love," Mrs Brown said, handing out hot drinks. "Isn't it, dear?" She eyeballed her husband, who nodded.

"We need to learn as much as we can about what happened to Lesley," Jay said.

Julia said, "It wasn't me if that's what you're thinking. We may have argued, but I'd never hurt her."

"I just need a summary from you of what happened last night. Who the pair of you were with, who you spoke to, when you left, why you left. Do you understand?"

Julia nodded, then said, "We went to town and met with Flora. We went to the cinema, then came back to go to the book club. Flora went to the shop, and Lesley and I got to the club early. So, we had a drink in the bar." Jay nodded at her and attempted a calming smile. He'd seen the DI do it before, which usually worked well. "The meeting started, and the author did his reading. He got a bit pushy, as you know from when you spoke to me last night."

Jay nodded again. She'd been one of the first he'd interviewed regarding Gin's murder. "And after we released you?"

"We walked some of the women home who live in the New Forest Village and the Heritage Village, and because we'd already had a few drinks, we decided to go to the pub."

"Who decided? Who walked?"

"Well, Lesley and I walked Aurelia, Bea and Sophie home. And then..."

Julia placed a hand to her mouth to stop herself from talking, but when she realised the three men were staring at her, she stopped.

"And then?" Jay asked.

"We went to the pub."

"Again, who is we?"

"Me and Lesley."

Jay frowned. "So, if I speak with..." Jay looked down at his notes "...Aurelia, Bea and Sophie, they will confirm it was just you and Lesley?"

Julia looked between her parents. "I don't know, do I?"

Mr Brown stood up. "This is getting a bit much for my daughter, Detectives. I must ask that you come back another time."

Jay stood up. "No. Your daughter is twenty-two years old. We can do this now and here," he said, spreading his arms out, "or we can do this down the station." He raised his brow, then sat down and finished his coffee. "It's your choice."

"You can't take her down to the station. Don't you need a warrant or a reason to arrest my Julia?"

"Whilst you're right, Mr Brown," Tashan said, "We have cause to arrest your daughter. She had an altercation with the deceased not long before she died. She was also one of the last people to see Lesley alive."

Both detectives let those words linger in the air and said nothing more. Jay had finished with his coffee, so he continued scribbling notes into his notepad, but Tashan slowly slurped his tea.

"Fine, Flora was with us, OK? But she was in the loo when Lesley and I argued," Julia said.

"Thank you," Jay said. "What were you arguing about? I assume you had plenty of alcohol in your system?"

"Exactly. Lesley was in a mood because she was skint and couldn't afford any..."

She placed a hand to her mouth again, and the mood in the room changed.

"You wouldn't make a very good poker player, Julia," Jay said. "And if it's about drugs, we already know. We've spoken with Mr and Mrs Ibbetson this morning."

Julia puffed out her cheeks. "OK, yes, I was going to say smack. But she couldn't afford any smack. It's what she was complaining about. I told her to stop relying on it and told her it was pissing me off."

She cringed at the swear word, as did her mother and father.

"Then what happened?" Jay asked.

"She slapped me. And I came home."

"Straight away?"

Julia nodded. "Straight away."

"How?"

"Daddy picked me up."

Jay turned to Mr Brown. "She's right; I did. I was annoyed she got me up out of bed."

"What time was that?" Tashan asked.

"Just after half-eleven." She pulled out her phone. "Look, that's the call."

Tashan asked if she would screenshot the log and then email it to him, which she did. Then he looked at Mr Brown. "May we see your log, too?"

Julia's father shrugged, pulled out his mobile and passed it over to Tashan. There was no pin protection, which Tashan wanted to lecture the older man about, but after receiving permission, he decided instead to screenshot the log and email it to himself.

As far as the two detectives were concerned, that was enough of an alibi to exclude her from the investigation, but that meant they now needed to speak with Flora Ogram. And they still wanted to know who this boyfriend was.

"Lesley's mum mentioned she had a boyfriend," Jay explained. "What information can you give us?"

"None," Julia said. "I don't think she did have a boyfriend."

"Mrs Ibbetson said it was the one who was providing her with drugs. Do you know of such a person?"

"I'm sorry, but no."

"And can you think of anybody who might have wanted to hurt Lesley? Somebody with a grudge, maybe?"

"She didn't get on very well with her manager at Greggs," Julia said. "She fired Julia because she started showing up late and stuff." Julia shrugged. "Can't blame her manager, though."

"How did her mood seem?" Tashan asked.

"It was awful. Lesley was up and down, up and down. The methadone worked for a while, but then she started wanting the real stuff. Like I say, that's why we argued."

"How was she paying, or attempting to pay, for drugs if she

had no job?" Jay asked. "Same for coffee in town. And cinema. And drinks. You must have spent a fair bit yesterday, so how was she affording that?"

Julia shrugged. "Universal Credit?"

Jay made a note. He'd ask DS Mason to check with the DWP. "OK, thanks," Jay said. "We'll end the recording. I'll get a typist to type it up and bring it to you to sign, OK? Otherwise, you can contact me via this number," he explained, removing a business card from his suit pocket, "or call Elland Road station and ask for DI Beaumont."

Both detectives stood up. "Thank you all for your time," Jay said.

"And for the drinks," Tashan added.

# Chapter Thirteen

Lisa Flack raised her brow at the Fiesta parked on the drive and pressed the green call button to call Freya.

Again, it went to voicemail. "I can see your car on the drive, Freya." She left the message going as she hammered on the door. "That's me knocking, so open up."

Nothing.

Lisa knew Freya's bedroom was the one that looked down upon the street. She saw no rustle of curtains, no movement of any kind.

She groaned and hung up. She looked through the letterbox but couldn't see much. Lisa also looked through the living room window but, again, didn't see anything.

Then she heard knocking. It was only faint. She turned to the right to find the side entrance to the back garden. The wooden gate was banging against the wall. Lisa thought back to yesterday. She'd shut the gate. Definitely. Lisa knew because she'd let Max out, and before letting the dog out, she always checked the side gate.

So, Lisa decided to look. But first, she called Freya again. "If you hear anybody at the side of your house or in your back garden," she told the voicemail, "then that's me coming to check on you."

The patio door was wide open, and the dog was nowhere to be seen. Lisa wondered if Freya let Max out, not realising the gate was open.

Entering the living room, Lisa was on tenterhooks. She observed every detail, but apart from the nearly empty coffee mug on the table; it was the same as she had left it yesterday afternoon.

Lisa picked up the mug and sniffed. Coffee. Freya had been home then. She always left the dreg-ends of her drink. Always.

Picking up the mug, she entered the kitchen and placed it by the sink. The first thing she saw was Freya's phone charging on the counter. She ran towards it and unplugged it. But there was a PIN. So she tried Freya's date of birth but got nothing. "Shit."

She tried Max's but also couldn't get in. "Fuck."

One more failed attempt would block the phone, so she placed it back on the counter. "Freya, it's only me, Lisa. Are you upstairs?" she shouted.

Then she listened for a reply that didn't come.

"Max?" she cawed. "Come here, boy."

Nothing.

Had she taken the dog for a walk and left the patio door open by accident?

It was the only scenario that made any sense. Freya hadn't told her she was on day off, though; otherwise, she wouldn't have come.

Lisa took another look around the ground floor and, after deciding everything looked fine, headed upstairs.

"Freya, are you up here?" Lisa asked as she walked up the carpeted steps. She got no reply.

"Max, are you up here, boy?" she asked. She got no response, not even a sniff.

Both bedroom doors were wide open.

Tiny flutters of fear flittered along the hairs on the back of Lisa's neck.

She had a bad feeling. A very bad feeling.

* * *

After Jay and Tashan left, Julia called Flora. The news of the passing of her best friend made it difficult for Julia to maintain composure, and she struggled with a shaking hand to contact the right person.

"The police have just been," Julia explained.

"How come, babe?" Flora asked.

"You don't know?" Julia muttered.

"Don't know what?"

"Lesley's dead. They think she was murdered."

"No fucking way! When?"

"Last night," Julia explained. "They came to see me because of the slap, which makes sense. I have a motive."

"Did they really say that?"

"Well, no, not exactly, but I could tell that's what they were alluding to. But I didn't do anything. I didn't kill her. I went straight home."

"What else did you tell them?" Flora asked.

"The truth, Flora," Julia explained.

"About me?"

"Well, yeah."

"Fucking hell, Julia. What did you tell them?"

"Just that you were with us, but when the slap happened, you were in the bog."

"Why would you tell them I was there? My fucking mum died yesterday! So they will think I'm a proper fucking arsehole for going out on the piss."

"Yesterday was hard for you, and you needed a drink as a release," Julia said. "Nobody's going to think you're an arsehole."

"You don't know the police. I do. You should have said nothing."

"But people saw you at the pub, Flora. So the police were always going to find out you were there."

"Right, OK. Let's pretend like this phone call never happened, OK?"

"OK, but why?"

"Delete the record from your phone once I hang up, OK?" Flora demanded.

When Julia said nothing, Flora said, "OK?"

"OK, fine. Why are you acting weird?"

"As you said, babe, my mum's just died. I'm feeling a bit paranoid, to be honest. So that's two of us now from the book club in two days. And I don't like it."

"Oh shit!" remarked Julia. "I didn't think of it that way. Do you think the two murders are connected?"

"Did the police say whether they think they are?" Flora cut in.

"They didn't say anything," Julia explained.

A loud knock interrupted Flora just as she was about to say something. She placed her phone down on the table and looked outside. The detective who interviewed her yesterday was standing there with a dark-skinned man with brown eyes and tightly curled hair on top of his head.

"Shit," Flora said. "They're here now."

"I'll delete the call log and pretend I didn't call you love, OK?"

"Thanks, babe. We'll be alright as long as we stick together."

* * *

DC Jason Scott knocked again, then turned to Tashan. "I'm sure I saw a shadow move."

"I saw it too, Jay," Tashan confirmed.

"Who is it?" came a voice from behind the door.

"Detective Constable Jason Scott and Detective Constable Tashan Blackburn. I'm Jay; we spoke yesterday?"

Jay heard the rattling of chains and what sounded like a key in the lock before an out-of-breath Flora Ogram opened the door. "Can I help you? I was just about to get in the shower."

She grinned at Jay once she noticed him blushing. She was wearing only a towel.

"Are you OK, Miss Ogram?" She looked distressed.

"I don't know if I am, to be honest." She paused. "Are you coming in?"

"Get dressed," Jay said. "We'll wait here."

"I tell you what, you get yourselves comfortable in the living room, and I'll go get decent, shall I?"

After ten or fifteen minutes, a fresh-faced Flora entered the living room.

"I'm afraid we have some bad news to share with you," Jay explained.

"Worse than my mum being murdered?" she asked.

Jay immediately felt stupid. "No, of course not. But your friend, Lesley Ibbetson, was found dead this morning."

She rushed her hand to her mouth. "Dead? What?"

"We're currently investigating, so we cannot share the details with you yet, but we do have some questions," Jay said.

"Questions for me?" she asked, and Jay nodded. "Why?"

"Because we know you were at the pub last night with Lesley and Julia."

"It's not a crime to have a drink, is it? I'm twenty-two." Flora then bit her lip firmly as if attempting to control herself.

"Of course not. We want to know what Julia and Lesley were arguing about when Lesley smacked Julia."

"I don't know, to be honest. I was powdering my nose." She paused as she said it, realising who she was talking to. "In a literal sense. I was putting some more makeup on as all I was doing last night was crying."

"That's understandable," said Jay.

"So, you didn't witness the slap or the argument?" asked Tashan.

"That's correct," she said.

Tashan scribbled some notes. It was tallying up precisely the way Julia had described it.

"Where did you go after the pub?" Jay asked. "My boss has seen the CCTV footage, and Julia leaves alone. She already told us she went straight home but couldn't tell us what you did."

Flora said nothing for a long while. Tashan could almost see the cogs whirling around her mind. "Flora?" he prompted.

"I called Nick to pick me up."

"And what time was that?"

"Half-eleven, quarter to twelve. I can't really remember exactly."

Jay pointed to her phone. "May we see your call log?"

"You can, but it won't show you anything. I did an update that screwed my phone this morning, so I had to factory reset it."

Convenient, Tashan thought. He shared a look with his colleague. They'd have to speak to Nick to confirm her story.

"You didn't see Lesley after Julia left?" Jay questioned.

"I didn't, no. I'd heard about the argument and couldn't be arsed with Lesley's shit. Please excuse my French, but since coming off the..." She paused—a deer caught in the headlights.

"We know about her heroin addiction, Flora," Jay explained. "We've already spoken with her mum."

"Oh, thank fuck for that," Flora said with a grin. "Since the methadone, she's been in a right state. After finding out about Mum yesterday, I didn't need more of a downer. So, I left." She nodded to signify the end of her explanation but then added, "Actually, one of the pool lads bought me a shot. I had that and then left."

Tashan scribbled more notes. They were heading to the pub straight after, and so would look out for any lads playing pool.

"I've noticed that with my mum, you mention the word murder, but with Lesley, you keep saying death. Am I reading into that correctly?"

The two detectives looked at each other.

"We don't know the full details yet, and won't until after the post-mortem, but she died of an overdose. Whether she overdosed herself or somebody else did, we don't know. What we do know is that she spent another half an hour at the pub after slapping Julia. She may have had her drink spiked."

"So, it could be murder, then?" Flora used the palm of her hand to rub her eyes. There weren't any tears, Jay observed.

"Why do you ask? Do you know somebody who'd want to hurt her?"

"No, Lesley was nice. She had her issues and her vices, but

otherwise, she was a nice woman."

"What about Lesley's boyfriend?" Jay asked.

"What boyfriend?"

"Her mum suggested Lesley had a boyfriend, one who was providing her with drugs."

"If she did have a boyfriend, and if he was providing her with drugs, then I don't know anything about it." She smiled at Jay. "I'm sorry."

Jay stood up. This had been a waste of time. "Here's my business card again. When you have time to think, call me. If you think of anything else, contact me. That goes for your mum's case, too. At the moment, we're treating them as separate cases, but because of the links between them, we're looking into both deaths.

Her fingertips lightly touched his as she took the business card from him.

He felt a spark at the contact. Flora must have, too, because she had to take a deep breath.

Tashan nodded in appreciation as he tucked his notebook into his pocket.

As the pair exited the flat, Tashan couldn't help but wonder why Flora Ogram hadn't cried despite her apparent distress at her friend's death.

She also hadn't inquired as to when or where.

Because of that, he knew Flora was hiding something.

## Chapter Fourteen

Not much fazed Detective Sergeant Isabella Wood, but as she walked up the drive to find Lisa Flack waiting, the look of terror in her eyes caused the detective to pause.

"I'm relieved you came," the woman said to Wood. "I don't know whether I'm being silly or not, but I can't find her, Detective."

"Why did you call nine-nine-nine?" Wood asked.

"Freya isn't in the house." She pointed at the car. "Her car's still here. Her phone's charging in the kitchen, and her bag is by the front door, too." Again, Lisa pointed. "I checked in case a robbery had happened, but the bag has a purse in it with her bank cards and cash in it."

"So Freya's missing, but you've found the dog?" Isabella questioned. "What about her keys?"

Lisa Flack nodded. She'd called triple nine, and the Control Room of the West Yorkshire Police had sent a uniform over to speak with her. After explaining that it seemed like the detective constable was missing, the control roll liaised with Laburnum Road, where Freya worked, and DS Wood was sent out immediately.

"He's asleep under the spare bed, which is really unusual," Lisa explained. "I've called his name repeatedly, but it's like he's been drugged."

"I'll take a look," Isabella said, pulling on her CSI gear. If a crime had happened here, then she didn't want to contaminate the scene more than what it already was.

Isabella looked around the living room first and then headed upstairs, taking each step one at a time, scrutinising everything. The house was decorated vividly and hurt her eyes. At the top of the stairs, she noticed two doors were wide open, confirming Lisa's story. The one at the end of the hall was the spare bedroom, whilst the one to her left was Freya Bentley's.

She ambled towards the spare bedroom, hoping she didn't have to deal with a dead dog. Unfortunately, her pregnancy meant she couldn't handle strong scents any more. Though, in truth, she was missing being at the crime scenes with her fiancé.

After slowly getting on her knees and peering under the bed, she found Max, whose black and tan fur was rising and falling.

She gently grabbed the cocker spaniel by the collar with a gloved hand and pulled him out.

He was out cold. Lisa was right.

Cradling him, Wood carried the sleeping dog in her arms into the kitchen to find Lisa staring at her, wide-eyed and open-mouthed. They'd asked Lisa not to contaminate any other rooms in the house. Lisa was made aware she needed to give samples and prints if necessary.

A trickle of worry pricked at the skin of Lisa's neck again. Where was Freya? From what Lisa knew of Freya, she never would have left Max alone. It was why she called on Lisa to help when Freya was at work.

"Don't worry, Lisa; he'll be fine. But he needs to see a vet. Which vet does Freya use?"

## CHAPTER FOURTEEN

Lisa told her about the vet on Middleton Park Road. Wood knew of it. They'd once scanned a dog for them on a case.

"OK. Let's phone the vet. Whilst I do that, I need you to draw up a list of Freya's family and friends. They might know where she is."

Wood called the vet, who told her to give the dog water and a little food. The lady on the end of the phone advised her to call back if there was no change in a couple of hours.

"Who's Freya's next of kin?" Wood asked.

"I've no idea, sorry," Lisa said.

"OK, who's Freya's best friend?" Wood asked.

"Other than me?" Lisa asked, and Wood nodded.

"I don't know, to be honest. Freya doesn't really go out. She prefers to be at home with Max."

"OK, no worries. I'll speak with Freya's colleagues."

"I found her phone," Lisa said. "I tried her date of birth and Max's date of birth, but neither worked."

"That's fine; I'll bag it up and take it to the station. Our IT techs will be able to get into it. Meanwhile, I'll speak with Wakefield HQ, where she was based, and get more information about her."

"Was she supposed to be at work then?"

"I can't comment," Wood advised.

"She must have been; otherwise, they wouldn't have sent a detective, right?"

Wood smiled. The woman was sharp. "Can you think of anybody Freya was in contact with other than yourself?"

"Not really. Freya was a lover of novels and was going to join a book club at the Corinthians rugby club. I know she was talking with one of the women there," Lisa explained.

Wood was nodding as she searched the living room. Beneath

the coffee table was a small notebook. In the back was a list of handwritten phone numbers. A few were crossed out, but one was highlighted. She called it, but it was switched off.

Below that was another number, this time with a name next to it. Wood called Lisa over. "Do you know this Ellie Addiman?"

Lisa shook her head. "I've no idea who she is, sorry."

Wood dialled the number, and when a woman answered, she said, "This is Detective Sergeant Wood from West Yorkshire Police's Homicide and Major Enquiry Team. I found your name and number in a notebook belonging to Freya Bentley. Do you know her?"

"Yes," the voice said. "I know Freya. Is everything OK?"

"Are you Ellie Addiman?" Wood asked.

"Correct. Is everything OK?"

"When was the last time you heard from or saw Freya?" Wood asked.

"I've only spoken with her once. She was interested in joining the New Forest Village Book Club I run. Why?"

Wood recognised the name because George was working on two murder cases involving the book club. "So, Freya wasn't a member?"

"Not yet; why? Is Freya OK?"

\* \* \*

When the bag containing Gin Creaser's remains was abruptly dumped onto the mortuary slab, Dr Christian Ross had watched in respectful silence. He greeted the paramedics before directing them out the door after signing for the delivery as though it were a Royal Mail delivery.

## CHAPTER FOURTEEN

The early morning start, and the fact that he'd have another body on the slab later, meant he needed coffee. And strong stuff at that.

After finishing drinking the coffee, he poured himself another one and was getting ready to put on his rubber gloves when he heard footsteps. "Hello?"

"It's only me, Dr Ross," a voice said.

"Ah, DI Beaumont. I did wonder whether I might see you here or not."

George grinned. "I considered sending one of the lads, but I've got them working on other stuff." He cricked his neck. "Sitting at the office all day isn't really my style, so I thought I'd stretch my legs."

"It's good timing on your part anyway, son." Dr Ross pointed to the body of Ginny Creaser on the table, exposed and waiting for him to start. The dead were always waiting. One aspect of the job the pathologist enjoyed was precisely that. Dead bodies were significantly more accommodative than their still-living counterparts, never in a hurry and didn't require awkward small conversation. Then again, the pathologist didn't mind small talk now and then. Of course, that didn't mean he didn't like being alive, nor did he particularly dislike the population who were still breathing, but working with live individuals was more difficult than doing it with dead ones.

Most of them were OK. But not all. Like the person who had caused poor Gin Creaser's death. Dr Ross wondered for a moment what the person was like and why they decided to kill Gin Creaser. What was their goal, and what was their intention? Was it planned, or was it random? They were all questions detectives asked, but Dr Ross liked to formulate these questions early and then try to answer them as he peeled each layer back.

The dead were like onions, he supposed. Onions that had no plans, no queries, and caused no harm.

Christ, he was getting old. And rather loony. Maybe it was time to retire.

"Are you OK, Doc?" George asked.

"Sorry, George, just thinking about the poor woman." Dr Ross pointed at Ginny. "She probably only lived about half her life, and I was wondering why."

"I'm wondering the same if it helps?" George said.

Dr Ross grinned. "Though you probably know a heck of a lot more about her than I do, son. For all I know, she was a cruel monster. Or a complete saint. I know nothing of that. I only know what story my blades and tools tell me."

"They're helpful stories, though, Doc," George said. "We wouldn't be able to do what we do without you."

"True enough," the pathologist replied.

The doctor closed his eyes briefly, apologising for what he was about to do to the woman's body but explaining how it was essential.

It was a ritual he did before every post-mortem, one he would continue until he retired. Or worse.

After a quick nod to George, who stood back, Dr Ross began to circle the body, inspecting it for any apparent wounds or evidence of damage. And then he noticed something and stopped stone-still, and his mind raced to weigh the ramifications of what he had just caught.

"She was forty years old, correct?" Christian Ross asked George.

"Correct, Doc."

He gave a calm, "My God," and closed his eyes. Then, he turned to DI Beaumont. "Detective, I have some rather unexpected and unsettling news for you."

## Chapter Fifteen

"Does Freya have a partner?" Wood asked.

Lisa shook her head. "As far as I know, she's single."

"OK, I'm going to look in her room now to see if anything's out of place. You need to stay here, OK?"

Lisa nodded her head. She knew she'd already fucked up by trampling through the house, but at that point, she hadn't thought her friend was missing.

Before heading upstairs, Wood spoke to the uniformed constable and asked her to start taking statements from the neighbours. One of them may have seen something.

Isabella pushed open the door of the main bedroom. The double bed was made up, indicating it either hadn't been slept in or Freya had made it when she got up.

The wardrobe door was open. Wood glanced at the vast array of clothing. Freya was a detective constable, yet the detached house was pretty new and probably very expensive. Detective constables didn't make a lot of money; hell, detective sergeants didn't either. The Ford on the drive was definitely new.

Wood looked around the bedroom. The furnishings looked expensive, also.

Where was she getting her money from?

Nothing looked out of place, so she turned to leave. But as she did, the change in light highlighted a damp patch on the carpet by the bed. She slowly got down on her knees and stared at it. Had the dog been in and had a wee? After sniffing it and confirming it was wee, she wrinkled her nose and shuffled backwards.

Everything else in the room was pristine, but right there, at carpet level near the stain, she noted scuff marks on the cream carpet.

Was she reading more into it than she should?

Had Lisa been in the bedroom with her shoes on, causing the scuff?

She'd ask her.

As she descended the stairs, she couldn't shake off the feeling that something sinister had happened in this house.

\* \* \*

Where the hell was she?

Flora couldn't stop the shakes. "I'm never drinking again," she vowed aloud.

She'd asked Julia Brown to meet her here, away from prying eyes.

Middleton St Mary's churchyard was always deserted at this time of year.

Eventually, Julia showed up. "Oh, thank fuck for that." Flora raised her brow. "I thought you weren't coming."

"How are you?" Julia stared at her. "You look as rough as I feel."

"I feel like shit. Last night is coming back to me piece by piece. I drank way too much."

Julia smiled. "Despite being slapped, I actually enjoyed last night." Then the memory of being interviewed about Gin Creaser entered her mind. "Shit, sorry. Your mum's just died, and I'm bragging about how much I enjoyed myself."

"It's fine. I enjoyed myself, too. Paying for it today in a big way, though."

"I'm a bit fragile myself," Julia said, laughing. She looked around at the ancient gravestones. "Are you going to bury your mum in here?"

"Not a chance of that!" Flora said. "Apparently, my grandma always said, 'You bury your loved ones, not burn them like rubbish.' But my mum always told me to cremate her and scatter her ashes at the seaside. So that's what I'll do once the police release her body."

"You'll have a service, though?"

"Of course. Cottingley, probably."

"You'll invite me, yeah?"

Flora frowned. "Why wouldn't I?" She shrugged. "I'll invite all the book club members, too."

Julia nodded. "Why did you want to see me?"

"Did Gaynor seem strange to you last night?"

"No, why?"

"She and Mum fought earlier this week. It's unlike them, so I was a bit worried," Flora explained.

"You don't think your aunt's involved, do you?"

"I'm not ruling anybody out, love," Flora said.

"What, even me?"

Flora nodded.

"It wasn't me, Flora, honest. I've no reason to kill your mum."

Flora met Julia's eyes. "What about Lesley."

"What about her?"

"Did you kill her?"

Julia pursed her lips. "What the fuck, Flora!"

"She hit you last night, and you stormed off. The next minute, she's dead. I'm the one who should be saying, 'What the fuck'."

"So what." Julia shrugged. "She was drunk, and we had a row. It was hardly a hit, just a stupid slap. We'd be laughing about it right now, with a voddy in the pub."

"Except now we can't because she's fucking dead." Flora paused. "What did you tell the police happened last night?"

"That we walked some of the women home who live in the New Forest Village and the Heritage Village, and because we'd already had a few drinks at the rugby club, we decided to go to the pub."

Flora nodded but said nothing, inviting Julia to continue. "I tried to keep your name out of it as much as possible. But they said I was probably the last person to see Lesley alive. The detective threatened to arrest me. Practically said I had a motive."

"Then what?"

Julia puffed out her cheeks. "I told them Lesley was mardy because she couldn't afford any smack. It's what she was complaining about. I told her to stop relying on it and told her it was pissing me off. That's when she slapped me."

"Did they ask anything else?"

Julia paused and bit the inside of her cheek. "Only about Lesley's boyfriend, which was news to me."

"Yeah, me too."

Flora immediately felt guilty. Julia had kept her name out of the conversation because it didn't exactly look good. Flora knew she shouldn't have gone drinking the night her mum was murdered. But she'd needed the drink.

Julia shivered. "You look like you could do with a strong coffee. Shall we go to the café up the road?"

"Honestly, I'm fine. I think I just need to sleep."

"Are we OK?" Julia asked.

Flora grabbed her friend and kissed her on the cheek. "We're more than OK, babe." Flora then lightly punched Julia on the shoulder. "Still haven't ruled you out of my investigation, though."

\* \* \*

At DCI Alistair Atkinson's order, Detective Constable Reza Malik arrived at Freya Bentley's house to assist DS Wood.

She was on the phone to CSI.

"Are you being a bit premature, sarge?" Malik said when she finished the call.

"I don't like the feeling I'm getting about this, Reza, so no. While waiting for you, I spoke with her superior, DCI Spector. He told me she was the most punctual detective on his team and the most hard-working, too. So if she were supposed to be in today, which she was, then she would have been in. So I believe that Freya's missing. I hope I'm wrong, but..."

Reza shrugged. "She might have gone out for a walk this morning and bumped into someone. Maybe they got chatting, and she didn't realise the time."

"Without her phone, keys and bag?" She frowned at him. "Come on, Detective Malik. It's past dinnertime."

Wood opened the patio door with gloved hands, stepped outside, and made her way to the wooden shed nestled in the

## CHAPTER FIFTEEN

back corner of the garden. The door was unlocked. She stepped inside.

A mower and a strimmer greeted her. There were a few spades, and a rake sat alongside a wheelbarrow with a watering can in it.

Not finding anything out of place or disturbed, she returned to the house.

"Anything?" DC Malik asked.

"Nope, but the SOCOs can check."

"What do you think happened to Freya?" he asked.

"The link to the book club raises questions I don't have answers to yet." She held out the notebook. "I need to know whose number this is." A uniform had already been to the house and taken the phone back to Elland Road for processing. "All I know is that her personal belongings are here, and her car is still outside. Wherever she went, she'd have had to walk or go with somebody."

Reza called the number using his own mobile, but it wouldn't connect.

"Call the DCI, Reza and ask him to give that number to one of the techs. Then, if it's not a burner, they'll be able to work their magic on it."

"On it, sarge," Reza said, popping back outside.

Wood desperately wanted to be back at the station. That, or she wanted to be at Laburnum Road. DCI Spector had told her she could speak with any of his detectives whenever needed. She thought it showed how valued Freya was. Their new DCI barely gave any praise. Wood didn't like DCI Alistair Atkinson all that much, but then, she was biased. George should have gotten the job, which still irked her.

"I've done as asked, sarge," Reza said, entering the living

room. "The DCI wanted a bit of an update, so I advised him of what you said and your theory that she's missing. He said to speak to the neighbours."

"I already have Uniform on it," Wood explained. "And you and I are going to head out in a minute, too. Look for CCTV or those doorbell cameras. Look through car windscreens for any dashcams." She thought of George. "We've managed to crack cases with footage from them before. She's missing, and so someone has to have seen something."

"What if she left in the middle of the night, sarge, or was taken then?"

"That's why we need footage, Detective Constable." Wood pointed towards the female uniform, only just remembering her name. "That's PC Candy Nichols, Reza. Whilst I speak with Laburnum Road, liaise with her, and canvass the neighbours, OK?"

The older DC nodded and headed to speak with the young PC. Wood stared out at the garden, gathering her thoughts. She didn't feel optimistic. Her gut told her that either Freya Bentley had been frightened of something that had made her leave her home or, more realistically, that she had been abducted.

# Chapter Sixteen

Before going to Wakefield HQ, she headed back to Leeds HQ and knocked on DCI Atkinson's office door.

"Come in."

Inside her boss' office, she refrained from rolling her eyes. The DCI had moved the furniture around again. Apparently, it was something he did to relieve his anxiety. Feng Shui or something. But it didn't seem to quench his thirst for sarcasm. Or for being blunt. It appeared the new DCI only cared about his own anxiety and not that of others.

Yet another tick in the box for DI Beaumont.

"You better be here to tell me you've found that DC, DS Wood."

"I'm afraid not. I suspect Freya is missing."

Atkinson shook his head and slapped a hand on his desk; a little too hard, Wood guessed, noticing that he flinched at the impact.

"I think I need to liaise with DI Beaumont," Wood said.

"Oh, do you now?" Atkinson said, cocking his brow. "And why is that?"

"Freya Bentley," Wood persisted, "the woman who may be missing has a connection to the New Forest Village Book Club."

Atkinson shrugged his shoulders. "What connection?"

Wood was about to speak when Atkinson interrupted her. "I didn't see her on the list of members that DI Beaumont gave me, so I assume there's a trivial connection somewhere. Did DC Bentley meet up for coffee with one of the women once upon a time?" Atkinson mocked. "Or did they attend the same school, sixth form or college? Did they play netball together? Or rounders? Go on, what's the connection? Because I know for a fact she isn't a member!"

He took a deep breath.

"I put George in charge of the murder of Gin Creaser and put you on a different case to separate you. You all know how I feel about two police officers working together who are in a relationship. I'm already under pressure from the super because of Lesley Ibbetson's death. So I don't need this from you, OK?"

"With all due respect—"

"Don't 'all due respect' me, Detective Sergeant Wood." DCI Atkinson stood, shoving his chair back with his legs which hit the wall with a wooden clunk. "Follow orders, OK. George has his, and you have yours."

"I am following orders, sir," she said. "There's a tangible link. I've spoken with Ellie Addiman on the phone earlier, who confirmed Freya intended to join the book club. And now she's missing."

"You haven't even found her next of kin yet, Detective Malik informs me."

Wood shook her head. She knew Reza wanted a promotion, but sucking up to the DCI was just ridiculous. "It's just me and him, sir," Wood explained. "Freya's phone has a PIN on it, so IT is working on that as we speak. After this conversation, I'm heading to Wakefield HQ to speak with her colleagues. DC

Malik is canvassing the area with help from PC Nichols and other uniformed officers. What else am I supposed to be doing other than investigating?"

When Atkinson said nothing, Wood went further. "Tell me, sir. What else can I possibly be doing?"

She could see Atkinson was turning red but didn't back down. Her own anger was boiling over now. "What if Freya Bentley is missing because of her connection to Ellie Addiman and the book club, sir? Will you pass it on to DI Beaumont, or will you let me liaise with him so he can concentrate on the other two murder cases you've given him?"

Atkinson went to speak, but Wood wasn't finished. "Or you know what? Let us work together starting now, sir. When DI Beaumont and I worked together, we had the highest success rate at solving major crimes in the entire force. We work well. Together. Not fragmented like this!"

DCI Atkinson was shaking his head. "For now, you both work separately." He rummaged through his drawer and pulled out some pills. He swallowed one dry. "If anything changes, let me know. I'll be the one to make the decision, OK?"

DS Wood nodded and turned on her heel, and left before she lost more of her temper.

* * *

Jay met Tashan at the Falconers Rest. The place was pretty busy if the car park was anything to go by, which would help them with their case. Then again, he imagined the regulars would live nearby and usually walked.

The pair went inside and looked for the landlady, Angela Hobson, who, as promised, identified the patrons who had been in the pub the previous night. The detectives took stock. A few lads were playing pool; two men sat around a table, a couple with what looked like beers and packets of crisps, and a group of older gentlemen by the bar.

"I say we interview them together," Jay said, and Tashan nodded.

"Want me to take notes, Jay, whilst you ask the questions?"

"Good plan, mate. And then we swap for the next lot?"

"Sounds good to me, Jay."

The DCs moved to sit on bar stools next to the four gentlemen. They each nestled a pint, were probably close to seventy years old, and were dressed outrageously in colourful T-shirts and shorts. Jay loved it. The men reminded him of his own grandad. He grinned broadly and produced his warrant card. "Good afternoon, sirs. Would it be OK if I asked you some questions about last night?"

"What time last night, son? By half-nine, I was pissed as a fart."

The other three men began to laugh, and both detectives joined in.

"I'm Detective Constable Jason Scott, and this is Detective Constable Tashan Blackburn." Jay grinned and looked at each man in turn. "Any of you not pissed as a fart by half-nine then?"

All four men erupted into more laughter.

"What do you want to know, lads?" one of the gentlemen asked. Despite being sat on a stool, Jay noticed the man was tall. He was pretty stocky for his age, too, and Jay wondered whether he'd been a weightlifter in the past. "I'm Arthur, by the way." He held out a hand, which was firm when both detectives shook it. "Do I know you, lad?" he asked, looking at Tashan.

"I don't think so, sir," Tashan replied. "Why?"

"You look familiar," Arthur explained. "Like a grandson of mine."

"You related to any Blackburns?"

"No, lad."

"Did you see the argument that happened last night between two lasses?" Jay asked, interrupting.

"I didn't, lad, but maybe Aidan, Thomas or Paul did." Arthur smoothed the black waves atop his head.

"It was just a slap, mate," Aidan, Thomas or Paul said. Jay wasn't sure who was who.

"What's your name, mate?" Jay asked. There was a nuance to his accent that Jay couldn't quite grasp.

"Aidan," he grinned. "You're trying to place my accent, aren't you, mate?"

Jay nodded.

"I was born in Australia and lived there until my early twenties. Lived in Miggy ever since."

"That's a bit of a contrast. Miggy or Australia, I know where I'd want to be."

"Met the love of my life, mate. It doesn't matter where you live when you're in the company of a good woman."

Jay'd had the pleasure of being in the company of a few Miggy women before and had a massively different opinion of Aidan. "So, it was just a slap, you say?"

"For sure," Aidan said. "Bird who got slapped fucked off, but the angry lassie stayed for a bit. That right, Paulie?"

"Fucked if I know," Paulie said. "Pissed as a fart, remember."

"And what about you, Thomas?" Jay asked, finally working

out who was who. He was a short, fat man with no hair and hardly any teeth.

"I noticed the argument, glanced at the girls, and immediately returned to my beer. It was something of nothing," Thomas said.

"Did you hear what they were arguing about?"

"Nah, it was proper busy last night, mush. Proper busy, like." Then with a smile devoid of teeth, Thomas said, "Didn't hear a fucking word. Couldn't even hear these three bastards, though that was probably a blessing in disguise."

Jay pulled a business card out of his inside jacket pocket and slid it across the bar. "Thanks, gentlemen. We'll let you finish your beers, but please let us know if you remember anything. Enjoy your day."

Next, they approached the couple, seated in the other corner from where the altercation had occurred. They were in their thirties and had finished their crisps by the time the detectives sat down. The man was dressed in beige shorts and a short-sleeved, open-collar white shirt, while the woman wore a pink strappy dress. It was a strange sight for a Friday evening, but then again, it seemed the entire pub liked to dress strangely.

"Hello there." Tashan flashed his warrant card. "I believe you were in the pub last night?"

The woman looked up. "We were, yes. Is everything OK?"

"Absolutely," Tashan said. "I'm Detective Constable Blackburn, and this is Detective Constable Scott. So the landlady tells us you witnessed the argument last night?"

"With the two birds?" the man asked.

"Correct. May I take your names?"

"I'm Sandra, and this is Jim. Our surname is Cafferkey," she said.

"So, what did you see last night?"

"Why?" Jim asked.

"We are investigating a suspicious death and an incident that happened last night to see whether they are related."

Sandra placed her hand on her chest. "I'm sorry to hear that. Do we know who? Was it one of those lasses?"

"We can't share specifics, I'm afraid, but it's those two women that we're most interested in. At around eleven thirty, a fight apparently started, and I was wondering if you heard or saw anything."

Jim nodded. "I saw it, but our lass was in the loo." He turned to her. "Right?"

"Right."

"What did you see?" Tashan asked.

"I was on the way back from the bar, and the lass who stormed off after being smacked almost knocked the voddys from my hands. I didn't see the smack exactly but heard it."

"Did you hear what they were arguing about?"

Jim shook his head. "Sorry, no."

"It's always way too loud in here on a night," Sandra said. "I'm not complaining, like, but you can barely hear each other, never mind anybody else."

"So, you didn't hear anything at all?"

"I didn't say that," Sandra said.

"Please explain," Tashan said.

"The two lasses were actually a trio."

"A trio?" They knew about Flora already, but it was nice to have an independent witness confirm she was there.

"Yeah, they were with Flora Ogram. I know her because I went to school with her…" She gesticulated, attempting to find the correct words. "Her stepdad, I guess. He was a few years below me, but he went out with my little sister, so I got to know him quite well."

The detectives said nothing, inviting Sandra to continue.

After an awkward silence, Sandra broke it. "Flora was upset. Crying her eyes out."

Tashan nodded. It was understandable. Her mother had just been murdered.

"Did Flora say why?"

"No, and I didn't ask." Sandra paused.

"She hasn't got the best reputation," Jim explained. "Flora's a bit of a firecracker—a proper rough un. You know what I mean? She's well known around these parts for causing trouble."

Tashan looked at Jay, who was furiously scribbling notes.

"Can you think of anything else?" Tashan asked.

After looking at his wife, who shook her head, Jim said, "Sorry, but no. We don't know anything else."

"Well, I'll leave you to it. I appreciate your time. Thank you, and have a good evening."

By the time they'd finished interviewing the gentlemen at the bar and the couple, the men playing pool were gone. Tashan was annoyed with himself. He'd wanted to ask about the shot one of them apparently bought Flora. So instead, they headed towards the two men sitting at the table, but as they approached, they got up.

"Sorry, fellas, but we've gotta go. We saw the slap but didn't hear why it happened."

The two DCs took their places. "We're not getting anything here," Jay said. "People remembered them, saw the slap, but don't know why they were fighting."

"We need to speak to Nick," Tashan said. "He'll be able

to tell us what time he picked Flora up and what time she called." Tashan paused. "I can take the lead on that because I interviewed him last night."

Jay checked his watch, desperately wanting to see Candy Nichols. "That sounds good to me, Tashan, but how about we leave it here for tonight and go see Nick in the morning?"

## Chapter Seventeen

In her car and on the way back from Laburnum Road, West Yorkshire Police's central HQ based in Wakefield, Wood answered a call over the speaker. "DS Wood."

"I've finished canvassing, sarge," Detective Malik said. "There's still no sign of the missing woman, Freya Bentley."

"What information have you gathered?"

"PC Nichols collated the questionnaires," DC Malik said. "I'm only part way through, but with information from Candy, it looks like all we've gathered so far is that Freya kept to herself. One neighbour said she was almost invisible. She didn't even know Freya's name. Another remembers her getting home late last night. A Mr Charles Small. He was brushing his teeth and noticed her pull up. It was about one-ish." There was a short, awkward pause. "What did Freya's work colleagues have to say, sarge?"

"She was a strong, likeable, professional character who recently passed her exams. Freya was expected to be the next Detective Sergeant: no complaints, no drama, no nothing. Unfortunately, Freya didn't socialise outside of work, so nobody could give me much insight into who she was as a person. It was a bit of a waste of time, to be honest." She looked down at the folder on the passenger seat. "I do have a copy of her employee record, though."

"Did you speak to DCI Atkinson about treating the investigations as being related?" he asked.

"I did. We're to keep them separate for now."

"Yes, sarge," DC Malik said.

She indicated right on the roundabout to get onto the M1. "Freya did not leave her home voluntarily. That's clear. But how is she related to Gin Creaser's murder and Lesley Ibbetson's suspicious death?"

"Just the book club," Reza said.

"Exactly. I think we should talk to Ellie Addiman and see what she's like in person." Wood preferred interviewing people in person as they'd give off little tells. She had always been very good at catching out liars. "It could be she's been in touch with other members, and we don't know anything about it."

"OK, sarge," Reza said. "Are we doing that tonight, or are we heading home because my shift ended an hour ago."

"Get yourself home, DC Malik, but be in at seven tomorrow morning, OK?"

"Yes, sarge."

Isabella didn't want to go home quite yet, so she continued towards Elland Road station, hoping George and the rest of the team were still there.

As far as she believed, what the DCI didn't know couldn't hurt him.

\* \* \*

The Picture House in Morley was an airy, modern pub built from the remnants of a former cinema. Or that's what Google had said. In truth, the place was a bit of a shithole, but it was cheap. And the two officers could see each other in secret.

Jay glanced at his watch. It had just gone past half-seven. He was disappointed not to find Candy waiting for him. He had sent her a WhatsApp message after managing to get rid of Tashan half an hour ago, and she'd replied with a thumbs-up emoji. He'd presumed that meant she was OK to meet him.

"A pint, please, mate," he told the barman. Then, after a few seconds of hesitation, he added, "Fosters." It was the cheapest.

Amber nectar, they called it. It was like piss water. But Jay was skint, and it'd do.

Jay looked around the place whilst he waited. A few older gentlemen sat beneath the television, chatting. Two women were in one of the corners, laptops out, seemingly discussing business. An older couple were eating fish and chips.

Picking up his piss water, Jay headed towards the other back corner to wait for Candy. A ping from his pocket sent fear through him.

Was she not coming?

Did she have to work late?

He placed his beer down on the table and pulled out his phone.

'Be five minutes. X'

Jay smiled and sat down. Despite being a 'good-looking lad', he never really had much luck with the ladies. His job didn't help. Being a detective meant he couldn't be readily available.

The door opened, and Candy entered, looking gorgeous. She looked around the room, and after spying him, she looked at him and smiled, slipping her phone into her bag.

He sat down before his knees buckled. How had he managed

to get so lucky? She has such kissable lips and massive hazel eyes. Her dark curls fell in waves down her back.

"Hello, beautiful," he said, standing back up to embrace her.

She eyed the lager on the table. "Surprised you can drink that after last night," she said, grinning. "I don't think I could drink any more this month!"

"I've got a tough stomach," he explained. And then shook his head. Tough stomach. What the fuck, Jay! He groaned inwardly. Get a grip, he warned himself.

"What's up? You've turned beetroot."

"I thought you were texting me to stand me up," he admitted.

"After last night, I don't think I'll ever stand you up, handsome," she said and blushed herself.

The silence soon became awkward when Jay didn't quite know what to say.

"I didn't want to get up for work this morning," she eventually said, sitting down. Jay sat, and she snuggled into him.

"Aye, me neither," Jay said. "Boss got me up early. There was another death."

"Yeah, I heard. I've been busy with DS Wood. Unfortunately, a woman's gone missing from the New Forest Village."

Jay raised a brow. "Missing?"

"Yeah, and get this, they think it might be connected to your cases."

"How so?"

"The missing woman was interested in joining that book club."

Jay shot back up and pulled his mobile from his pocket. "Does George know?"

"I think so." She shrugged. "Isabella said she was going

back to the station, so I guess she'll let George know. Plus, they live together, right?"

"Right." He sat back down.

She smiled and eased back into the leather upholstery. She picked up Jay's lager and took a sip. Then she grimaced. "I don't know how you manage to drink that."

"I don't, either." He pointed towards the bar. "What can I get you?"

"Just a coffee," she said.

When he returned from the bar with two coffees, one in each hand, she was on her phone. She put it away and smiled up at him. "Is everything OK?"

"Yeah, it's just been a bit of a whirlwind recently."

"The job or us?"

"Both," he explained. "I don't want to slow down, don't get me wrong, but I really like you, Candy. I want to get to know you more."

"I guess we did kind of put the cart before the horse." She winked and offered Jay her hand. "My name is Candy Nichols. I'm twenty-two. I work for West Yorkshire Police as a police constable. I was in foster care as a child, and no, I don't talk about it. I was also in a home. Again, I don't want to talk about it." She smiled at Jay, who was nodding. "I've never been in a serious relationship, which is OK as I'm only twenty-two. I've no kids. I love work. I love life." She took a long drink of coffee. "Your turn."

"I'm Jason 'Jay' Scott. Yes, I'm named after a Power Ranger. And no, don't ask. Please." He grinned. "I also work for West Yorkshire Police as a constable. My parents are wonderful, if not slightly overbearing. Work is hectic and stressful. My boss is tough but actually very nice. We didn't get on at first. It was my fault, I think. My sarge, Luke, is the same. I learn a lot from them." He paused and took a drink of his coffee. It tasted shit. He looked over at the lager and salivated. "I, too, have never been in a serious relationship, though I'm hoping that's going to change soon."

Candy blushed.

"How is work?" she asked.

"It's harder than I ever expected it to be. As I said before, I made the relationship difficult initially. George is a good man. He gave me chance after chance to prove myself, and yet Tashan seems much further ahead of me. I'm worried he will get a promotion before me, yet I've been in the job longer."

"Promotions don't mean everything, Jay," she said, placing her fingers atop his hand and delicately stroking. "If you're happy where you are, then that's enough."

"But I'm not sure I am." He took another sip of coffee and winced. "I'm good at my job. I think I'd make a good detective sergeant. And then we've got Malik, too. He's in his late thirties and is still a detective constable. I don't want to end up like him."

"Why not?"

"Because he's bitter. He's been through God knows how many divorces. He's got kids everywhere."

"Don't you think you're being a bit harsh?"

"Maybe," he said, pulling the Fosters closer.

Another silent void slid between them, and Jay struggled with what to say next. Candy clasped her hands on her knee and stared straight ahead.

He gulped down the pint, set the glass back on the table and wiped his mouth. "I'm sorry."

She furrowed her brows. "What for?"

"For being so awkward and not knowing what to say."

"Jay, can I ask you a question?"

"Go ahead."

"What's it like being a detective?"

"It's tough. But tough in a way that only other detectives know. And then you feel isolated because you can only talk to other detectives about it. But at the same time, most of them are so far up their own arses that they don't want to admit how tough it actually is." He went to take another sip of lager and realised it was empty. "Our team isn't like that, though. It's more..."

"Go on, Jay let it all out."

"The new DCI. He's a prick. And the super has changed. He isn't himself. I know he's avoiding George because he got Atkinson in instead of promoting him. But there's a strange atmosphere."

"Well, I think you're doing great," Candy said. "I see it from the outside. As a PC, I have a different role. You look like you're smashing it to me."

"Thanks, Candy," he said, pulling her in for a cuddle. "You won't believe just how much I needed to hear that."

\* \* \*

"Where's Jay?" George asked Tashan.

DS Mason and DS Williams were clacking away at their laptops in the incident Room. They both stopped and looked at the young DC.

"I don't know, sir," Tashan said.

George furrowed his brows. "He was with you at the pub, right?"

"That's right, sir," Tashan said. "We didn't get much info from the regulars and decided we needed to speak to Nick Creaser again."

"Why's that?" Mason asked.

"He'll be able to tell us what time he picked Flora up and what time she called him, sarge." Tashan paused. "I told Jay I'd take the lead on that because I interviewed Nick last night."

"So why didn't you go interview Nick?" George asked.

Tashan looked down at the floor. "Jay advised it would be better to see Nick in the morning, sir." Then he shrugged. "I thought I'd see him back here, but..."

"It is getting late, boss," Mason said.

"No such thing as late when you're investigating a murder and a suspicious death," George said. He'd have to have a word with the young, blond DC in the morning. Something was bothering him. George could feel it deep down in his bones. "Anyway, I have some news from Gin Creaser's post-mortem."

George thought back to the moment Dr Christian Ross had told him about the foetus.

"Shit," he'd said, and the pathologist had nodded his head.

"I have the foetus over here if you'd like to see it," the pathologist had explained, heading for a different table.

George wasn't sure he wanted to, especially considering his fiancée was pregnant, and stood still. "How far along was she when she died? And is it possible to get DNA from the foetus?" He wondered if they were dealing with a reluctant father brandishing a knife or if Gin Creaser cheated on her husband. His gut told him it was something completely different, and most of the time, he trusted his gut.

"Gin Creaser's baby is over here, Detective." Dr Ross had slowly drawn back the sheet, and George had gasped at the sight of a tiny but fully developed baby curled on its side on the cold, hard steel. Dr Ross had then given George the sex and estimated gestation at the time of death.

Both men had to compose themselves at that information. In all the time George had known the older pathologist, he'd never known him to show any emotion at any of the post-mortems.

"I've carried out a lot of post-mortems in my time, George, but this – this is evil...' The older man had eventually composed himself. "Sometimes I think there's nothing left to surprise me, but then something like this happens." The pathologist shrugged. "There's always one more horror awaiting discovery, I suppose." He turned, picked up the reports and handed them to George. "Please, George, find whoever did this, and throw the book at them," Christian had said, his voice soft and flat.

George watched the various looks of surprise and shock registering on the faces of the other detectives as he explained.

"Shit," Mason said.

"Shit indeed," said George.

"Oh, God. That's... That's awful," said Tashan.

"She was pretty far gone by all accounts, too," George explained.

"We really do need to speak with Nick, don't we?" Tashan asked.

"Yep."

"What are we gonna tell him, sir?"

"The truth, Tashan," George said. "Even if it's fucking awful news, we still need to deliver it. But not yet. We need to wait for the DNA to come back."

"I can't believe it," Mason muttered. "Did the doc say how

## CHAPTER SEVENTEEN

far gone she was?"

"He said something about measurements and how they suggested he was about thirty-two weeks old."

"He?" Mason asked.

George nodded. "He."

"Fuck."

"Fuck indeed."

Yolanda drew in a deep breath. "Wow, that poor woman."

"It makes sense now why her hands were cut to ribbons, though," George said.

"She was protecting her child," Yolanda said.

George nodded before turning to Mason. "I checked the transcript you uploaded and the statement he gave. He made no mention of the pregnancy."

"Gin hadn't told him then, sir?" Tashan asked.

"My thoughts exactly, Detective Constable. It's why we need to hold off talking to him until we get the DNA back from the lab."

"Shit," said Mason.

"Shit indeed."

George's phone began to ring, the shrill tone shattering the silence.

"Hi, George, it's Dr Christian Ross. I have some news for you regarding Lesley Ibbetson's death. I've just finished the post-mortem."

"Evening, Dr Ross," George said. "I've put you on speaker, and the team can all hear you."

"That's fine. They're going to want to know about this, too." He paused, and George could hear the sound of paper being scrunched. "Lesley Ibbetson was murdered."

## Chapter Eighteen

"Murdered how, Dr Ross?" George asked.

"The lab found Fentanyl-laced heroin in the syringe, George," pathologist Christian Ross explained.

"What's that?"

"Fentanyl is a powerful synthetic opioid that is thirty to forty times more potent than heroin. Many dealers sell fentanyl-laced heroin or fentanyl alone under the guise of highly potent heroin because fentanyl is relatively cheap to produce and easy to source."

George turned to Tashan. "Get on the database and see if we have any known dealers who sell fentanyl-laced heroin."

"On it, sir," Tashan said, clacking away on his laptop.

"But why is it murder, Dr Ross? Surely she could have bought the heroin herself."

"Because of the angle of the syringe, George. We did some geometric tests under a microscope, and with a mathematician's help, we understand that Lesley Ibbetson could not have injected herself. It's the bones, you see. They get in the way."

"So somebody injected her?" George asked. He thought about Ida Bruce and the black-cladded figure with the balaclava.

"That's right, son," Christian said. "It's why she died so

quickly." He paused. "I'll send my report over so you can browse it at your leisure, but I thought you'd want to know."

"Thanks so much, Dr Ross," George said before hitting the end call button. Then he turned to the team. "Shit."

"Shit indeed," retorted Luke.

"OK, next steps." He pointed at Tashan. "Keep researching dealers, and let either of us know if you get a hit."

"Will do, sir."

George turned to Luke. "Anything from uniform and house-to-house?"

"Nothing, George," Luke said. "It was late. The doorbell cam footage we have is useless due to the fencing, and the CCTV we've managed to procure is useless. So you can't see anything."

George nodded. "OK. So we have nothing at all."

"That's right."

"Shit."

"Shit indeed."

"This isn't going so well," George said. Luke left to help Tashan with his research, and George racked his brains. Who did he know who was a heroin dealer? Then it clicked. There was Jürgen Schmidt. He and Jay had been part of the raid on one of his suspected warehouses on Thursday night. He was also a notorious loan shark.

He called the two detectives over. "What about Jürgen Schmidt as a suspect?" he asked. "We know he deals with heroin, and we know he is a loan shark." The super was currently heading a task force trying to get evidence to put Schmidt away, but they weren't getting very far.

"I don't think it's his style," Luke said.

"Jay would know," Tashan explained. "When he was a PC,

he dealt with Schmidt's goons a lot."

George thought back to last month. Jay had got them in touch with one of Schmidt's lackeys, Colby Raggett. The DI got up and wrote Colby's name on the Big Board, then turned to his team. "Luke, I want you and Jay to interview Colby tomorrow. OK?"

"Fine with me, boss. I'll text Jay and get him to meet me there early tomorrow."

"Not too early, though," George said. He looked at his watch. "It's getting late as it is, and I need you all energised. Eight in the morning should be early enough. Colby probably doesn't get up until noon."

"Right you are, boss."

\* \* \*

After sitting on his office chair, DI Beaumont pulled out his mobile and called DCI Alistair Atkinson.

"Everything OK, George?" the DCI asked after picking up the mobile.

"Sorry to bother you, sir, but we have some news."

"I wanted to contact you, anyway," the DCI explained. "DS Wood is busy working on a missing person's case, so I'm giving Gin Creaser back to you, OK?"

Whilst he could have done with knowing about it sooner, George took a breath and said, "Not a problem. I was going to ask for it back, anyway."

"How come?"

"Because Dr Ross has just called."

George explained about the fentanyl and how they suspected Jürgen Schmidt. He also explained about the lack of CCTV and the dodgy witness who didn't really know what she saw. "It was dark, but she swore she saw a person wearing full black and a balaclava following Lesley."

"Sounds like one of Schmidt's lackeys to me. They were all dressed that way at the raid."

"So I'm OK to look into Schmidt despite the super's task force?"

"Yes, George, but try to question him only on Gin Creaser and Lesley Ibbetson, OK? Don't mention anything about the raid."

"Of course, sir." *I'm not a fucking idiot...*

\* \* \*

At the knocking noise, George looked up and shouted, "Come in."

Isabella Wood entered the room looking absolutely gorgeous. "You're glowing," he whispered.

"Oh shut up, you flirt," she said.

"I missed you."

"We missed you more." She cradled her tummy.

They hadn't told work just yet. Well, the superiors. George had told Luke, and Wood had confided in one of her best friends. They'd agreed to tell only one person each.

The pair knew they would have to tell people soon, especially as the baby grew. It would mean more time at the station for Isabella rather than being out in the field, but she'd told George that was OK.

The only stipulation she required was that they got married before the baby arrived, which was OK with him. They hadn't set a date just yet, but they both really wanted a summer wedding.

"Had a good day?" he asked. "The DCI told me you're SIO on a missing person's case?"

"Yeah, Freya Bentley," she said.

George recognised the name and said this to Isabella.

"She's a Detective Constable at Laburnum Road, so maybe you've heard her name because of that."

"Must be that, yeah," George said. "Atkinson's given me Gin Creaser back."

"Yeah, he texted me earlier about it. He left early because he wasn't well. I think it's because I had a bit of a to-do with him earlier."

George cocked his brow. "Oh, aye?"

"Yeah, I gave him what for. He was being a prick."

"What else is new?" asked George.

"I think our cases are related."

"How so?" George asked. He took a sip of his coffee. It was cold and bitter. He winced, and Isabella giggled.

"Freya Bentley wanted to join the New Forest Village Book Club. She spoke with Ellie Addiman, the organiser, about joining."

"Interesting," George said. "So we have two members murdered and a suspected member possibly abducted?"

Isabella shrugged. "Maybe."

"I'll leave Ellie and Freya to you, then," George said.

Isabella frowned. "Why?"

"No reason."

"I know you better than that, George." She cocked her brow. "What aren't you telling me?"

"Ellie and I used to be a thing," George explained. "It's why I got Jay to interview the members on Thursday night." He pondered for a moment, trying to figure out how much to share. Finally, his brain told him to share everything, especially considering they would be married soon. "I lost my virginity to her. We went to secondary school together."

"So I gotta watch out for her then?" Wood said, a grin spreading across her face.

"Yeah, maybe. I didn't see Ellie as I was avoiding her purposely, but if she's still good-looking, you may have something to worry about."

She leaned in and kissed him.

"Or maybe not," he said, breathless.

\* \* \*

"Did you interview Balthazar Crane today?" George asked.

"I did, yeah, unfortunately," Wood said.

George grinned. "Jay tells me he's a bit strange."

"He is, but he was cordial enough. He gave us his prints, and we took a DNA swab. He also let us look at his phone. We copied all the data from it, and IT is giving it a once over as we speak."

"How much contact did he have with Gin Creaser?" George asked.

"Not much, to be honest. It was mostly through social media. He has an author Facebook page and a private one. Gin spoke to him on his private one, but they did swap numbers in case his data didn't work. He was quite keen on attending the book club meeting, to tell you the truth."

"You think he's involved?"

Isabella ran a manicured hand through her brunette waves. "I don't think so, no. He's a red herring." She grinned.

"Even though the intro to his newest book is exactly how Gin was murdered?" asked George.

"I thought about that. Crane's going to email me a list of people he gave ARCs to."

"What the hell's an ARC?"

"Advanced Reader Copies, apparently," said Wood. "A month before release, he gives out digital copies for free in exchange for a fair and honest review. He talked my ear off about independent publishing, and I must say, it's rather interesting." She smiled. "Much more interesting than him, anyway." Isabella yawned and rubbed her right eye. "I'll send you the list once I get it, and you can get Tashan or Jay to follow it up." She then winked at her fiancé. "We could have another Blonde Delilah on our hands."

\* \* \*

DI Beaumont and DS Wood left the DI's office and headed for the incident room.

DC Blackburn and DS Mason were clacking away on their keyboards. DS Williams was in the corner, her eyes glued to two monitors.

All three detectives looked up and said hi to Isabella.

The team had worked together for so long and cleared so many cases together that being split up was challenging. George understood, despite hating every minute of it.

The pair sat down, and Wood pulled out Freya's file. She slid across a picture of Freya. "This is Freya Bentley. Twenty-two. She's a bit of a genius, a high-flier. She's a Direct Entry Detective Constable, which tells you everything you need to know about her."

"Her record's clean," George said.

"As a whistle. But Freya's only been a detective for a year."

"She looks really familiar," Tashan explained, picking up Freya's picture. He was passing by on the way to the coffee machine.

"You know her?" George asked.

"I'm not sure. It's the face. I feel like I've seen it recently."

"She's a DC from Laburnum Road, so maybe you did some training together?"

Tashan shrugged. "If it comes to me, I'll let you know."

"You do that, DC Blackburn," Wood said, grinning.

"Any next of kin details in there?" George asked.

"Nope. Well, yes, but it's Freya's friend, Lisa Flack. From what Lisa tells me, they're just good friends, and Lisa helps walk her dog at lunch. But for her to be next of kin is strange, right."

"Right."

They continued routing through the files, and George picked up what looked like a certificate. George read it and then found the report it had initially been attached to. "This explains it," he said.

"Go on," Wood said.

"Freya was in care," George explained. "And this is an adoption certificate."

"So she does have a family, after all?" Wood asked.

"A mum from the look of it." He looked at the address. "A mum who at one point lived in Middleton." George pointed. "Maybe she's still there?"

Wood snatched the document from George's fingers and then grinned at him. "I know where I'm going in the morning."

## Chapter Nineteen

Nick was looking forward to a quiet evening at home after an arduous day. He'd identified Gin that morning and had been to Elland Road to give an official statement and provide his prints and a DNA sample.

Then he'd spoken with Sky, British Gas, and Yorkshire Water to let them know about Gin's death. They'd been nice with him, which he hadn't expected.

He desperately needed a stiff drink and wanted a greasy doner but couldn't afford either.

Flora rushed him as soon as he opened the door to the flat.

"Hiya, love, are you OK?" he asked, seeing the worried look on her face.

"About half an hour before the police detectives arrived, somebody came to the house and threatened me!" Flora sobbed. "I thought it was you. You always forget your bloody key! But when I opened the door, a man pushed his way in."

"Who was it?" he asked. She shrugged. "What did he look like?"

"About your age and stick thin. Skinhead. Lanky with a snake tattoo on his neck. A proper arsehole!"

Nick knew who it was, one of Schmidt's goons, Lanky Jake. He had the money owed to Schmidt upstairs in the bedroom but was going to message him and explain about Gin.

At arm's length, he drew her away from him and looked at her face. "He didn't hurt you, did he?"

"No, but as I said, he forced his way in." She paused. "He said you and Mum owed him money. Is that right?"

Nick shut his eyes, and he paled. He said nothing.

With a shudder in her voice, Flora said, "He said he'll be back soon. And that he will pursue payment in various ways if you fail to provide the money. Those were his words."

Nick's heart raced. "Did he say when?"

"Monday to collect the cash for this week. And because of late payment, the loan has increased by another fifty quid."

"Fucking hell!" The last thing he needed right now was Lanky Jake causing trouble, especially if he got Schmidt involved. He was lucky they still lent money to him after being so terrible at paying it back in the first place. Then again, they probably lent him the money because he was a shite payer, which meant more interest.

He didn't know what to do but was constantly sick of being broke. He needed a job; especially now Gin was gone. But then again, they might start and pay him more Universal Credit now that she was gone. And if Flora stuck around and claimed too, they wouldn't have to give up the flat.

But most of it was Gin's debt anyway, debt accumulated from her first marriage to Flora's dickhead dad. The three credit cards, plus the HSBC loan, took a massive chunk out of their benefits each month. But now that Gin was gone, they wouldn't be his problem, would they?

But he needed time, so he decided to contact Lanky Jake, explain the situation.

When Jake eventually picked up the phone, Nick barked,

"Stay the hell away from my house, you fucking dickhead!"

"Easy, Nicholas, my friend," Jake retorted. "I'll stay away once you pay!" He snorted at his rhyme. "Remember that this isn't my fault, but yours."

"Well, I suggest you stop threatening people. Flora isn't involved."

"Ah, is that what they call that cute piece of ass!"

He explained what had happened to Ginny and how if they gave him a few weeks or even a month, he could give them what he owed in full.

"Whey! Moving on already, son? Wife isn't even buried, and you've moved on to a scantily clad twenty-something."

"Fuck off, Jake!"

"I'm going to pretend you didn't just tell me to fuck off and give you a bit of leeway. I want all the money in two weeks. Every. Fucking. Penny. Otherwise, what happened to your wife will happen to you! It'll make my warning to your squeeze seem like a friendly gesture. Do you understand?"

When Nick said nothing, Jake screamed, "DO YOU FUCKING UNDERSTAND?"

"Did you kill my wife, Jake?" Nick asked.

"Fuck you, you little prick," Jake said. "But take my warning for what it is. Do you understand?"

"I do, Jake, yeah. But please don't involve Flora in this. I'm the one that owes it to you."

Then the line cut and he smashed his fist onto the table.

Flora rushed to his side. "Are you OK?"

"Just angry," was his response. "He could have hurt you, and it would have been all my fault."

She placed a reassuring hand over his and massaged his bruised knuckles. "Hey, I'm good." She gave him a comforting smile. "Maybe I overreacted, and he wasn't that bad after all," she said with a shrug.

He returned the smile, but it was forced. There was no way he could escape this situation.

"I didn't know you and Mum were struggling," Flora said. "Can I help?" She tried to put her arms around him, but Nick put out his elbow to stop her.

"I'll deal with that bastard, OK?"

"I'm just worried he's going to come back when you're out again. I didn't like the way he was looking at me."

You should have heard how he was talking about you, he thought.

He took her in. She was wearing pyjamas, or that's what she would say if he asked her. Nick didn't think a crop top and shorts were suitable pyjamas, but what did he know? He raised his brow. "I mean, look at what you're wearing."

"I wasn't wearing this when he was here," she said, stepping closer. "I put them on for you. Do I look sexy?"

"Stop, Flora."

She shrugged and put her hands on her hips. "Stop what?" She moved closer and began unbuckling Nick's belt.

"This is not the time, Flora," he said.

She slid the leather belt through the loops and dropped the belt to the floor with a sultry grin on her face. She knelt down and was about to undo the buttons on Nick's jeans when she said, "I can't think of a more perfect time. You're stressed. Let me help you."

Nick stood there as she pulled down his jeans. "I told you I didn't want this to happen again, Flora."

"Mum's not here any more."

Nick said, "That's not the point."

"Speaking of Mum," Flora said, "I need your help with something." She pulled down his boxers. "I help you, and you help me, right?"

Ignoring her advances, Nick pulled Flora to her feet and asked, "What help do you need?" He pulled up his boxers and then his jeans.

"If anybody asks, you picked me up from the pub last night."

Nick raised his brow. "Why would I lie?"

Flora pouted. "You're not lying, not really. You are just bending the truth. I walked home, but I know people won't believe that. If you say you picked me up, then it saves hassle." She took a deep breath. "Plus, me and you need to stick together."

"Why's that?"

"Because people think we're involved in Mum's murder."

"What the fuck? How could people think–"

"Imagine what they'd do if they found out about our affair."

"It was a drunken night, Flora," Nick said. "A mistake."

She pouted again. "It wasn't a mistake, Nick." She tried to embrace him, but he held out an arm. "Anyway, I've been thinking."

"Go on."

"What if Lanky Jake actually killed Mum? I heard the threats down the phone, Nick." She took a deep breath and said, "I think we need to tell the police about the loan. And about him. She had rolled up bank notes in her mouth."

"I don't think that's a good idea."

"It's illegal to be a loan shark, not to borrow from one," she retorted.

"But I borrowed the money, not your mum." Then he thought back to the cash in her purse and ran into their bedroom, Flora hot on his tail.

"What are you looking for, Nick?" Flora asked.

"Dosh." He emptied Gin's underwear drawer but found nothing. He pulled the shoe boxes from under their bed but also found nothing. "Your mum had quite a bit of money in her purse when she was found.

"And she was found with money in her mouth," Flora explained. "The detectives think it was a sign."

"Then maybe she has more money?" Nick asked as they met eyes. "Maybe she did take out a loan, too?"

"Maybe, but I gotta go out. I'll see you later maybe," Flora said.

Nick spent the next half an hour searching, and just when he was about to give up, he struck gold! "I fucking knew it!"

# Chapter Twenty

The entirety of George's team was gathered in the incident room. He was about to start the briefing when Detective Superintendent Jim Smith poked his head around the door.

"Just letting you know that DCI Atkinson has rang in to say he needed to take a sick day. So if you need me, DI Beaumont, or any of you, you all know where I am."

The super closed the door and scurried away.

George was glad the DCI had called in sick. It meant he could liaise with DS Wood without the prick interfering.

Standing with the Big Board to his back, he looked at the team. Expectant faces stared back at the DI. They didn't know that he was about to give them a shit-ton of information they already knew and then provide them with a shit-load of questions with no answers.

So he took a deep breath, pointed to the photograph of the first murder victim, and proceeded to outline the facts.

"Thursday. The first victim was discovered at Corinthians Rugby Club in Middleton, hidden in the dark and found by a late-comer member of the book club. From the post-mortem results, we know the victim was pregnant and was stabbed in the stomach repeatedly with a hunting knife. The culprit left the victim's phone and purse behind. Inside the purse was a hundred pounds, and there was another hundred pounds rolled up and stuffed in her mouth." He looked at the expectant faces. "Why would the culprit do that? Is the money a message? And why did the culprit stab the victim's stomach repeatedly? Did the culprit know the victim was pregnant?"

"To exert control over her?" Mason suggested.

"The money is definitely a message," Yolanda said.

Luke looked at Yolanda and nodded. "Nick and Gin were having obvious money problems. He wanted the money back immediately, but we advised him we needed to send it off for testing first."

"Who do people go to when they have money problems?" asked George.

"Family, friends, or the bank?" Jay offered.

"Think outside the box, Jay," Luke said. "Gin was unemployed. And, looking at Gin's friends and her lack of family means she got the money elsewhere."

"A loan shark?"

Luke grinned as George said, "That's what we think. She owed money to a loan shark. Perhaps they didn't pay, and Gin's death was a message."

"To Nick?" Tashan asked.

George shrugged and said, "The killer took a great risk killing Gin Creaser outside the club. What does that mean?"

"It means they know the area well," said Tashan.

"Bingo," said Luke.

"It could also mean they're integrated into the community," Jay offered.

"I agree, DC Scott," George said. "It could well be one of the book club members." The DI looked down at his notes. "According to Dr Ross, no DNA was found under nails, despite her trying to defend herself."

The team nodded at him.

"How important is the pregnancy?" George asked.

"I say very important," Yolanda said.

"I agree," said Mason. "Do we need to look further into Nick? He doesn't exactly have a solid alibi for the night Gin was killed."

"He does, actually," Jay cut in. "I forgot to tell you, but after leaving Tashan at the pub last night, I went to the takeaway Nick ordered from. The delivery driver remembers handing the food over to Nick personally."

"What time was that?" George asked.

Jay showed the DI a picture of the receipt the owner had given him. Then, Jay showed the DI a picture of the GPS timestamp of when the delivery driver had delivered the food.

"This is good work, Jay, but because we don't have an exact time of death, we can't fully rule him out."

"Fair enough, boss."

George turned to Mason. "He didn't mention the pregnancy?"

"Not at all, no. I think Nick would have been more emotional if he knew, too."

George nodded. He understood. He loved the foetus in Isabella's belly so much despite the child not yet being born. He'd be heartbroken if anything happened to it.

"You think Gin Creaser was cheating on Nick, then, boss?" Jay said.

"Yeah, I think so. It's the only thing that makes sense, especially as Dr Ross said the wounds on her hands were defensive as if protecting her stomach."

"Do we think she told anybody, boss?" Jay asked.

"We need to interview Gaynor, Gin's sister. And we could do with visiting Nick and Flora too, considering she is a huge link to Lesley Ibbetson."

"Is that our task today, sir?" Tashan asked.

George nodded. "Yes. But first, we need to discuss Lesley's murder."

"Murder, boss?"

"Yes, murder." George cocked his brow. "If you'd been here last night, then you'd have known that Lesley Ibbetson was murdered."

"Shit."

"Yep, but it means we now have two murdered book club members–"

"And don't forget the missing potential book club member," Luke Mason cut in.

"What potential book club member?"

"Freya Bentley," Tashan said. "She went missing yesterday. Last night, before going home, the DCI issued appeals through social and national media. The same goes for Lesley Ibbetson. So far, though, we got nothing."

"I know that name," said Jay.

"She's a DC who works at Laburnum Road, Jay," George explained.

"She's the hotshot who skipped being in uniform, right?" Jay asked. "Never met her, like."

George nodded. "DS Wood is SIO on that case but will liaise with us if necessary. Meanwhile, we need to concentrate on Lesley and Gin."

Expectant faces stared up at the DI. George took a sip of coffee and continued.

"On to Friday when Lesley Ibbetson's body was found on a

farmer's field opposite the Heritage Village in Middleton. We initially thought it could be an accidental overdose, but now we know, due to Dr Ross' diligence, that Lesley was murdered. The culprit injected fentanyl-laced heroin into Lesley, which would have killed her practically immediately." He paused and took another sip. "We still haven't found any information relating to her supposed boyfriend. What we do know is she had an altercation with her friend, Julia Brown."

"Julia Brown has a solid alibi, right?" asked Mason.

"Correct," said George. "We also found out that Flora Ogram was in the pub that night. She told Jay and Tashan she left before Lesley did and that her stepdad, Nick Creaser, picked her up. We haven't spoken with him yet to clarify that, but we will today." George pointed at the pictures he'd printed from his phone. "I visited Ida Bruce, who is our only witness. She states she saw a person dressed fully in black with a balaclava following Lesley after leaving the pub. Ida has a good vantage, as seen in the photos I took."

The team looked at the images and then nodded. "So I ask you, who do we know who supplies heroin and wears all black?"

"Jürgen Schmidt and his goons," offered Jay.

"My thoughts exactly, DC Scott," George said. "I wanted you and Luke to visit Colby Raggett this morning and interrogate him, but I texted Luke last night because I thought this briefing was necessary."

"So Schmidt is our number one suspect, then?" Mason asked.

"I feel that both murders link heavily to somebody like him, a loan shark slash drug baron. The book club link could be a red herring." George turned to Tashan. "Any luck on the database last night?"

"Just Schmidt, sir," Tashan said.

"Who's going to ask him for his alibis, boss?" Jay asked.

George grinned. "You are!"

"I'm not liking this, boss," Jay said.

"Schmidt's all bark and no bite, Jay," George said.

"I don't mean him, boss. I mean it all. Everything. It's a mess. We have a ton of questions and no answers."

"Be positive, DC Scott," Mason said. "We don't have many answers yet! But, we could find something today and crack both cases."

George closed his eyes and let the stress settle. Jay was right. The investigations weren't going smoothly. The only good thing was that Atkinson wasn't around to witness it. He turned to Luke. "Give out tasks, please, Luke."

"DI Beaumont and DC Blackburn will interview Nick Creaser and, if around, Flora Ogram. DC Scott and I will interview Colby Raggett and then visit Jürgen Schmidt."

"I've got to ask, boss," Jay said, turning to George. "If it is Schmidt, then what's his motive?"

George deliberated over this. "I don't know. It might not be Schmidt; it could be one of his lackeys." George shrugged. "But everything we know seems to be leading to him or the book club, and we need to know why."

George looked around the room at the small team assembled. "Any questions?"

Yolanda stood up. "What am I doing today, sir?"

"What you do best, DS Williams," George said. "Search for more footage and trawl through it."

"I've already spoken with the various bus companies," Yolanda explained. "There wasn't any running late Thursday night, so they won't help with the Ibbetson case, but I have some footage to look through from earlier that Thursday. I'll see if I can spot Gin Creaser and her killer."

"Thanks for that, Yolanda; good thinking. Keep me informed, OK?"

She nodded and headed towards her monitors in the far corner of the incident room.

George spent some more time reviewing all the details; then, with the chatter rising and the detectives raring to go, he sent everyone to work. But a nagging doubt prickled beneath his skin. George was missing something; he was sure of it.

# Chapter Twenty-one

Luke banged on the terraced house's frail, rotting front door, and barking and snarling greeted him. Luke banged again. "Answer the bloody door, Colby; we know you're in there. I saw you peeping out between the curtains." Luke banged again.

The dog stopped barking, and Jay looked up at his boss. But still, there was no answer.

"It took him a while last time, boss," Jay said. He stepped forward and was about to bang on the door when he heard the sound of a lock turning, and the door opened slightly.

Jay listened to the distinctive metal rattle and assumed the security chain was being pulled tight when a spotty face appeared in the gap. "Help you?"

Mason thrust his ID in front of the spotty face. "DS Mason, and you know DC Scott. Let us in; it's pissing it down."

"You're not coming in without a warrant," Colby said. The man had clearly learnt from last time, and Luke wondered who had taught him that valuable lesson.

Luke grinned at the cretin. "You're awfully suspicious, Colby. We're not here to nick you; we just want to talk."

"I'm recording you on my phone, so you can't lie about why you're entering, OK."

Luke grinned again. This one was fake. "No problem, Colby.

Whatever makes you feel safe."

Eventually, the door was opened, and the two detectives were invited into a literal shithole.

Colby didn't blush but said, "I was just about to clean that pile of shit up when you knocked on the door. Give me a minute, yeah?" He pointed towards the living room. "Make yourselves comfortable." He went to move, then added, "But don't fucking steal owt!"

Both detectives entered and attempted to find a pew but decided to stand. The threadbare carpet was covered with empty beer bottles and cider cans.

Luke thought the whole place stunk of cigarette smoke, which was only slightly better than dogshit. Nicotine had yellowed the magnolia walls and turned the white skirting boards into an off-white.

Luke coughed and got a taste of strong alcohol. He turned to find a bottle of vodka open on a coffee table. He shook his head. The whole place was fucking filthy.

Colby eyed the two detectives, then looked around the living room and smiled. He jumped into an armchair facing the TV and sipped from the vodka bottle. He then offered the bottle to both detectives, who shook their heads and held up their hands.

Jay said, "Can't drink on duty, mate."

"What a shit rule, man," Colby said. "Anyway, what the fuck do you both want?"

"We're here to ask you some questions about Ginny Creaser, also known as Gin, and Lesley Ibbetson," Jay explained.

Luke took the Dictaphone from his pocket. "We're going to record this conversation. OK? You can record it on your phone, too, OK?"

Colby nodded his consent, and Jay made the necessary introductions. He was about to get started on his questions when Colby jumped in.

"I'd like to clarify now that I'm not in trouble, right?"

If Jay remembered rightly, Colby had asked the same question before. He confirmed that Colby was not in trouble but added, "Unless you've done something wrong, that is." The spotty man shrugged. "Tell us about Ginny Creaser and Lesley Ibbetson."

"Don't know either of them. Next question."

"Are you sure?" Jay asked.

"I'm sure. Next question."

Jay turned to his boss. "Am I wrong in thinking that Colby didn't really think about the questions I asked, boss, or is it just me."

"Aye, son, I think you're right," DS Mason said. "He didn't even think. That makes me suspicious."

Jay licked his lips. "Me too, boss." He looked at Colby, who shrugged. "Do you know those women?"

Colby said, "I know Lesley, but not Ginny."

"I don't think I believe you; after all, you've already lied to us," Luke added.

"Honest." Colby grinned. "Scout's honour."

Jay turned to his boss. "Colby looks like he's telling us the truth now," he said.

"Aye, OK, Detective Constable."

"Innocent people don't lie, so why did you lie, Colby?" Jay asked.

"I panicked, OK."

Jay knew most people got nervous around authority figures, but Colby was brought up differently. "Why panic?"

"I suffer from anxiety, OK? I'm even on tablets for it." He pointed at Jay. "I fucking told you last time about these pills, you prick."

"I meant no offence, Colby," Jay said. "I just want the truth, OK?"

"OK."

"Where were you between 5 pm and 8 pm last Thursday?"

"Where I always fucking am," Colby said.

"And where's that?"

Colby looked at the detectives, exasperated. "Here, of course. I suffer from chronic anxiety. I haven't been out of the house since you got me sacked from my last job!"

"And what job was that?" asked Luke.

"You know what job that was."

"So you haven't seen Jürgen Schmidt?" Jay asked.

"No comment."

And it starts, thought Luke. "Talk to us, mate. Schmidt won't find out from us."

"No comment."

"Let's talk about Lesley, then," Luke said. It was clear the man wouldn't say a word about Jürgen Schmidt.

"What do you want to know about her?"

"Well, how do you know her for a start?" Luke asked.

"She went to school with my little sister, Larisa." Colby said. "Lesley's a proper smackhead."

"What, and that's it?" Luke asked.

The spotty man shrugged.

"Where did she get her smack from?" asked Jay.

Colby sunk back into the armchair. "I don't know, do I? It wasn't me."

"What wasn't you?" Jay asked.

"The dealer who sold her smack."

"And you promise you're not lying to us."

Colby blinked. "What?"

"I want you to promise us you aren't lying to us," Jay said.

Colby rubbed the stubble on his chin. "OK. I promise."

"Where were you between 11 pm and midnight on Thursday?"

"I'm getting fucking sick of this, detectives," Colby said. "I was here. OK. I haven't left the fucking house! It's like you don't want to listen to me." He stood up and pointed towards the door. "Out! I want you out right now!"

"Who takes your dog for a walk, Colby?" Luke asked as he stood up.

"You what?"

"Answer the question, Colby," Jay demanded, but the man stayed silent.

The two detectives allowed the silence to deafen the spotty man. They knew Colby would crack before they did. It was only a matter of time.

Colby's face tightened, his mouth becoming a thin, narrow slit. "No comment."

Jay grinned. "Kindly provide footage from your doorbell camera, Colby, and we will be on our way." He let gravity take hold.

"What footage?"

"Unbelievable!" Luke roared. "Do we need to take you into the station, Colby?" He stepped closer. "Because we will. And it's not a nice experience. Trust me."

"There's no need for that, Detective Sergeant."

"Tell us what we want to know," Jay said.

"I can't."

Jay asked, "Can't or won't?"

"Both. Either. Does it make a fucking difference?"

"You're damn right it does because Lesley Ibbetson is dead. She was murdered with fentanyl-laced heroin." Luke let the news sink in. "I read your record on the way over." Luke grinned. "Give us the footage, and tell us who walks your dog!"

"If you want the footage, get a fucking warrant," Colby insisted. "And I want you to leave." He picked up his phone. "I'm filming you, remember."

"I don't give a shit!" Luke said. "Two women are dead, Colby! You've admitted to knowing one of them, and considering your record; we have all we need to drag you into the station for at least twenty-four hours." Luke paused. "I'm sympathetic to your disability, which is why I'm interviewing you in the comfort of your own home. But my sympathy is going to run out!"

"I want you both to leave."

"Fine. We'll be back with a warrant, and we'll drag you to the station in a meat van!" Luke threatened.

\* \* \*

"Sorry to show up like this unannounced," George said to Nick Creaser after he'd opened the door to the flat. "I'm Detective Inspector Beaumont, and this is Detective Constable Blackburn. May we come in?"

"I was wondering when the boss would show his face," Nick said, his brow raised.

You could cut the atmosphere with a knife.

"I remember you from school, you know," Nick said to

George.

"I'm quite a bit older than you, aren't I?" George plonked himself down on the three-seater and nodded for Tashan to sit next to him. That left the armchair for Nick, who hovered.

"You were leaving when I started. You were like a god to us young uns. Somebody to look up to. And then you kicked the shit out of me."

George frowned. "Excuse me?"

"You heard. It was my own fault, though."

George exhaled. Adrenaline had started to flow through his body. The tension was still palpable. "Your fault; why?"

"I was a cocky twat back in school. I thought I wa' 'ard. I wanted to be cock o' the school. So taking you down was my only option. But you kicked the fucking shit out of me." He stood up and crossed over to George. "Thank you."

He held out his hand. George ignored it. "Do you know why we're here?" the DI asked, looking up. He felt defenceless and had his fists balled up inside his trench coat pockets.

"To talk about Gin, I presume?"

Tashan nodded. "We're very sorry for your loss."

"Are you?" Nick asked. He looked at George.

"We are, yes. Very sorry for your loss."

"Thank you." Nick thrust a thumb over his shoulder towards the kitchen. "Would you like a drink?"

"No, thank you, Nick, we're swamped," George said. Then he looked at Tashan.

"We're here to ask you some questions about your late wife, if that's OK," Tashan said.

"Go on then."

"But first," George said, receiving a shocked look from his younger colleague, "I want to apologise for how long the forensics is taking on the cash found. Are you struggling, Nick?"

"Who isn't," Nick said. "Cost of living is ridiculous. I can't wait for summer when I can turn the bloody heating off." He swivelled his head. "If Flora weren't 'ere, I wouldn't 'ave it on, but she's no meat on her bones. She needs the 'eating on."

"Is Flora here now?" George asked.

"No, she's out." Nick shrugged. "I don't know where she is. She could be anywhere."

"OK, Mr Creaser, are you ready to answer questions now?"

Nick pointed at Tashan. "You were here last time, right?"

"That's correct, sir."

"Stop calling me sir or Mr Creaser. It's Nick, OK?"

"OK, Nick." Tashan took a deep breath. "Where were you between 11 pm and midnight on Thursday."

"The other day?" Nick asked, and Tashan nodded. "That's the night Gin was murdered, right?" Again, Tashan nodded. "Well, I was here. You know I was here because you interviewed me with that other fella."

"Did you go anywhere after we left?" Tashan asked. It was an open question, one he hoped would trip Nick up.

"I can't remember. My head was such a mess that night." Nick shrugged. "I can't even remember what I did last night. Or even this morning." He paused again. "I mean, what fucking day is it even?"

"OK," Tashan said, making notes. "Did you pick your stepdaughter up in your car at all this past week?"

"As I said above, I can't really remember, mate. It's been a shit time for me, and I don't even know what fucking day of the week it is."

Tashan flipped back in his notebook. Flora had said Nick

picked her up around 'Half-eleven, quarter to twelve.'

The young DC shared a look with George. The plan was to get the alibi question out of the way and then go straight into the difficult questions.

"Were you aware that your late wife was pregnant?"

Silence.

The intense atmosphere dissipated.

George tried to give the man a consoling smile.

Eventually, Nick said, "Ask me that question again, lad."

"Were you aware that your late wife was pregnant?" Tashan asked.

"I was not." He ignored Tashan and looked at George. "Is it... Was it mine?"

"We're currently comparing the DNA swab you provided against the foetus' DNA. I'm so sorry for your loss, Nick."

"Fuck."

George said nothing.

"We'd been trying since the wedding." Tears began falling in large bulbs from his eyes. Then he started shaking. "I'm sorry, I haven't really cried since she died. I guess I was saving it for this."

George nodded at Tashan and then nodded towards the kitchen. The DC got up to get Nick a glass of water.

"She was thirty-two weeks along, Nick," George explained.

"Holy fuck, it's worse than I thought." He wiped his snotty nose on his sleeve. "Girl or boy."

"I'm not sure–"

"Just fucking tell me, mate. It can't get any worse."

It can, George thought. It can get much worse. "A boy."

"Fucking hell, I always wanted a boy."

Tashan gave him the glass of water, which he gulped down

in one. "What the hell did I ever do to deserve this, eh?"

"Last time my colleagues spoke with you, they asked you whether Gin had any enemies. Do you have anything new to share?" George asked.

"No." Then he asked, "Why?"

"Because of the way your late wife was murdered," George explained. "She was stabbed in the stomach. Repeatedly. There's also evidence of defence wounds to the hands as if protecting her stomach from the knife blows." The words were just rolling off George's tongue, despite him cringing at every second. The poor man was going through enough.

"And she was lured there, right? That's what that family liaison person told me."

"Correct."

"So you're saying she was lured there, and then the culprit purposely targeted Gin's stomach?"

"Correct."

"And next you're going to ask me whether she was cheating on me, right?"

"Correct."

## Chapter Twenty-two

Freya Bentley still hadn't come home, nor had she been found.

DS Wood parked outside Constance Bentley's house and quickly checked her phone for emails. Nobody had answered her initial knocks, and it was pissing it down. The initial results on the stain found on Freya's carpet were in, which was surprisingly fast work by the lab. Urine. Human. Not the dog, then. Was it Freya's?

As Isabella was about to enter Freya Bentley's house, she received the dreaded call. A body had been discovered on the wasteland where New Forest Way met Sharp House Road. It wasn't far away from Bentley's house.

She sped out there and, after being allowed through the outer cordon, parked by the kerb. Pausing to gather herself, she gazed around the area. Sharp Lane was right ahead of her, a bustling and hectic road, which they'd also closed off. Wood was already thinking about appealing for dashcam footage and potentially looking at cameras on buses.

After producing her warrant card, the PC guarding the inner cordon signed her in and provided a Tyvek suit, mask, gloves and shoe covers.

The inner cordon was alive with activity as SOCOs set up. Peering through the leafless trees, Isabella could see the SOCOs in their white suits working like a colony of ants. She saw DC Malik talking with CS Manager Lindsey Yardley as she donned her SOC gear.

She headed towards them, her boots sinking in the mud, and then asked, "What have we got?"

Lindsey pointed a little further up the path, where a tent was being hastily erected in an attempt to preserve potential evidence from the rain. Bit late for that, she thought. A line of stepping plates highlighted the way up.

"I want to get closer to see who it is," Wood said, praying it wasn't Freya.

Lindsey led the pair of detectives up the hill, and as they neared the tent, DS Wood's heart began to race. This was the part of her job she enjoyed the least, but she knew she had to see the body for herself and make her initial assessment.

They entered the tent. The body was face down, fully naked, and looked as if it were asleep. She was a brunette, just like Freya Bentley. More and more, Wood was convinced the body was Freya's.

"She wasn't killed here," Lindsey Yardley explained.

Wood looked up at her and nodded. "Because of the lack of blood?" She'd already noticed. "Could it have washed away in the rain, though?"

"Maybe," said Lindsey. "I'm sure it rained during the night, and it's currently throwing it down. Despite that, I'd still expect to see some discolouration of the soil."

"Do you know how she died?"

"Not yet," Lindsey advised.

"Time of death?"

Lindsey said, "She's in rigour. I'd say she's been dead between two and eight hours."

## CHAPTER TWENTY-TWO

It was 9 am now. "So between what, 11 pm and 7 am?"

"It's the best I can give you until Christian arrives."

"Is it Freya Bentley, sarge?" Malik asked.

Wood shrugged.

Despite being unable to see the face, nausea rose up from her stomach and into her throat. She was sure it was Freya Bentley. It was the hair. And the body type. "When can we turn her over."

"Only when I've finished, Sergeant," Yardley said.

Wood took a breath of fresh air to compose herself. "OK, let me know, as I need to take a closer look."

"I've got to wait for Dr Ross," Lindsey explained. Then she asked, "Have you got a photo of the missing woman? Does she have any identifying marks or tattoos?"

"No tattoos that I'm aware of." Wood thought about the photos. "I have two—one of her head and shoulders and one of her wearing her detective clothes. But from what I see, the hair looks similar. Why?"

"If you look from the right-hand side, there's a scar on the lower right-hand side of her abdomen."

"This woman had her appendix out?" Wood asked.

"Exactly."

"I'll check that out. Thank you, Lindsey. Anything else?"

"Nothing yet."

Wood returned to Malik, who was talking to a flustered young woman with a dog.

"There were birds on top of her. They flew off when I got closer." The young woman's body convulsed in a long shiver. "I just wandered over to see what it was. I never expected... you know..." She gulped. "Sorry."

"That's OK; it's always a shock when you find a dead body."

Malik gestured with his hand. "See anyone else around?"

"It's a Saturday and kids play football on that field," she explained and pointed. "It gets pretty busy."

Wood thought it was a blessing in disguise that the body was found by the dog walker rather than by a young child. "Do you know her?" Wood asked.

"The dead woman?" the woman asked, and Wood nodded. "Well, I couldn't see her face, so..."

"Fair enough," Wood said. "We will need a formal statement, fingerprints and a DNA sample."

"I never touched her, though."

"I appreciate that, but it's for elimination purposes."

"I really have to go now," the woman said to Malik. "You have my number. Call me if you need anything else." Then she looked at DS Wood. "I'll come by later tonight. Elland Road?"

Malik answered for his sergeant. "Elland Road, yes. That's fine; thanks so much."

As the woman hurried away towards the outer cordon, Wood raised a brow.

"She stumbled on the body walking her dog."

Wood nodded. "She seemed keen."

"Not my type."

"I didn't know you were into men, DC Malik," Wood said, pleasantly surprised.

He looked angry at that. "I'm not, but she wasn't..."

"She wasn't what?" Wood pushed.

"Just leave it, OK?"

Wood held her hands out, palms facing him. "OK, sure." At the call of her name, Wood looked up. Lindsey was calling across to her. "What is it?"

"There's a black substance around the victim's wrists,"

Lindsey explained.

"What do you think it is?"

"I'd say she was bound with tape. Because it's black, I'd say insulation tape. We might get lucky and be able to lift some fingerprints from the residue.'

"That would be amazing," Wood said. "Why was she dumped here?" she pondered aloud. "Does this place hold some significance for her murderer?"

"No idea, Sergeant," Lindsey said. "But as I explained, it's obvious she wasn't killed here. Instead, someone went to the trouble of transporting her body and leaving it out in the open to be found."

"Why would a person do that?"

"That's why you're a detective, and I'm not," Lindsey said.

"How long's Christian going to be?" Wood asked.

"I don't know, Sergeant."

Once outside the cordon, Wood asked Malik to meet her back at Elland Road. There was no point in staying at the crime scene when she could be back at the station looking through Freya Bentley's medical notes.

At her car, Wood tore off the protective suit and stuffed it into an evidence bag. Then she followed Malik's car back to the station.

* * *

"Gin wasn't cheating on me," Nick said. "I'm sure of it."

George nodded his head. "Did she have access to a second mobile phone?"

"Not that I'm aware of."

"We're going to have to do a search of your home, Nick,"

George advised.

Nick narrowed his eyes. "Why?"

"Whilst we believe you, and what you're saying, that Gin wasn't cheating on you, we need to know for sure."

"Because if she was cheating on me, then that could be who killed her?"

"Exactly," George said. He also thought that Nick could have killed Gin and her baby out of spite if she was cheating on him, but obviously didn't say that aloud. "We've got into her phone, and there's nothing on there to suggest she's cheating on you. But there is one number we don't recognise. The number was messaging her the night she was murdered, asking to meet early at the club." He handed Nick a piece of paper with the number on it. "Do you recognise it?"

Nick shook his head. Then he pulled out his own mobile and looked as if he were typing the number in to call it. It beeped and then disconnected. "It's switched off," Nick said. "And it's not in my contacts." He showed George the phone. "Look."

George took it from him, and whilst Tashan was watching, he scrolled down on the call log. There was no call from Flora on Thursday night. The two detectives shared a knowing look, and Tashan scribbled more notes.

"We could do with speaking to Flora about this, too," George said as he handed the phone back. "Are you sure you don't know where she is?"

"I've no idea, but I'll tell her to contact you when she gets back home, OK?"

"Thanks for that," George said, standing up. They had one more question to ask, and George found by pretending to leave that any shields or barriers that were put up usually fell. Tashan followed suit, pen and pad poised.

They let Nick walk them to the door, but before Mr Creaser opened it and let the pair out, George asked, "Do you know a man named Jürgen Schmidt?"

\* \* \*

DC Scott and DS Mason pulled up on New Lane in Middleton, a few houses down from Jürgen Schmidt's.

They eyed the camera as they walked up the drive and passed the Range Rover parked there.

Mason knocked on the door, and when Schmidt opened it, he said, "Come back with a warrant."

"That obvious?" Mason asked, pulling out his warrant card.

"I was going to say something nasty, but I'm in a bit of a good mood, so I'll just tell you to fuck off instead." He went to shut the door in Luke's face and grinned when the detective sergeant stuck out his foot to keep it open.

"I guess it's lucky for me that I don't need a warrant to ask you a few quick questions, Jürgen, which you know as well as I do is the truth of it all." Mason looked around at the neighbours' houses for twitching curtains. Despite there being none, he nodded at them anyway and then grinned at the man. "Do you want me to ask questions outside or in the comfort of your home?"

"And the quicker we ask our questions, the quicker we leave," Jay added, holding up his warrant card.

Dangerous, dark eyes narrowed at them both. Jürgen Schmidt was a very terrifying man. A very dangerous man. They knew that. The fact that he lived so openly testified to that. Most people knew of Jürgen Schmidt and what he was, though Luke struggled with the German's vocation. What was he, a gangster? A mob boss? Whatever the German was, he was extremely dangerous.

"You've got five minutes," Schmidt eventually said, stepping backwards, keeping his eyes firmly on the two men.

The two detectives nodded and then squeezed inside, careful not to brush against Schmidt. By the door was a baseball bat wedged beneath an expensive-looking alarm system. A monitor showed four images of the front garden. It was clear Schmidt had known about them as soon as they'd passed the threshold.

The sound of scratching and barking came from the detective's right, and Jay shit himself, jumping back at the sounds. Schmidt laughed and shook his head.

"Is this what passes for a detective these days?" he asked, gesturing for the pair to head towards the kitchen directly at the end of the lushly carpeted hallway.

"After you, Mr Schmidt," Luke said. There was no way he was going to lead the way, not with that terrifying bastard behind him. It would be all too easy for Schmidt to smack one of them across the back of the head with that bat.

When they reached the kitchen, Jürgen turned and ordered them to "Sit!" When they both did, Jürgen asked, "What can I help you with?"

## Chapter Twenty-three

DC Malik ambled over to Wood's desk. "Sarge, how are you getting on with Bentley's medical records."

"As usual, I'm waiting." She shrugged. "You know what it's like. Data protection and all that. DSU Smith's getting a warrant signed as we speak. I'm just sending an email to the bus companies, requesting footage from all buses that ran between 11 pm Friday and 7 am Saturday."

"That's a lot of footage, sarge," DC Malik said.

"I know," Isabella said with a grin. "You'll be a very busy man." She paused to let the message sink in. "I've also emailed social and national media appealing for any information and dashcam footage between 11 pm and 7 am."

"There's nothing in her work file about any tattoos or scars," Reza advised, putting the folder on Wood's desk.

"She could have had the operation done as a child." Wood told Malik about the adoption certificate and how she was outside the Bentley house that morning when she got the call about the body. Wood also told him she'd spoken with DSU Jim Smith about a warrant for information from the Adoptions Section in Southport. "According to council tax records, Constance Bentley lives there alone. But I'll go and see her later."

"Maybe she knows about the appendix operation?"

Wood stood up. "Why the hell didn't I think of that?" she asked. "Great thinking."

"You heading there now?" Reza asked.

Isabella looked down at her desk. They had a missing woman, a dead woman, and she had a shitload of paperwork to complete. "It might be better to see Lisa Flack first, see if she knows anything," Wood said.

"Want me to follow this up, sarge? I can give her a call."

"Face-to-face is best. I'll go with you."

* * *

"Do you know a woman named Ginny Creaser?" Luke asked. Jürgen gave him nothing. Not even a flicker of recognition. "No, what about Lesley Ibbetson?" Again, Schmidt gave them nothing. He was good. Too good. "Come on, Jürgen. What about Nick Creaser?" The German still didn't react.

"We know for a fact you know Mr and Mrs Creaser," Jay said. "They're clients of yours, right? You lent them money."

"Just like you lent Paxton Cole money."

"Ah, that's where I fucking know you from," the German said, pointing at Jay. "Where's your little black friend today? Tasha, was it?"

"DC Blackburn is working on a different case," Jay explained.

"Oh, so you're here about a case?" Schmidt asked.

"Don't play games," Luke said. "Everybody has heard about Gin Creaser's murder, even you."

"Well, if her murder is such common knowledge, why are you here?" The German then cocked his head. "Found her killer yet?"

"We think we have, yes," said Jay.

"Then why are you here?" asked Jürgen. And then it clicked. "You think I killed her?" The German started laughing. "I think I said this to you before, but I'll repeat it. If she owed me money, what would I gain by killing her?"

"To send a message to her husband," Luke explained.

Jürgen looked mildly entertained. "That's an excellent motive. But nothing to do with me, OK." He stood up. "If that's all, I'm a very busy man."

"Where were you between 6 pm and 9 pm Thursday?" Luke asked.

There was an awkward silence, and the detective sergeant wondered if Jürgen was considering how best to reply. "I was here, actually. I got home around 6 pm and didn't leave until the next morning."

"Do you have anybody who can corroborate your story?" Luke asked.

Schmidt's jaw clenched, and then he grinned. "A person cannot, but my CCTV can." He pointed towards the front door. "I'll provide you with the footage if you like. It proves I returned around 6 pm and didn't leave until 6 am the next morning." The German looked between both detectives. "I trust that will suffice?"

They knew he wasn't captured at the raid; otherwise, DSU Smith would have said something. "It will. What about your lads?"

"Lads?" He stared straight at Luke. "What, lads?"

"We know you fired Colby Raggett, but I'm sure you have others lining up to take his place. What about one of those."

Schmidt said nothing.

"My boss, Detective Inspector Beaumont, promised to make

your life hell if you didn't help him. I'm going to say the same, Jürgen." Luke paused and stared directly at the German. "You help me, and I help you. OK?"

Schmidt's scowl deepened, and the atmosphere in the kitchen darkened. "I am only responsible for myself, Detective. And I have offered you my alibi. So take it or leave it."

Luke felt defeated. Schmidt was good. Too good. The CCTV footage would exonerate the German from both murders. "Do you have CCTV out back?" Luke asked.

"No, but how do you say it over here?" Schmidt paused. "I have two huge-fuck-off-dogs that patrol my backyard. I do not need CCTV." He licked his lips. "Do you have more questions, or are we done?"

"How much money did the Creasers owe you?" Jay eventually asked.

"I've already answered that question, and if you keep repeating it, I will have no choice but to get my solicitor involved." Schmidt said. Jay looked confused, so the German added, "I did not lend them any money."

"Fine," said Luke. "If you think of anything helpful, call me, yeah?" Luke offered Schmidt his card, but the German made no move to take it. So instead, Luke dropped it onto the kitchen counter. "Make sure you call me Jürgen."

Luke gestured for Jay to lead and turned to leave. "A uniformed officer will be by soon to collect that footage." On the long walk down the hallway, he felt eyes on the back of his head.

He wondered how desperately Schmidt wanted to hurt him.

He also wondered just how much they'd rattled him.

\* \* \*

## CHAPTER TWENTY-THREE

The bell tinkled over Wood's head as she entered Soaps Galore. "This is a nice place," she said to Reza. "I pass this way so often; how have I never noticed it?"

"Hello." Lisa exited from behind the counter and paused when she recognised the detectives. She wore a long, yellow dress and Dr. Martens, her ginger hair piled up on her head.

"Is this about Freya?" Before Wood could say anything, Lisa Flack seemed to deflate. Bulbous tears fell from her eyes. Her breathing became frantic. "Is she dead? She's dead, isn't she?"

"Calm down, Lisa," Malik said. "We don't know; we just have some questions, OK?"

"Is there somewhere we can talk?" Wood prompted.

"I'm—I'm sorry, but I'm on my own here. I have no staff."

"It's important, Lisa."

"I guess I can shut up the shop for a few minutes if you like."

"That'd be great," Isabella said. "We won't keep you long."

It took ages for Lisa to lock up the shop. She was struggling to breathe between the crying and the shaking. And once she was back at the counter, Lisa leaned against it as if she needed propping up.

Eventually, Lisa asked, "How can I help?"

Wood said, "We wanted to get a few more details about your friend."

"OK."

They needed more information on Freya to conclusively identify the body. "Has Freya any distinguishing marks or scars? I didn't see any tattoos, but does she have any she usually covers up?"

Lisa shrugged. "I don't know to be honest. And no tattoos; she hated them. Why are you asking that? Is she—"

"Do you know whether she ever had her appendix out?" Wood interrupted.

Lisa scrunched up her eyebrows, thinking. "Oh, I'm not sure." She paused. "I guess I never asked, and she never volunteered. Why?"

"Has Freya any distinguishing marks or scars?" Wood repeated.

"Is Freya OK?" Lisa asked, ignoring the question again.

"Has Freya any distinguishing marks or scars?" Wood persisted.

Lisa scratched her head. "I don't know about her appendix, but I'm sure I saw a scar when we went swimming. If that's what you mean?"

"On the right of her abdomen?" Wood asked.

Lisa shrugged, then looked down at the floor. "I can't remember, but it was just above her panty line."

Wood turned towards Malik. He acknowledged this information with a slight nod.

Lisa looked from one to the other, her face paling. "You've found her, haven't you?"

"We found the body of a female, but we haven't been able to identify her." Wood wished they'd been able to turn the body, but Lindsey had insisted on waiting for Dr Ross. However, she had little doubt now. Freya Bentley was dead.

"Oh my God," Lisa cried. "That's awful."

"We really need somebody to identify her formally."

A look of horror spread across Lisa's face. "You mean me?" Another bulbous tear fell from her eye. "I don't know if I—"

Malik held up his hands. "Has Freya any family?"

"Not that I know of, no."

Wood wondered why she hadn't mentioned Constance Bentley. Did Lisa really not know? Would Freya really have kept that from her?

"That means you believe this dead woman is Freya, doesn't it?" Lisa said, disrupting Wood's thoughts.

Wood nodded. Lisa was both sharp and persistent; she had to give her that. "We suspect so, but please don't say a word."

"OK," Lisa said. "And I'll do it. I'll do the identification if you think it's important."

"Thank you," Malik said.

"It might be later today or maybe tomorrow. Does that work for you?" Wood said.

Lisa Flack looked around the shop and then at the front door. "I'll make it work." Lisa's eyes clouded over. "I'll be brave."

"We really appreciate you doing this for us, Lisa," Reza said.

"How did she die?"

"We can't divulge that at the moment." Wood couldn't even if she wanted to because she had no idea.

"Where was she found?"

Malik shook his head softly and smiled. "We'll release a statement shortly, so keep an eye out."

"Then you may as well tell me," Lisa said.

Wood nodded at the DC.

"The body of a female was discovered this morning in Middleton just off Sharp Lane."

"Oh my god! How awful."

Wood asked, "Is there anything else you can tell us about Freya that might help?"

"I've already told you everything I know." She paused. "Did you find out who that number belonged to?"

Wood smiled. "I can't divulge that information either. I'm sorry." She took a deep breath. "Where were you between 11 pm last night and 7 am this morning?"

As if someone had dropped a heavy weight on her shoulders, Lisa's body slumped. And her eyes had darkened, which puzzled Wood. "You can't possibly think I killed her?" Lisa said.

"It's just for elimination purposes," Reza explained. "We ask everybody."

"I was at home," she explained. "I didn't open the shop until ten."

"Can anybody corroborate?" Malik asked.

Lisa paled again. Then she shook her head. "No."

Isabella didn't think Lisa had abducted and then murdered Freya Bentley, but she had been wrong before. "Is there anything else you want to add?"

Lisa lowered her eyes, and silence filled the small shop. "If I think of anything, I'll let you know."

"Thanks for your help, Lisa."

Wood turned and made her way to the door with Malik in tow.

"What do you think?" she asked when they got to her car.

"I don't think she's involved," he said.

* * *

Dr Christian Ross, the pathologist, had just arrived back at the morgue from his preliminary examination of the scene when DS Wood reached him on the phone.

"Hello, Isabella. I've managed to take a quick look and figured you'd want some info."

"Thank you. How long has she been dead?"

"The weather has been wet, but not freezing. We also don't

know how long she's been outside. But I'd say six hours, but don't quote me. From visual inspection, I didn't notice any frostbite."

"So between 11 pm last night and 5 am this morning? Or between midnight and 6 am?"

"I'd say the latter, Detective," Dr Ross advised. "I'll send over my initial report."

"Do you know who it is?" Wood asked the pathologist. "Did you get to have a look at her face? I need confirmation that it's Freya Bentley."

"PC Candy Nichols showed me the missing woman's photograph." Dr Ross paused. "I don't know who it is, but it's not Freya Bentley."

## Chapter Twenty-four

"Your Jane Doe's lips were blue, as were her extremities," Dr Ross explained. "That's her hands, fingertips, and toes. Do you know much about cyanosis?"

Wood confirmed she did. George had spoken with her about Lesley Ibbetson.

"Cyanosis happens when there's not enough oxygen in your blood or there's poor blood circulation. In this case, it's peripheral cyanosis."

"What does all this mean, Dr Ross?" Wood asked.

"It means your Jane Doe overdosed on drugs, my dear," Christian explained. "That's the official cause of death. Her mouth and nose were stuffed with powder. I've managed to get samples and have sent them to Calder Park Lab for immediate inspection. You should have the results in the morning."

"So, like Lesley Ibbetson, you think she died because of an overdose?"

"Exactly."

"Murdered?"

"I'm sorry, Isabella, I can't answer that. She could have put the powder in her mouth and nose herself."

"Or somebody could have forced it there," said Wood.

\*\*\*

Nick Creaser stood dumbfounded. "Who?" he finally managed to ask.

"Do you know a man named Jürgen Schmidt?" George repeated.

"The name sounds familiar. Is he a football player? Or a manager?" Nick asked.

"No, he's a loan shark," Tashan explained.

"Why would I know a loan shark?" asked Nick.

"You tell us," said George.

"I don't know any loan sharks."

Plural. Why did Nick say sharks instead of shark, George wondered.

"I'll be frank with you, Nick," George said. "We have access to Gin's bank account." Nick was about to protest when George held up a hand. "Your wife was murdered, and you have separate accounts. So we have every right to access hers. And boy, were we glad we did."

George let the words linger and stared straight at Nick.

"So, what did you find?" Nick eventually asked.

"Debt. And a lot of it." George shrugged. "Perhaps you don't know any loan sharks. Perhaps you don't know Jürgen Schmidt. But we think your wife did." He pulled out a piece of paper from his pocket and unfolded it. George then handed it to Nick. "She deposited five grand in cash."

"Where did she get that money from," Tashan asked.

Nick thought about Lanky Jake and Jürgen Schmidt. He owed them. There was no way he could grass on them. Not now. "I didn't know she had that money," Nick explained. He looked down at the floor and tried to cry, but the tears wouldn't come. He'd never been a good actor but hoped he could fool the detectives. "We're struggling so much, yet she had that much cash. Why didn't she help us?"

"So you didn't know about this money?" George asked.

"No, sorry."

The man didn't convince George, but they had zero proof that either Creaser had loaned from Jürgen Schmidt or one of his lackeys. "Call me if you think of anything, Nick." George turned to leave through the open door, then turned. "I just want you to remember that we're here to help you. OK?"

* * *

Luke and Jay entered the incident room to find George and Tashan in deep discussion.

George turned to his old mentor and his younger colleague. "Did you get much?"

Luke shook his head. "Schmidt has an alibi for Gin Creaser's and Lesley Ibbeston's murders. He practically lauded it over us. Uniform's there now getting the footage, the fucking prick!"

"He's slimy, isn't he?" asked George.

"Aye, son, he is."

"Did you get owt from Colby Raggett?"

"Nothing, boss," Jay confirmed. "He denied knowing Gin and Lesley at first. Then he confirmed knowing Lesley through his younger sister, Larisa. Confirmed that Lesley was, in his own words, a 'proper smackhead'."

"No confirmed alibi, but he doesn't look to have left the house in ages," Said Luke. "He's got crippling social anxiety, apparently. Jay spoke to the super on the way back. Smith's getting a warrant for us so we can access his medical records."

"He also got shifty when we asked him about his dog, boss," Jay said. "He wouldn't confirm who takes it for walks. You know because Colby apparently doesn't leave the house. He wouldn't give us his doorbell cam footage, either. Like Schmidt, it'd prove his innocence, so that sounds dodgy to me."

George nodded his agreement.

"Colby also wouldn't talk to us about Schmidt," said Luke. "No comment this, and no comment that, the bastard."

"All this means that Schmidt has somebody else working for him that we don't know," explained George.

"That was my thinking, too, son," Luke said. "Did you get much from Nick Creaser?"

"No, not really. Nick genuinely seemed upset by the news of the baby. And he was convinced he was the father and that Gin wasn't cheating on him," George explained.

Tashan added, "We also spoke with him about the number texting Gin the night she was murdered. He didn't recognise it. Nick even called it whilst we were there, and then he showed us his call log." The young DC paused to take a sip of his drink. "He wasn't aware of Gin having a second mobile and was against us searching the house."

"Nick also denied knowing Jürgen Schmidt and having taken a loan. He looked shocked when we showed him Gin's bank statement, too, so we got nothing, really," explained George.

"We did get something useful from the visit, sir," Tashan said.

"Oh yeah, it turns out Nick couldn't remember if he picked Flora up the night Lesley was murdered," explained George. Luke's eyes went wide. "There's no proof on his phone of any calls like Flora advised, either."

"So she has no alibi?" Jay asked.

"Correct," said George.

"Did you interview her?" asked Jay.

"Flora wasn't there, unfortunately. But we'll find her soon. I think she's a suspect."

"Really, boss?" Jay asked. "She seemed nice to me. Really down to earth. I didn't get any vibes from her."

DS Wood entered. "I've got some news for you." She shared the information Dr Ross had provided about her Jane Doe and expressed her opinion that this death was probably linked to their cases rather than her own.

George agreed with her. "It's because of the death by drug overdose, isn't it?"

Wood nodded. "She's not on the database, though. PC Nichols used a lantern device."

"Do we have a photo?" George asked.

Wood nodded, pulled out her phone and forwarded Dr Ross' report to the team's shared inbox. The DI saw each team member pull up the email and check the images attached.

Not one detective recognised her.

"OK," George said and turned to Tashan. "DC Blackburn, I want you to look at the missing persons' database and see if anybody has been reported missing recently. Keep me informed."

"Will do, sir."

George turned to Isabella. "Did you get much from house to house?"

"Nothing at all. I've spoken with the bus companies, and DC Malik is going through the footage as we speak. I've also spoken with social and national media who are putting out appeals for information." Isabella took a sip of water. "DNA profile won't be back until tomorrow or even Monday."

"And she might not be on the database, anyway," said George. "We tend to take both prints and DNA."

"My thoughts exactly."

## Chapter Twenty-five

That afternoon, after receiving a message from the Facebook group the night before, the New Forest Village Book Club members met at the Corinthians Rugby Club to discuss Flora's proposition.

"Do the police have any idea what happened to your mum?" Sophie asked, looking at Flora.

"I don't know," Flora replied. "And Lesley dying has made it even more complicated. Is anybody else worried?"

"Gotta be a coincidence, right?" Sophie asked.

"Two members in two days, though," Ellie said. "I can kind of see where Flora is heading. And why she called this meeting." Ellie didn't want to mention Freya Bentley just yet so turned to Flora. "Have they updated you on the case at all?"

"Only that Mum was in contact with somebody who asked her to meet with them here earlier. The police are trying to figure out who the number belongs to," Flora explained.

Rebecca said, "So somebody lured her here and then..." She stopped at the look on Flora's face. "Sorry, love. That was terrible of me."

"It's fine, Bex. I need to get used to people talking to me about my mum that way."

Bex watched as Flora brushed her hand against an eye but

was unsure whether she'd actually seen a tear form.

"That's terrifying, though, love," Sophie said. "Do they have any CCTV?"

"Lots of CCTV," Flora said. "It's blurry, though, as most of it belongs to the council. There were quite a lot of people around, too, so they can't be sure the killer is even in the footage."

"I saw the appeal," Ellie said. "They're wanting people who recognise themselves on the footage to come forward."

"I think it's a waste of time," Flora explained. "People won't want to put themselves forward even if it means they will be excluded from the case."

"She was in contact with that shifty author, wasn't she?" Aurelia asked. Flora nodded. "That opening passage was brutal, love. Maybe it was him?"

"They've spoken with him and released him on bail pending further inquiries," Flora explained. "Or that's what the family liaison told Nick, anyway."

"Got to be somebody close to her then," Aurelia said. "I mean, I've known her for years, and even I don't have her mobile number."

"Which implies that the person who killed her must have known her on a personal level," said Aurelia. "Ooh, we're quite good at this, aren't we?"

"Good at what?" Flora asked.

Anxious not to be outdone by Aurelia, Rebecca said, "Good at this detecting malarky." She handed Flora a notepad and pen from her bag. "Here, write down all the names of people close to yer mam."

Flora frowned but did as Rebecca asked.

"I've got an idea," Sophie said, raising her hand.

Ellie grinned and nodded. "Go on."

"The police should look for people entering and leaving the club. There's only one way in and out. Therefore, the person who enters and leaves around the time of death is the killer."

"Ooh, we are very good at this," Rebecca said, flashing her thumbs at Aurelia and Sophie.

"Do you not think the detectives have considered that?" Flora asked.

Ellie nodded. "DI Beaumont, the man in charge, has a wealth of experience. It's the first thing he'll have done."

"So, we have a killer running around in Middleton?"

"Who knows," Sophie said, "the killer could even be part of this group."

"What the fuck, Soph?" Flora said.

"Look, I watched a movie recently, right, where a masked killer was running around. The group were warned the killer was among them, and they kept ignoring it until they were picked off one by one." Sophie shrugged. "I hate to say it, but first your mum, and then Lesley..." She let the sentence ring out.

"Maybe you're the killer then," Flora said.

"It's not me," Sophie said.

"Not me either," Flora said.

"Nor me," Aurelia added.

Each member shook their head and swore it wasn't them.

"One of us is lying then," Sophie said.

"Not necessarily," Flora explained, sliding the list across the table to Ellie. "These are the people closest to Mum. I've obviously left my name out of it."

Ellie looked at the list and found herself nodding. "Do we give this to the police, or do we investigate ourselves?"

"Wait, you were being serious about investigating?" Flora

asked.

The members began nodding at each other.

"We can't leave a murderer running around Miggy," Sophie eventually said.

"I want to help," said Florence, the landlady of the club. The club hadn't noticed her presence. "I've known Lesley since she was little, and I've known your mum for a long time, too."

Flora nodded at Ellie, who looked down to find Florence's name on there.

Ellie clapped her hands. "Fine, but I think we need to elect a leader," she explained. "The police had distinct ranks when it comes to detectives, with each following orders from above."

"I vote for Ellie," Sophie said.

"Me too," added Rebecca.

"Me three," said Bea and Tasha, almost in sync.

"Sorry, love," Aurelia said to Flora, "but you're too close to the investigation because of your poor mum. I think Ellie should lead, too."

"OK, so Ellie's in charge. She's Detective Inspector. Who is going to be her Detective Sergeant?" Flora asked.

Sophie, Rebecca, Tasha and Bea looked at Aurelia. "Fine," the older woman said. "I guess a woman with experience is necessary, eh?"

"So, the rest of us will be Detective Constables, then?" Flora stated.

The group started talking between themselves, and Ellie looked at Flora, who appeared to be once more on the verge of tears, and her heart softened. Sod it, she thought. The young woman needed answers, and if the police weren't going to give them to her, then they would do what they could.

Plus, if it meant a chance to speak to Detective Beaumont,

then Ellie was up for it.

"OK, here's what we're going to do." She looked at the young woman. "Flora, you and Rebecca go to your house and look for clues." Rebecca opened her mouth to object, but Ellie forestalled her. "We're playing to your strengths here, Bex." They all knew she was a nosey cow. "With your skills and Flora's knowledge of the home, if something's out of place, you two are most likely to notice."

"What exactly are we supposed to be looking for?" asked Rebecca.

Ellie turned to Aurelia, hoping for some help with an answer. Then, realising that Aurelia wasn't listening, she turned to Sophie. Sophie was obsessed with reading crime thrillers and police procedurals. So she knew what to do. "Has your flat been searched?" Sophie asked Flora.

"No," Flora said. "She wasn't murdered at home, so they..." She winced and then closed her eyes.

"It's OK, love," Aurelia said, placing her hand atop Flora's.

"You're looking for notes or pieces of paper, which might shed some light on who your mum was meeting, then. If we figure that out, we could crack the case almost immediately. Wear gloves, though, as the police may search the flat eventually. The police will go mad if they think you've messed anything up."

"Anything else?" Ellie asked.

"Did she have a laptop or a tablet?" Sophie asked.

"She had a phone," Flora said.

"The police will have that, though, right?"

"Right."

"Can you access her email account? Maybe she was in contact with the culprit via text and email."

"I think Nick gave the detectives her login details, so the police will already have looked," Flora explained.

"Doesn't mean we can't give it a once over," Ellie added. "You and Bex OK with that?"

Flora and Rebecca nodded.

"Good, we could also do with looking at the CCTV footage ourselves," Sophie added. She looked at Florence. "You know most people from Miggy, right?"

"I wouldn't say most, but enough, aye."

"You might recognise some of them." Sophie looked at Tasha and Bea. "Can you help Florence with that?" The pair nodded. "Good; I think those three jobs are a priority for now."

Flora looked slightly sick, and Ellie worried for a moment. The poor lass was only twenty-two and had to deal with all this.

"What are you and Aurelia going to do, Ellie?" Flora eventually asked.

Ellie pointed at the list. "I'm going to speak to the people on this list and find out what they know." She couldn't help but grin at the progress they were making. "Shall we meet back here on Monday to discuss what we've found?"

"Sounds good to me," said Sophie. "It's the weekend, so it'll mean we have time to do the three jobs." She looked around at the book club members. "Do we all know what we're doing?"

They all nodded, got up, and left the function room one by one.

\* \* \*

Flora Ogram was shocked to find DC Jason Scott waiting for her outside the rugby club. He was very handsome, and she had a bit of a crush on him. He was goofy but professional. But that's what she liked in a man.

"Are you here to see me, sweetheart?" she flirted.

"I am, actually," Jay said. The DI had been disappointed in Jay's tardiness, so the young DC had decided to take the initiative and see if he could find Flora himself. He'd gotten lucky, though. The landlady of the club, Florence, had been his first call, and she'd confirmed Flora was there as they spoke.

"Oh, I was kidding." She nibbled her lip.

Jay wondered whether it was a nervous tick or an attempt to look sultry.

Either way, Jay thought she looked stunning. "I need to talk to you about Nick and your mum." He pointed to the rugby club and then to his car. "We can talk upstairs, or I can take you down to the station." He paused. "Your choice."

"Can we do it in your car, Detective?" she asked, batting her eyes and grinning.

"This is serious, Flora," Jay said.

"I'm sorry, joking like this is one of my coping mechanisms." Tears began to drip from her eyes slowly. "My mum was murdered, remember."

Jay closed the distance. "I'm so sorry about that," he said. "You could help find her murderer by answering some questions."

"Fine." She pointed upstairs. "I think Florence will let us use the room for a bit."

Jay followed her up the steep stairs, suffocating on her sweet-smelling scent. They turned left and into the smaller room. Florence was cleaning glasses behind the bar. The DC explained the situation, and Florence left them.

"I'm going to record this conversation," Jay said, pulling

out a Dictaphone, "OK?"

"Fire away," Flora said.

Jay wanted to start with small talk and then ramp the questioning up. "Did you have a good book club meeting?"

"Yeah, it was OK. They asked about Mum and the case, and I told them I didn't know much." She paused. "Do you have any updates?"

"We have a few suspects and are interviewing them and collecting evidence. I can't say much."

"Who do you suspect?"

"You know I can't tell you," Jay said. "How long have you known Lesley?"

"All my life. I'm so sad. I miss her so much."

"We can help with all that, you know?" Jay explained.

"I'm sure you can, but I'm better on my own." She coughed and wiped away a stray tear. "Let's stop with the small talk. Start questioning me because I really want to go home, Detective."

"You told me that Nick picked you up the night of Lesley Ibbetson's murder, but that's not true, is it?"

Flora began to cry. "I think Mum borrowed money from some terrible people," she said.

"What money? What people?"

"I don't really know him, but Nick calls him Lanky Jake."

"Lanky Jake?" Jay knew him from his time as a Bobby on the beat. He was sure Jake Cappleman was a good mate of Colby Raggett. "Are you sure they didn't owe money to Jürgen Schmidt?"

"I'm not sure. I didn't know anything about any loans until the other day. Honest." She looked at him with pleading eyes. "But that Jake pushed his way into the flat on Friday and threatened me. I thought it was Nick coming home. He always forgets his bloody keys. When I opened the door, Lanky Jake pushed his way in."

"Can you describe him for me?" Jay wanted to make sure they were looking for the right man because Jay knew for a fact that Jake was a known dealer of heroin and cocaine. The issue was proving it in court.

"Tall and stick thin with a skinhead. A snake tattoo on his neck."

That sounded like a perfect description of Jake, Jay thought. "What did Jake do next?"

"After forcing his way in, he said Nick and my mum owed him a lot of money."

"How much money?" He thought about the £5k deposit they'd found on Gin's bank statement.

With a shudder in her voice, Flora said, "I don't know. He said he'd be back soon, though, and that he'd pursue payment in various ways if Nick failed to provide the money."

Jay nodded his head. Could Jake have killed Gin? He was the violent type. And stuffing Gin's mouth with money certainly seemed like somebody was leaving a message. Was that Jake? "What happened next?"

"Nick called Jake and asked him to leave me alone, but Jake threatened Nick. I'm worried for him if I'm being honest." Then Flora's breathing started to become ragged, and she began to cry again. "What if Jake killed my mum, Jay? And what if Nick's next?"

Jay placed his hand on Flora's. "We'll look for him, OK, and make him answer for his crimes."

## Chapter Twenty-six

Nick received a text message that had him all fired up. Quickly, he washed his pits and face splashed some aftershave on and jogged down the stairs.

"I'm just nipping to the shop," he said to Flora. "Do you need anything, love?"

"No, I'm good," she said, her head buried in her phone.

He shook his head, not surprised. Flora was obsessed with it. She'd just lost her mother, yet she didn't seem affected by it.

At least she wasn't obsessing with him tonight, though. Ever since their drunken one-night stand, he'd been walking on eggshells around her and Gin. It had been a mistake, of course—a huge one. But Gin had become so dull. All she talked about was having a baby, yet the sex had completely dried up. He'd broached the subject, pointing out that to have a baby, sex was required. But she'd dismissed him and had gone out with her friends from the book club.

Flora had been home. They'd opened a bottle of wine and put a film on. Unfortunately, one thing had led to another.

Asda was open, but he preferred the paper shop in the district shopping centre. The rain was pissing down, which would keep lots of people in and would work to his advantage.

Whistling, with a spring in his step, he crossed the ring road at the traffic lights and ducked under the canopy, pulling his jacket tight against the bitter wind.

Halfway along, just past the discount shop, he jumped as a shadow caught his eye.

"Fucking hell!" He laughed and clutched his chest, feeling the hammering of his heart. "You scared the shit out of me."

She laughed. "Yet it was your idea to meet here."

"I've been thinking about you all day." He stepped in close, and suddenly they were in each other's arms, frantically kissing. He ran his hands up and down her back, lingering on her firm ass before squeezing it. "Did I ever tell you how fucking sexy you are?"

She grinned and then nibbled his lip. "Once or twice."

When they finally came apart, Nick's excitement was there for all to see.

"I thought you said we shouldn't do this any more?" she whispered.

Panting, he replied, "I lied. I can't fucking live without you." He looked around. Other than a few teenagers entering the Grille & Co and Caesars takeaways, the place was dead. Iceland and B&M were shut. He pulled her close once more and whispered in her ear, "I'm addicted to you." Nick felt the smile on her face as he kissed her neck beneath her ear. Sometimes she would stop him, but this time she didn't, not even as his hands explored her curves. "Meet you 'round back in two minutes?"

She shook her head, grabbed him by the hand, and they jogged like young lovers past the gym and the shoe shop, then around the back, towards the old entrance to the rugby club. It had grown over since being disused as an entrance and was perfect for what they both wanted.

Soon, she was bent over the barrier, her leggings and thong around her ankles, and he was deep inside her.

And then they drew apart. It was over far too quickly. It never lasted long. In fact, it took longer for them to rearrange their clothes.

"This isn't enough for me," Nick said. "I want to be able to do that to you every night."

She paused before replying. "I want that too," she eventually said. "But you said we'd never do this again."

"I made a mistake." He held her face in his hands and kissed her on the forehead. "I told Flora I was going to the shop, so I can't be too late back."

"Go then," she said.

"I don't want to." He leaned forward to kiss her on the lips. Who knew when he'd get another taste? He was desperate for one last kiss before going back to normality.

"I'm sorry about Gin," she said.

"So am I, but it means we can be together now."

"So that's why you changed your mind?"

It wasn't. He'd been trying to devise a plan to separate from Gin for a while. It was why he'd loaned so much money from Jake. But each estate agent he went to needed references, and some even required confirmation he was working. Which he wasn't.

Before Gin died, he was trapped. But now that she was gone, he was free.

Nick shared his thoughts with her, and she grinned.

Why did she make him feel so good? He knew what they were doing was wrong, but it felt so right. Nick asked, "When can I see you again?"

"Next weekend, maybe? Same time, same place?"

"I'm not sure I can wait that long," Nick said. "I could come to yours?"

"It's too risky."

"True, but it'd be fucking worth it."

She smiled. "I'll text you."

"You'd better."

Nick watched her walk away, happy but disappointed that was all the time they could have together. Seeing her again, and fucking her, wasn't part of the plan, but he'd spent the entire waking moment of the last month thinking about her.

He knew if it came out, people would be hurt. Families would be destroyed. He knew it was wrong. But he found he didn't give a fuck.

Turning, Nick headed towards the paper shop, thinking about her. Then, he turned left, not hearing the footsteps behind him. He was just about to turn the corner when he felt an impact on the back of his head.

Nick saw spots of light as he fell to the wet ground, unable to spread out his hands to catch his fall, his chin hitting the pavement.

As he tried to turn over to see his attacker, he received another blow to his cheek and saw more stars.

Blinking, Nick eventually got up to his knees but received a kick in the ribs. He spat out blood and could barely breathe. "Stop," Nick sputtered. But the blows kept coming, and he curled up into a defensive ball.

Eventually, he heard a voice. "Don't you ever fucking threaten me again, you prick!"

It was Lanky Jake, and with each word he screamed, he punched and kicked Nick until Jake himself was out of breath.

For what felt like a lifetime, Nick stayed there on the wet

ground, curled up, and the blows eventually stopped. He was sure Jake had broken some of his ribs, and one of his teeth felt loose in his mouth. "I'm good for the money, Jake," he eventually said.

When Jake didn't reply, Nick attempted to sit up and winced at the pain. The tall, thin man looked down at him with a sneer. He went to punch Nick again, who flinched, and Jake laughed as he stopped his punch just a couple of inches away. "Fucking pussy!" He shook his head and turned. "Let that be a lesson to you, Nicholas. I'm not the type of person you can fuck with, OK?"

"OK," Nick eventually whispered. Despite the beating, at least he wasn't dead.

Lanky Jake hawked up and then spat at Nick. "I'll see you next week for my money, you prick."

Holding on to his side, Nick staggered his way home, dreading having to explain to Flora. What on earth was he going to tell her? They did live in Miggy, though, so telling her he'd been mugged wouldn't be so unusual. But then, she was shrewd, and Nick didn't think Flora would fall for that after Lanky Jake's earlier visit.

Flora was in the living room when Nick got home. She was still on her phone, so she didn't notice the blood and the bruises as he headed into the bathroom. Then, checking his reflection in the mirror, he saw the full extent of the damage Jake had done to his face.

His eye was already bruising and swelling by the minute. His chin was bleeding from a flap of hard skin that he knew would kill when he eventually had to peel it off.

Flora's jaw dropped when he went into the living room.

"Holy fuck!" she said, putting down her phone but not

standing up. "What the hell happened to you?"

He considered lying still, but her narrowed eyes were already scrutinising him. "Lanky Jake attacked me on the way to the shop," he said.

"I told you, didn't I?" she said. "I fucking told you to go to the police about him!"

"I know, I know," he admitted.

She picked up her phone, and he saw her checking her pockets.

"What are you doing?" he asked.

"Looking for that detective's number. Lanky Jake could have killed Mum. He could have killed Lesley. He could have bloody killed you!"

"Why Lesley? I thought the police were going down the accidental death route. Or do you know something I don't?"

"Lanky Jake's a drug dealer as well as a loan shark. Everybody knows that. His drugs could have killed her, whether intentionally or not!"

Nick winced, feeling more pain in his ribs. He'd have to raid Gin's medicine cabinet for Tramadol so he could sleep tonight. "I'm not letting the police know about Jake," he eventually said. "I shouldn't have phoned him up kicking off. It's my own fault, but hopefully, he'll leave us alone now."

Flora said nothing about her interview with Jay earlier. "So, you have his money, then?"

"You know I do, Flora," Nick said.

"But that's Mum's money. Maybe she owed it to him, too." She thought about the money left inside her mouth. It could have been a message. She told Nick her thoughts.

"I'm not sure, Flora," he said. "Anyway, I'm not telling the police, and that's final!"

"But he's hurt you, Nick." She tried to put her arms around him, but he held out an arm to stop her. He didn't want her smelling perfume on him. Or the smell of sex.

"Do me a favour and just leave it, OK?" Nick asked. "I feel shit enough from taking a beating without having to talk about money."

She tried once more to console him, but he stormed out of the living room and into the bathroom.

Nick locked the door, sat on the loo, and whimpered. How could tonight have gone so wrong? One minute he was having fun, and the next, he was on the floor getting his arse kicked.

And it was all his fault, too.

Just like it always was.

He wondered whether people's lives would be better without him being in them. There would have been no cheating, no lying, and no debt.

Nick took a deep breath.

He pulled out his phone and dialled.

"What do you want, Pussy?" Lanky Jake asked.

"I want Schmidt's number," Nick said.

"Why the fuck would I give you that?"

"Because I could do with earning some money. I can kill two birds with one stone if I work for him, right?"

"I'm not sure if he'll want you working for him after what happened last time, ya dickhead."

Nick winced.

"Will you ask him for me?" Nick eventually said. He didn't want to get into all that shite again, but what choice did he have?

## Chapter Twenty-seven

Jay's head boomed, and his mouth felt like Gandhi's flip-flop. The hangover from hell had taken hold, and Jay couldn't lift his head from the pillow.

What the fuck had he done last night?

He tried to swallow his spit in an attempt to moisturise his throat, but all he could taste was Jägermeister. Jay ran a hand over his face. He'd drank a shit load of Jägerbombs.

The need for water was immeasurable, but he couldn't get up. It was impossible.

He reached for his phone on the bedside table. As his fingers scrabbled around for it, he knocked it to the floor. Leaning over the edge of the bed to look for it, he squinted with one eye; it was too painful to open both. Light streamed in through the window. He'd forgotten to draw the curtains last night.

Once his eye managed to focus, he saw his phone had landed beside a black, lacy bra.

Both his eyes shot open. A black lacy thong then came into focus.

"What the fu–?"

Each word thumped behind his eyes as if a jackhammer was going at his skull. It was agony. He fell back, his delicate head hitting the pillow.

## CHAPTER TWENTY-SEVEN

Jay felt sick. He felt dizzy. He felt horny.

His morning wood was crippling him.

And then he felt a hand snake across his washboard abs.

"And the pretty boy is finally awake," she said.

At the sound of the voice, he turned and stared at the top of a blonde head, face down on the pillow beside him. Slowly she looked up at him and grinned.

She was fucking gorgeous! But it wasn't Candy. She had brown hair.

Fuck!

Jay shook his head, causing more shooting pain.

What had he done? Who had he done?

He recognised her but couldn't remember why.

"Hi," was all he managed.

"You don't remember last night, do you, Jay?" A little smirk curved towards her eyes.

"I do. Absolutely!" He was lying. He hadn't a clue how she came to be in his bed.

She laughed and buried her face in the pillow again. Her outstretched hand reached lower and lower, and gasped at his morning wood. "Was I not enough for you last night, Jay?" she purred.

But Jay couldn't concentrate. His mind was flitting between controlling his nausea and controlling his penis. He didn't want to explode from either end, but the amount of booze he'd obviously consumed last night was making that difficult.

He needed to get up. He desperately needed a piss, a drink of water, and to brush his teeth. But what she was doing felt so good.

After a minute, if it was even that, and he'd exploded over the bedsheet, he got up. "I've got to go to the loo, but I'll be back in a minute or two." He grinned at her. "Don't go anywhere, OK?"

She laughed, the sound music to his ears. "OK." The sheet had slipped down, and he saw her magnificent bare breasts. Her nipples were pierced. A flash of memory appeared in his vision, and he was aware of what he'd done to them last night. What she'd allowed him to do to them.

Stark bollock naked, he looked around for his boxers.

She started laughing again. "Looking for these?" she asked, holding up Jay's underwear. He nodded, but she kept them. "Don't worry," she said. "I saw everything last night."

With a face as crimson as a ruby, he quickly headed for the bathroom, had a piss, flushed the toilets and began to wash.

Looking in the mirror, he looked a right mess. His blond hair was spiking up at all angles, and his skin looked pallid.

Time for a quick shower? No, she might disappear on him. And he owed her an orgasm. Or attempt at one, at least.

All thoughts of Candy were gone now; they were just wholly on the blonde bombshell lying in his bed.

He ran a toothbrush over his teeth, splashed cold water on his cock and balls and rinsed sleep from his eyes. After drying his face and body, he rooted in the cabinet for some lynx. All he could smell was alcohol, sweat and sex, which may have been sexy last night, but was disgusting this morning.

Then, after fiddling with his package to make it look bigger, he returned to the bedroom.

He had only been gone two minutes, but she was up and dressed, tying up her hair.

"I thought I told you to stay where you were?" he asked, grinning.

She was wearing a low-cut top, and he was starting to get a

semi. He wasn't sure where he was getting the stamina from, but if he didn't use it now, he'd never fucking use it!

"Your phone keeps going off," she said. "Looks like you're needed, Detective Scott."

He felt the blood drain from his face. Had she been on his phone? He didn't have a passcode on it. Had she seen the messages from Candy? Did she know he was now a cheater?

Fuck.

"I didn't check your phone if that's what you're thinking. It was vibrating like mad against my bra and thong, so I had to move it to the bed. It says DI Beaumont."

"No, no," he said, holding his palms up. "I wasn't accusing you at all. I'm just hungover, that's all."

"That's no problem at all, Jay," she said, heading towards the door. "I'll see myself out, OK?" She turned and kissed him on the cheek. "It was nice meeting you." Then she paused and held out her hand. "Now, if you could just pay me what you owe, I could get going," she said.

DC Scott paled further. He hadn't been that stupid, had he? He took her in. Tight skirt, low-cut top, stilettos. Lacy bra and thong.

Oh fuck.

Then she moved towards him and lightly jabbed him on the shoulder. "I fucking got you!" she said, transitioning into laughter. "You should have seen the look on your face!"

She continued pissing herself laughing whilst Jay stood there in shock.

Eventually, Jay managed to ask, "Will I see you again?"

She shouldered a handbag she'd picked up from the floor and slipped on a jacket. "You asked me out on a date. It's tonight, remember?"

He winced. "Of course I do. Remind me where and when." He bit his lip. He hoped he looked cute.

"Don't worry. We were both pretty wasted when you asked me." She licked her lips, then paused. "You still want to go out with me, right?"

"Abso-fucking-lutely. Where and when?"

"Tonight, at seven. You're going to pick me up. Don't be late." She winked and moved to the door. "Oh, in case you've forgotten, Jason Scott, the man with two first names, I'm Flora, the girl with the awful second name."

Jay sat on the edge of the bed for a good five minutes after she'd left, his face in his hands, trying to dredge up some memory of the evening. Flashes came and went. After interviewing Flora, he'd offered to take her home, which she'd accepted. He'd given her his card and said, "If you need anything, then contact me."

And that's what she'd done. A couple of hours later, she'd called Jay up, inviting him out for a drink. And like an idiot, he'd accepted.

They'd gone to Westy's Bar in Morley first, then Eighteen90, and then the Tipsy Cow. There was a lot of dancing and a lot of drinking. Too much drinking. Then they'd got a pizza from up the road from the takeaway next to the vets.

Fuck. He daredn't check his bank account.

The state of his bedroom, his sheets in particular, and the snippets he could remember told him there was yet more to remember, but he needed to check his phone and get to work.

What time is it anyway? he questioned, holding his head and dragging the phone from the table. "Oh fuck!"

He had over twenty missed calls and five text messages.

He was definitely in the shit, especially as one of those five

## CHAPTER TWENTY-SEVEN

messages was from Candy Nichols.

'I thought we were meeting up tonight?' The message had started. 'Oh well, I guess I'll see you at the station tomorrow.'

Jay lay back down on the bed, made his pillow comfortable and closed his eyes.

Flora fucking Ogram. Fuck. Not only had he shagged a witness, but he'd cheated on Candy.

Fuck, fuck, fuck!

\* \* \*

"Look what the cat dragged in. Good of you to join us, Jay, for part of the day at least," George said when Jay entered the incident room.

"Sorry, boss," he said. "My phone was on silent."

George turned to Tashan, Luke, Yolanda and Isabella and said, "Give me a minute alone with DC Scott, please."

One by one, the detectives left the room.

Jay knew what was coming.

"You've been late for work three days in a row. I understand you're young, but we're in the middle of a double murder case, Jay." George paused. "Please don't continue in that vein; otherwise, it will end up outside my control, and you may well be suspended."

"Suspended? That's so unfair, boss."

"I don't make the rules, Jay." George shook his head. "It's a good job you're dealing with me, not the DCI. You're lucky he's still off sick. But I am disappointed in you. You're better than this, Jay."

"Sure, boss, whatever you say."

George watched his shoulders drop and his head droop as he

walked to a desk in the corner, shaking his head. He could see in the young man's eyes how disappointed he was in himself, which was enough for now. But the DC couldn't keep continuing in this vein.

The DI headed for the incident room door and was about to usher the rest of the team back in when he heard Jay shout, "Fucking hell!"

Jay had drawn out his chair too quickly, the wheels catching on the desk's leg, causing a folder filled with sheets of paper to crash on the floor and spew out its contents.

* * *

Nothing had yet come in overnight, which was disappointing. They desperately needed to identify the Jane Doe. Waiting for forensics and the lab was always tricky because of how long the jobs took. George knew it wasn't their fault, of course. It wasn't as if they were going slow on purpose; it was just how long the jobs took.

It still frustrated George, though.

Luke stood up and gave out tasks. The appeal for dashcam footage for the death of their Jane Doe had resulted in tons of footage. He was going to work with Tashan and Yolanda to syphon through them. DS Wood was still looking into the missing Freya Bentley. Jay was told to keep checking the missing persons' database, and George was going to speak with their press officer to circulate the image of their Jane Doe on social media.

But before the detectives left the incident room to get on with their jobs, Jay stood up. "I have an update, actually. It's quite important."

## CHAPTER TWENTY-SEVEN

George frowned. "What update?"

"Last night, I found Flora Ogram and interviewed her." He pulled out his Dictaphone. "I recorded it."

George headed towards the young DC and clapped him on the shoulder. After bollocking him this morning, Jay probably needed it. "Nice one. Good job."

Tashan hooked it up to the whiteboard speakers, and they listened to the interview.

After it had finished, George felt conflicted. They'd found out about Jake Cappleman, and George immediately put out a BOLO, a 'Be On the Look Out for' which was the warning flag used to describe when a suspect is circulated on the Police National Computer (PNC) as wanted. Still, at the same time, Jay hadn't insisted on her answering the question of who picked her up the night Lesley Ibbetson was murdered.

George was about to say something to Jay when Isabella nudged him. She held up her mobile and passed it to him. It was an email from Calder Park Labs. They'd managed to identify their Jane Doe because she was on the DNA Database.

They'd also managed to identify what had killed her. Fentanyl-laced cocaine that had been stuffed inside her mouth and nose.

The DI stood up and called his team together. "Listen up. We have an ID on our IC1 Jane Doe." He paused and looked at their expectant faces. "It's a woman named Larisa Raggett."

# Chapter Twenty-eight

"Missing persons' report." Tashan tapped his pen against the desk. "It was filed late last night, so it wasn't uploaded until just now."

George read quickly. "Larisa Raggett, aged twenty-three. Possibly missing since Friday, according to her mother, though only now being reported. I wonder if—"

"She's quite clearly our Jane Doe," Jay cut in.

George raised his brow. "I wonder if she's related to Colby Raggett." He eyed Jay. "Do you know her?"

"I knew he had a sister, but I don't think she's known to us. I also don't know her personally, if that's what you meant."

The DI turned to Tashan. "Give me the address, and I'll talk to the mother. Where's DS Wood?"

"I'm here, George."

Isabella appeared with hot drinks that were clearly not from the station. George's eyes lit up. He'd bloody missed working with her.

George turned to Jay. "I want everything we know about Jake Cappleman on my desk by the time I return, OK?"

"OK, boss."

\* \* \*

## CHAPTER TWENTY-EIGHT

George was familiar with Acre Road. It was a rough part of Middleton with a reputation to match. Though despite that, George had never really had many issues. He'd even had a couple of mates who'd been brought up there.

The Raggett house stood in the middle of a terraced row opposite the church, brightly painted. It stood out from its neighbours, who were probably once cream in colour, and now a weather-beaten brown.

The curtains were closed.

George pushed the rusted gate inward. There was dogshit littered on the ground.

"This place is a bit of a mess," Wood said.

George rang the doorbell.

Isabella had noticed the door was slightly ajar. Tentatively she pushed it inwards, then said, "Hello? Ms Raggett?"

Nothing.

Grey lino covered the floor, faded where people had walked over it. The stairs were to the left, covered with a brown carpet, the bannister littered with coats and jackets of all shapes and sizes. A doorway Wood assumed was the living room was to the right.

"Hello? Mrs Raggett?" Wood repeated.

George entered behind her. Both then heard a cough come from the door to their right. The DI knocked and then entered.

"Mrs Raggett? I'm Detective Inspector Beaumont, and this is Detective Sergeant Wood. Can we have a word, please?" George flashed his warrant card.

The woman sitting on the ancient sofa nodded and, with a cigarette lodged between nicotine-stained fingers, beckoned for them to sit down.

On the short drive over, George had tried to imagine what

type of mother Colby Raggett had. Now the answer sat in front of him.

Clearing jackets and coats from a chair, George sat, glancing at his surroundings. Wood grimaced and remained standing.

Behind Ms Raggett was the kitchen. From his vantage, George saw the fluorescent tube flickering overhead. Flies drifted around as if drunk. Then there was the awful smell of rotting vegetables. George assumed it was coming from the dishes piled high and caked in dried food.

"You're here about Larisa, I assume?" Wood looked perplexed as Mrs Raggett poured a liberal amount of vodka into a mug. Then, without adding any mixer, she took a large gulp, burped, and grinned. The shake in her hand was clearly visible when she put down the mug.

"You reported your daughter's disappearance last night." George breathed through his mouth. "Can you fill me in on the details, Mrs Raggett?"

"Call me Elaine, love. And details? What details?" Her words slurred into each other.

"When did you last see Larisa?"

"God knows." She burped again. Or at least George hoped it was a burp. He wasn't looking at her.

"But it's not the first time the ungrateful little bitch has run away."

"Why would Larisa want to run away?" asked Wood. She was struggling to remain focused on Elaine Raggett because her eyes were constantly drawn to the chaos surrounding them.

On the table in front of them was an ashtray brimming with cigarette butts. The floor was littered with empty cans and bottles. In front of Elaine was a bowl with congealed beans stuck to the rim. She remembered the way George had

## CHAPTER TWENTY-EIGHT

described Colby's house, and she guessed the mother was exactly the same as the son.

Wood hoped they'd find Larisa's killer quickly, so they wouldn't ever need to enter this hovel again. She was sure he could hear rustling coming from the kitchen. Wood shivered at the thought.

"She's never been away this long before," Elaine said, lighting a cigarette. She tossed the old one into the bowl. "Sometimes she stays with friends." Elaine shrugged. "Larisa tells me anywhere is better than here." She gestured with her hand towards the door, dropping ash everywhere.

"When exactly did you last see her?" George felt his patience waning.

"Friday morning. She went to college. She's trying to better herself. I told her it was in her genes to fail, but she didn't fucking listen. Education is a waste of money if you ask me."

But alcohol and smoking weren't a waste of money? George wanted to argue with the woman, but she was clearly too drunk to care. It was like pulling teeth.

"Today is Sunday," George explained. "Why wait until late last night to report it?"

Elaine lowered her eyes, looking down at her shaking hands. "Got to wait twenty-four hours, right?"

"That's a misconception!" It always pissed George off when that was their excuse. This isn't a film; this is real life! "There's no such thing as waiting for twenty-four hours, Mrs Raggett," George explained. "You should have called us immediately."

Elaine ignored George. She took another gulp. He watched her greasy hair fall over her eyes as she bent over for the mug.

"Did you even ring Larisa?" Wood snapped. "I assume she

has a mobile phone?"

Ignoring Wood this time, Elaine tapped her cigarette in the same bowl as before and sparked up yet another.

Then she picked up the mug and drained the contents. "I'm an alcoholic," she confessed. "That's not against the law, is it?" Elaine went to take another sip and was disappointed when she found it was empty. With a shaky hand, she returned it to the table. Then she looked at George and said, "Pass us that bottle, love."

George ignored her and repeated Wood's question. "Did you call Larisa?"

"I might be a drunk, but I'm still her mum. I've been ringing her every hour since putting in that report last night." She shrugged. "Her phone's dead. So I don't know where she is."

"I'm sorry to say that your daughter is dead," George said. "We are very sorry for your loss."

George had expected lots of tears. There were none. He wondered why.

"Can you pass me my voddy now?"

George still ignored her request. "I've just told you about your daughter's death, and all you want is a drink?" He narrowed his brows. "Don't you want to know how? Or where she was found?"

Elaine's eyes shifted upwards through the haze of cigarette smoke. "Yes, but I need voddy to get through it, OK."

George handed it over, watching as she spilt vodka all over the table. He shut his eyes and took a deep breath through his mouth. He could taste the alcohol and nicotine. He grimaced. When he opened his eyes, Wood was also pulling a face.

"Tell me what I need to know," Elaine eventually said.

"She was found on some wasteland just off Sharp Lane,"

Wood explained. "We believe she was murdered."

"How."

"Fentanyl-laced cocaine had been stuffed inside her mouth and nose."

"Would she have suffered?" Elaine asked.

"No."

"Good."

"Did Larisa take drugs?"

"I've no fucking idea, love," Elaine said. "Ask me another."

"You honestly don't know?" George asked.

"I hoped she was on the straight and narrow, unlike me and her brother," Elaine said. Then she shrugged. "I guess she was as bad as us two." She stabbed her cigarette into the bowl. "Little bitch was always up on her high horse, judging us. I always told her addiction was a disease."

Fed up with the verbal diarrhoea, George said, "I want to see her room."

"Crack on, love," Elaine said. "Her door says 'Keep Out'."

"Does she have a boyfriend?" Wood asked as George headed into the hallway.

"Fucked if I know, love."

\* \* \*

Unlike the rest of the house, Larisa's room was relatively clean and tidy. The only issue was the clothes that littered her floor. Various bra and knicker sets of different styles and colours had been thrown about, and George wondered whether Larisa had been heading out on a date.

Wood pointed with a gloved hand to the outfits on the bed. "Looks like she was going out on the lash," she said.

George, his hands also gloved, pointed at the floor. "I thought the same."

"It doesn't seem like she was running away, does it?" Wood asked.

"Nope." He looked at the dressing table overflowing with perfume bottles, makeup, and every shade of eyeshadow and eyeliner. "Is that a normal amount of makeup?" George asked.

"Maybe for a twenty-three-year-old."

Wood looked around the room some more. Jackets hung from the back of the door. A pile of jeans was bundled up in the corner of the wardrobe. Boots and shoes were on the floor next to them. Dresses and other tops and bottoms were hung up on hangers.

She couldn't see anything unusual.

"I think Larisa worked for KFC," George said. Wood ambled over, and George pointed at the overflowing wash basket.

"Looks like it. I'll ask Elaine which one Larisa worked at on our way out."

Fed up and having enough of the house, George turned on his heel and knocked a stack of paperbacks hidden under the bed. Unfortunately, the shoe covers he wore tended to make his movements clunkier than he wanted.

They were all by Balthazar Crane. A bookmark was sticking out of one of them.

To Larisa, I'm so thrilled you enjoy my novels.

I, too, enjoy reading about the place I grew up in.

I'll send you an ARC of my latest novel. I hope to see you at the New Forest Village Book Club soon.

BC

After placing the bookmark in an evidence bag, George turned to Wood. "I had no idea she was a member."

Wood shrugged.

"Shit, that means I'll have to speak with Ellie Addiman," George said. He wanted to know if Ellie knew who else received these Advanced Reader Copies.

"You make sure you let me know when you're going to see her, as I'll accompany you," Isabella said with mischief in her eyes.

George shook his head and laughed.

\* \* \*

DS Wood begrudgingly nudged Elaine Raggett.

"Wha'? What d'ya want?" Elaine shook her head and then squinted at the detective. "Oh. It's you. Fuck me, are you still here?"

"Which KFC did Larisa work at?"

Elaine sat up straight, looking from George to Wood. "Why'd you want to know?"

"To see if work knows anything to help us find her killer".

"The one in Hunslet near the Morrisons."

"Thank you," said Wood.

"Do you know Balthazar Crane?"

Elaine started pissing herself laughing. "What a fucking name!" She continued until George cleared his throat. "Do I fuck."

"And where's Elaine's dad?"

"Fucking dead, I should think."

"We really need to talk to her friends," Wood added.

"What fucking friends?" Elaine started laughing some more. "She hasn't had any bleeding mates since she had imaginary ones as a kid!"

"Be serious, Mrs Raggett. Do you have any names for us?"

"Just some dickhead lad from KFC. Ahmed, I think. Fucking Paki! I told her not to bring him 'ere."

George winced at the racial slur, but Wood looked furious. "Did your daughter ever have her appendix out?" she asked.

"Yep."

"Do you want me to assign a family liaison officer to stay with you?" George asked. "You've just found out your daughter has been murdered."

"I'm fine on my own." Elaine sparked up another cigarette and then switched the TV on.

Shutting the door behind them, George breathed in the fresh, Miggy air. He was glad she'd said no to an FLO. They'd probably have sent poor Cathy, and nobody deserved to spend any time in that shithole!

# Chapter Twenty-nine

Pulling up at Elland Road, George sighed as Mia's name flashed up on his phone.

Wood noticed him physically deflate, kissed him on the cheek and said she'd meet him in the incident room.

He took a deep breath, gritted his teeth and answered.

"Ah, he answers," Mia snapped at him. "I thought you were ignoring me."

"Hi, Mia. I'm working on a murder case. Are you OK?"

"Are you still having Jack tonight?"

"I'm sorry I—"

"Work getting in the way again, George?"

She knew exactly which buttons to press and when to press them.

"It's my job, Mia," he said, trying to keep the anger that flared through him from lacing his tone. "I'm SIO. You know what my job entails. Jack will understand."

"But I have a date tonight."

"I'll pay for a sitter," George said. "Or I can have my mum come over."

Since finding out about Isabella's pregnancy, George and his mother had started meeting regularly. Of course, he hadn't told her yet, but she'd seen Jack. He figured life was too short, and in truth, she really seemed like she'd changed.

"Don't you worry, George Beaumont, I'll cancel my date because you can't keep your promises!" Mia screamed.

George took a deep breath to force away the venom building in his voice. "That's your choice, Mia. I've offered you two alternatives."

"It's a good job that Jack's not old enough to remember you are cancelling on him," Mia retorted.

Mia always used that line on him. She was being a bitch, and she knew it, but George was used to it by now. Biting back would only make Mia more difficult, most likely ignoring her phone as George attempted to make plans with their son.

So he said nothing.

"As you said, you're busy, so I'm going. Ring me when you're not so busy, yeah? Jack misses his father." And with that, the line went dead.

George stared down at the black screen of his mobile and forced himself to take slow, deep, calming breaths. When he was calm, he clicked the screen of his phone on, and a picture of him, Isabella and Jack lit up his lock screen. They'd taken it in Bridlington earlier in the year.

Isabella would have been pregnant then, too.

George smiled. Those three were his world, and he loved them more than anything.

*　*　*

Jay was in two minds about answering the call flashing on his phone screen. She was a witness. And he was seeing Candy, wasn't he?

But he pressed the green button, anyway.

## CHAPTER TWENTY-NINE

"How's the head?" Her voice was soft, almost lyrical. It made his stomach flutter.

"Hi, Flora."

"Busy day?" she asked. "Your head OK?"

"Busy, yes, head OK, no."

"I heard a woman is missing; is that right? And a body was found near Sharp Lane?"

Jay wondered whether she was calling him for him or because of his job. He paused for a moment. Did he still suspect her? He wasn't sure. "I can't comment on either, Flora. Sorry." He'd get sacked if he told her about the body's identity, or what they'd just learned about Freya Bentley.

"That's OK; I was just interested in your job," she laughed. "I was calling just to check up on you and to make sure you're still on for tonight."

"The cases are going well, so I should be able to get off at a reasonable hour," Jay explained. The boss had taken Jay aside earlier and given him a bollocking. He'd deserved it and just kept apologising. He'd never make sergeant with his current attitude. George hadn't even needed to say that because Jay already knew.

He only had to look at fucking Reza Malik to see what he could become.

"That's great, but I think you should pick me up at eight instead. That cool?"

"That would be better, actually," he said. It would give him time to wash his sheets and give his place a vac. It was a proper shithole. "I'm shattered. How are you?"

"Yeah, I'm OK, considering," Flora said.

In all the commotion of the morning, he'd forgotten her mother had been recently murdered. It hadn't even crossed his mind. What a selfish prick. "Well, I'm here if you need me."

"How's the case going? Any closer to finding my mum's killer?"

Jay winced. "I'm not supposed to talk to anybody about it." Had they assigned an FLO? He searched his memory. They had. Cathy Hoskins. "Speak to the family liaison."

"OK"

She sounded disappointed, and Jay hated that he'd disappointed her. "We're making good progress, Flora. We're following up on leads left, right, and centre, OK? Plus, we have a CCTV expert who is amazing. She might end up breaking the case."

"OK, that's good. I need to tell you something."

"What is it?" asked Jay. Then he added, "I'm sorry I can't tell you anything you don't already know."

"That Lanky Jake guy, he attacked Nick last night."

"What?"

"On the way back from the shop. But Jay, Nick told me not to tell you, so please don't do anything about it."

"I can't promise that, Flora," Jay said.

"But Nick will be really upset with me."

"I'll try and keep your name out of it." Jay took a deep breath. "We're so busy."

"But I'm still seeing you tonight?"

"Wouldn't miss it," he said. "I think it'll just be coffee for me." Then he thought about last night and what the alcohol had done to them both. He really wanted a repeat of what he could remember. And more. "I could probably be persuaded, though. I'm a glutton for punishment."

Flora scoffed. "Meeting me is punishment, Jay?"

"Oh, for fu–"

"I'm only kidding, Jay. You know, you take everything so seriously."

"It's the job, I'm afraid."

"True, I suppose." She paused. "So you'll pick me up tonight?"

"I will. See you soon."

"Why don't you text me when you finish work, and then if we can meet up earlier, we will?"

"I will." He paused, his heart racing. "Oh, and Flora, thanks for calling. You've made my shitty day a whole lot better."

He killed the call before he could ruin anything by being mushy, then racked his brains. George had already put him on a warning. There was no nine to five when working significant cases, but he was already thinking about excuses he could use to get out of work early so he could clean up his shithole of a house.

Jay put his head in his hands. Shit. He hadn't asked her for her alibi again. The DI was going to kill him.

Everything he did was stressing him out. It was so typical that he'd meet somebody like Flora when he was needed in a murder investigation. George had told him he 'needed all hands on deck' and that 'long hours meant long hours'.

The DI had been very disappointed. Jay could tell by both his body language and the tone of his voice.

But this was the first time in ages that he'd felt good about someone. About himself. He really liked Candy, but there was something about Flora.

Something enticing. Exciting. Sexy and alluring.

He thought he was addicted to Candy, but Flora was something else.

All Jay did as he entered the station was think about the curve of Flora's breasts, his brain struggling to come up with excuses to leave early.

Until then, he would keep his head down and work hard. That way, George couldn't possibly get mad at him.

Could he?

* * *

George parked the car outside a brightly painted house with a modern navy-blue door sporting golden accessories. The garden could do with better maintenance, but then it was still winter.

The door was opened by a thin woman, who stood tall on the step, her brown hair flowing down her front, turning reddish with the sun.

"How can I help you?" she asked once George had made their introductions and shown their warrant cards.

"Is Freya here?"

"Freya? No." The woman narrowed her eyes. "She would be at her own home. She doesn't live here."

George figured the woman was in her fifties, towards the younger end, rather than the older end. He couldn't place her accent, and he was usually good at that. "We know she doesn't live here, but she hasn't been home for a few days."

"What. Why wasn't I told?"

Isabella stepped forward. "I was here yesterday to speak with you, but nobody answered the door," she explained.

"I was at work. Why didn't you come later?"

"We're here now," explained George. "Do you know where Freya is?"

"Well, she's a police officer, so I expect she's at work." Constance shook her head. "You don't exactly have set hours, do you?"

"When did you last see your daughter?"

Constance's face paled. "Is she in trouble?"

"Not that I'm aware of. But as I said, Freya's missing. She hasn't been at work since Thursday."

"And I'm only finding out about this now."

On seeing the look of horror falling across Constance's face, Wood added, "She's twenty-two."

"Who has her mutt?"

"A friend, Lisa Flack, has him." George looked around and saw neighbours watching. "Can we come in?"

## Chapter Thirty

"I haven't seen her for over a week," Constance Bentley explained, ushering them into her living room. "She doesn't call that often. Her work takes up all her time."

George glanced at Wood, who smiled back. If anybody understood how hard a detective had to work, they did.

A feeling of claustrophobia engulfed George. The place was extremely overcrowded. Every available surface was covered with something. It looked as if Constance Bentley was a hoarder.

Suddenly, a pot of tea and three mugs appeared on the table, with milk in a carton and sugar in a white bowl.

"Do you know of anybody who could tell us where Freya could be?" Wood asked. "It's important."

"Why is it important?" Constance asked as she slowly sipped her tea.

"I can't tell you why," Wood explained.

With her hand shaking, Constance put down the mug. "So I have to help you without knowing any of the details?"

"Unfortunately, yes," George conceded. "Other than Lisa, does she have any other friends?"

"Freya is an only child. She found it difficult to make friends, and when she did, she found it hard to hold on to the few she had. Because of this, she sought comfort in imaginary friends."

George scratched his chin, perplexed by this information. From reading Freya's record, he got the impression she was a confident and friendly person who was well-liked by her peers. But, then again, Isabella told him she didn't socialise outside of work. "Can you think of anybody at all?" George asked. "Any partners?"

Constance was silent for a moment. "Sorry, no."

"Did she have any enemies?"

"She's a police detective; I'm sure she has many enemies. Have you spoken with her boss?"

Wood nodded. "What else can you tell me about her?"

"I think her issues stem from the fact that I adopted her."

George had waited for Constance to volunteer the information.

"What information can you give us regarding the adoption?" he asked.

"Not much, to be honest." Constance looked tired. "Her biological mother abandoned her at the gates of the Springfield Children's home on the A654."

George knew the place. It was a three-storey Victorian building that was rotting, just set back from the road. He was sure it had shut down because of reports of child abuse. He'd have to do more research.

"Freya knows all this?"

Lifting her mug, she held it in both hands, still shaking. "Yes."

"Could she have gone to find her biological parents?" Wood asked.

Constance looked horrified at the thought. "I doubt it." She took a sip of tea. "On her eighteenth, I gave her a box filled with stuff Springfield had found out about her biological mum. Freya didn't want it."

"Where's that box now?"

"Burnt." Constance grinned. "We burnt it together. She told me I was her mum, and she wasn't interested. I doubt anything has changed in the last five years."

"Do you remember anything from the box?"

Constance hesitated. Both detectives saw it.

"I'm going, to be frank with you, Mrs Bentley," George said. "We have two scenarios. One, your daughter has been abducted and is in danger. Two, your daughter is a serial killer."

Constance paled. "Excuse me." She looked devastated.

George repeated his sentence. "One, your daughter has been abducted and is in danger. Two, your daughter is a serial killer."

"We need to find her, Mrs Bentley," Wood said.

"I'm sorry. If she contacts me, I'll let you know."

"I'd appreciate that." George finished his tea and stood. He handed over a card with his contact details.

But Wood remained seated. "You hesitated earlier. Why?"

Constance smiled weakly. "Her biological father, Gary, tried to contact Freya when she turned sixteen, and I turned him away."

"Do you know his surname?"

"No."

"Is there anything else?"

"She has a sister."

George asked, "Does Freya know that?"

Constance shook her head. "She doesn't even know her father's name."

"What about your husband?"

"He passed away before I adopted Freya," she explained. "He was much older than me. So many people said I married him for his money, but they were wrong."

"And you're sure you don't know where Freya is?" Wood asked.

"No."

Wood got up, but Constance gripped her wrist.

George closed the gap immediately, his face contorted. He had his fists clenched.

Immediately, Constance let go. "Are you a mother, Detective Sergeant?"

"I am."

George smiled. Isabella told him the night they found out that she considered herself a mother from that point. "Why wait for a baby to be born? It's growing inside me right now."

"Then you know all about protecting what is yours," Constance said. "I'm sorry about grabbing you; I really don't know what came over me."

"It's shock, Mrs Bentley. She's your daughter." Wood got up, then turned. "But if you know where she is, you need to tell us. You might think you're protecting her, but if she's done something terrible, like we think she may have done, by not telling us where she is, you're putting other people's sons and daughters at risk."

Constance dropped her head before raising it with tears nestled in her eyes. "I really don't know where she is. I wish I did."

*　*　*

Detective Sergeant Yolanda Williams was waiting for George when he returned to the station. "Sir, I've got something you need to see."

"What is it?"

The DI followed Yolanda into her corner of the incident room and nodded to the screen on her left. "This is from the night Lesley Ibbetson was murdered. I believe it was you that got the footage?"

George took a look. It was paused just as Lesley was going to smack Julia Brown. "Yeah, I got it from the pub; why?"

She pointed towards two men watching. They had pool cues in their hands. "Recognise this man, sir?"

He shook his head. Yolanda sat down on the chair, leaned forward, and pressed a button on her keyboard. The video played, and that was when he recognised Jake Cappleman.

George looked at Yolanda, who smiled. She said, "This proves Jake was near Lesley Ibbetson the night she was murdered."

"This is great work, Yolanda," he said. "Have you found him at any of the other scenes?"

"Not yet, but we're working on it."

* * *

George finally managed to sit down in his office. DC Scott had done a great job in digging up everything they had on Jake Cappleman, and he wanted to go through it.

He still wasn't sure whether Freya Bentley was a victim or a suspect but knew figuring out Jake could help with that.

* * *

## CHAPTER THIRTY

The incident room was buzzing as George entered. He took a sip of his coffee, removed his suit jacket, and stood in front of the whiteboard.

With help from DC Blackburn, DS Wood wheeled three Big Boards, so they were flanking George.

"We currently have four suspects," George explained. "Flora Ogram, Nick Creaser, Jürgen Schmidt, and Jake Cappleman."

George pointed at the pictures on the Big Boards one by one.

"We'll start with Flora." He pointed at a picture they'd taken from social media. "Gin Creaser's daughter and Lesley Ibbetson's friend. Her whereabouts are unknown during Gin's murder, and regarding Lesley Ibbetson, Flora's alibi is non-existent. So other than the book club link, we can't currently link Flora to Larisa Raggett unless somebody knows something I don't?"

Nobody said anything, so George continued. "Then we have Nick Creaser. He links only to Gin Creaser, his wife. He ordered a takeaway the night Gin was murdered, and whilst we have solid evidence of what time he was home, we still can't fully rule him out." George scratched his beard. "He may have known Lesley Ibbetson through Gin and Flora and may have known Larisa Raggett through them and the book club, too. However, his memory is hazy, and he has no alibi for Lesley's death, either. We haven't spoken with him yet regarding Larisa Raggett."

Sweat started to dribble down George's back. The heating was on full whack. It was always like this. He took a sip of lukewarm coffee and continued. "The crime lord Jürgen Schmidt has solid alibis for Gin's and Lesley's murders, but it's all a bit sus. He was too happy to provide us with the footage, and when asked about his back garden, he became agitated." He looked at Luke, who nodded. "DS Williams checked ANPR data for that night, and it proves Schmidt's Range Rover didn't move until he said it moved."

"He could have been picked up, boss?" Jay asked.

"True, Jay, but we have zero proof of that."

"Why is Schmidt a suspect?" DC Malik asked.

"Rolled-up money was found in Gin Creaser's mouth, Lesley Ibbetson was killed using fentanyl-laced heroin injected into her bloodstream, and Larisa Raggett was killed by fentanyl-laced cocaine which was forced into her mouth and nose. Each murder gave off a clear message and is indicative of gang murders. Schmidt may not have murdered these women himself, but he has plenty of people on his payroll."

"Isn't that, to use your phrase, a bit, 'sus'?" Reza asked.

"Explain," George said.

"When something is too good to be true, then it usually is," DC Malik explained.

"Point taken," George said. "Let's discuss Jake Cappleman next." He nodded at Jay, who stood up.

"I've known Jake for years. He was in Colby Raggett's pocket, and whilst we've never been able to arrest him, we know he deals with drugs and offers loans to vulnerable people who need them. This suggests he could be working with, or most likely for, Jürgen Schmidt. He knows all three of the victims, has links to them, and has even recently attacked Nick Creaser for owing him money."

George cleared his throat. "He is currently our prime suspect, and we have put out a BOLO."

"He also threatened Flora Ogram because her late mum owed Jake money," Jay added.

"We know for a fact he was in the area the night Gin and Lesley were murdered. Gin's murder was probably a message aimed at Nick, and for all we know, Lesley scored some smack from Cappleman and didn't pay him back."

"If only the dead talked, eh sir?" DC Malik said.

"If only." George cleared his throat again. He hoped he wasn't coming down with something.

"What's Nick Creaser's motive?" Reza asked. "Or Flora's? Or Schmidt's?"

George furrowed his brow. He wasn't used to being challenged like this and wasn't sure he liked it. Yes, the DC was older than him, but George was two ranks higher.

"What's Nick Creaser's motive, sir," George said. "I may be younger than you, but I still deserve the respect of my rank."

"My apologies, sir; my previous DCI actively asked us not to use, sir."

"Any questions?" George looked between the detectives, who all shook their heads. "That's it for my briefing. Go home and enjoy the rest of your Sunday but be back early tomorrow morning."

## Chapter Thirty-one

Nick quickly looked around before knocking on the door. All it'd take was one nosy neighbour to spot him and get him into trouble.

It was late. The kids would be in bed, which only made their affair more thrilling.

She answered the door and quickly dragged him inside. Her smile made his heart hammer, and as soon as they were in the living room, his arms encircled her, and his lips found hers.

There was something exhilarating about having sex in someone else's home. It was probably because of the fear of being caught, which no doubt heightened the senses. But at the same time, it felt indulgent and risky all mingled into one. It made the pleasure come quickly; it was fast and frenetic but much more satisfying.

Nick's hands were all over her, pulling her t-shirt over her head first, then unclipping her bra. Her face displayed lust and excitement as he pulled down her panties. She got down on her knees and took him in her mouth. He felt like the only man in the world. He knew it shouldn't, but it felt so good. Not at all wrong, just fantastic.

They both lasted longer than they did outside, but it was over way too soon for Nick. But then again, they'd both got what they were after. Afterwards, they adjusted their clothes, and she grinned. Then, with a flush across his face, he returned it. He wanted to stay the night. They could have a repeat just before going to sleep, but he knew that could be risky.

"I missed that," he said as he pulled her near again. "I wish it didn't have to be so quick, but it was worth it. Right?"

As she thought about what he said, she bit her lip. He found the act irresistible, and he pulled her close. They kissed again, this time slow and passionate. They'd learned over the years of their affair to take their chances with the sex first. Being caught out was not an option.

"Gin's gone. That means we're both single."

"Stop talking like that, Nick," she said, getting up from the sofa. She entered the kitchen and returned two minutes later with two ice-cold bottles of cider.

He'd told her repeatedly that he was going to break it off with Gin, even before they were married, but had never been able to escape the relationship. Nick understood why she didn't entirely trust him to be with her, so he didn't broach the subject again that night. Instead, like two people in a relationship, they began to tell each other about their day.

There was something about their discussions that always made Nick excited about the future. She was truly into him, unlike Gin, who he felt had settled. He'd certainly settled with her, anyway. His love for the woman opposite him was different from that of his late wife.

It was evident from the number of times they'd ended the affair only to succumb to the pleasure of it all again. He'd watched her on his wedding day, watched as tears fell from her eyes. She'd looked sad rather than happy. She'd denied it, of course, but the pictures from the wedding told a clear story.

"You're like a drug," Nick said, interlinking his fingers with hers. "At first, I think I've cracked the addiction and given you up, only to become obsessed with you again after a tiny taste. So what are we gonna do now?"

"That's up to you, Nick. I've wanted to be with you for years. You know that."

Nick closed his eyes. Had she really been waiting for him all this time? He thought back to her last boyfriend. Damon. A Polish immigrant who worked at the car wash down in Hunslet. They'd got together just after he and Gin had got married. Had she been punishing him? Or had she been trying to move on?

"You said we'd never do this again after nearly getting caught the last time. Remember?"

Nick grimaced. They'd gone out for the day. It wasn't often they went out in case they were seen, but the kids had been at their dad's, and Gin had gone to Blackpool with Flora. They'd driven to Cleethorpes, a seaside town in North Lincolnshire, miles away from Leeds, where they could be themselves without fear of being seen.

The entire day had gone off without a hitch, and Nick had never felt happier. That was until they bumped into somebody Nick knew, an old friend who had moved away in year 11. Luckily he hadn't met Gin, so he had introduced her as his wife instead. It had been close enough for them both to think of what they would lose if their secret ever came out, but Nick found he didn't care. He'd felt happier on that one day than he ever had in his years with Gin.

Yet something was stopping him from leaving her.

She checked her watch and sighed. It was after midnight. "I guess you'd better leave, Nick. I wish you could stay longer, though."

"I can," he said. "I'll set an early alarm and leave before the kids get up."

She leaned forward and put a finger to his lips. "Don't do that, Nick," she cautioned. "You're not being fair."

He said nothing for a moment and then nodded before getting to his feet. He held out a hand which she took, and he pulled her up into his arms. "Fancy a quickie before I leave?"

She pulled out of his embrace and grinned. "They're always quickies, Nick." Then she slapped his arse, pushing him towards the hallway.

After putting on his shoes, his lips found hers one more time, and he, like usual, didn't want to let her go. But eventually, they broke apart.

"You make me feel so good; you know that?"

She laughed. "That's the sex talking."

"Well, I like it when sex talks," he said. "When will I see you again?" It was better than 'This needs to stop.' Or 'We can't do this any more.' Their parting words were usually a variation of the three.

She grinned. "You want to see me again?"

He was desperate to be with her for the rest of his life. To wake up next to her every morning, not only to enjoy her whenever they could fit the time in. It wasn't enough. It hadn't been for a long time now. When he thought about it, the night he'd met the pair, he'd chosen wrong. It was a fact. He'd known it from the second time he'd met her. "Stupid fucking question. I want to wake up with you. Every morning–"

"Don't make promises you can't keep, Nick," she said.

"But I can keep them now," he pleaded.

"I'll message you," she said, ignoring him.

"Fine, you'd better," he said with a grin the Cheshire Cat

would be proud of.

Outside, he checked his surroundings and, when he thought it was safe, strode down the drive. Even with his mind full of thoughts of being with her all the time, he still had Gin to bury. And despite his promises, getting with her now was probably not the right thing to do. For some reason, though, he felt as though they were on borrowed time. That, for her, it was only sex, and it was only him who wanted more.

Yet, as he walked home and tried to convince himself it was only sex, he knew deep down it was much more than that now.

He only hoped she felt the same way.

\* \* \*

Nick's heart hammered in his chest as he thought about what he'd just done. The Cheshire Cat grin was still on his face.

There were two ways home. One, he could cut down Oak Drive, but then he'd have to walk uphill on St Georges Road. Or two, he could continue up Waggon Road and meet St Georges Road nearer the roundabout. Either way, he'd then have to walk past the St George's Centre and then Asda, cutting across the Asda roundabout, and then down the Ring Road to his flat.

He chose the first option. It meant there weren't as many nosey neighbours to contend with.

Nick continued past the roundabout on St Georges Road and began the steep walk towards the crest of the hill where the St George's Centre was.

But he needed a piss. He didn't like going to the toilet in other people's houses.

A person watched Nick from the shadows, not that he knew. They'd been watching him since he left the house on Waggon

Road, their fists clenched tight, drawing blood.

The rain was lashing down, mixed with sleet that battered Nick from above. He was only wearing jeans, a T-shirt and a light jacket. It soaked him.

Nick slipped through the cycle gate into the field parallel to the secondary school. At the end was a ginnel where he'd once received a blow job as a teenager, not far from the Lingwells and Acres, where his gran had lived at the time.

After hiding inside a small grove of trees and checking nobody was watching him, Nick unzipped his jeans and pulled out his penis to relieve his bladder.

The person watching Nick had kept to the shadows. The sound of the rain battering the ground would mask their footsteps.

They thought Nick was stupid to leave the safety of the road and enter a dark, secluded area.

Still, their pace quickened. They kept their breathing light. They were sure Nick was nearly finished.

The figure's heart rate sped up, as did their pace.

Nick was right there, close enough that they could smell his cheap aftershave and the recognisable smell of sex.

Nick Creaser put his penis back inside his pants and zipped up. Then he turned to his right, his intention to head back to the main road.

But the figure had removed the hunting knife from the pouch of their hooded top, and both people crashed into each other.

The figure heard the satisfying sound of a sharp knife slicing through soft flesh, and Nick coughed up blood on his assailant's balaclava.

The figure removed its balaclava and looked Nick Creaser in the eye.

"It was you?" Nick questioned.

The figure nodded and put the balaclava back on. Then they stood back and grabbed the hunting knife tightly.

"You cheating bastard," the figure said as they thrust the knife deep into Nick's stomach.

The figure continued to do that until Nick could no longer hold his weight and slumped to the ground on his knees, his face meeting the blood-soaked grass.

## Chapter Thirty-two

After showing the uniformed officer his warrant card and driving through the outer cordon on St Georges Road, Detective Inspector George Beaumont saw blue lights blaring and a hive of activity in the distance.

He parked at the Willowdale junction and got out of his car. He'd tried to contact DC Jason Scott already, but the young man wasn't answering.

George walked down the hill towards the green where the body was found and was met by Candy Nichols, who was guarding the inner cordon just in front of the cycle gate. "Morning, sir," she said.

"Jay not with you?" George asked.

"No, sir, I haven't seen him for a couple of days."

"You weren't with him last night?"

Candy shook her head.

He tried the DC again, but the young man still didn't pick up.

Candy gave him a Tyvek suit with blue gloves, mask and shoe covers, which he put on over his suit.

The rain was still coming down, though not as much as before. In the distance, he could see a large, blue tent had been erected.

Saying thanks to Candy for signing him in, George slipped

through the cycle gate and stepped on the metal plates indicating the common approach path, a designated way all the officers used so they didn't accidentally tread on any evidence.

Lines of trees, to both his left and right, dripped water onto the grass below. George looked up at the flats to his left. People were watching. There was nothing he could do, not really. Even news companies were using drones now to get beyond extended cordons.

Lindsey Yardley met him at the tent. Next to her was pathologist Dr Christian Ross who acknowledged George with a nod.

George greeted the pair with a "Morning" as he moved closer. "Got much for me?"

Lindsey nodded towards the tent. "IC1 male who according to his licence was twenty-nine. Nick Creaser–"

"Nick Creaser?" George asked.

Lindsey nodded. "He was stabbed, just like his wife."

"More than his wife," Dr Ross said. "Much more, actually. It's too wet to measure the entry wounds here, but I'll do that at the PM to compare with the others."

"Thank you," said George.

"Time of death?" George asked.

Lindsey deferred to Dr Ross, who frowned. "Hard to say because of the damp and the cold. He's in rigour, so dead between two and eight hours at least."

"So killed not long after midnight?"

Dr Ross nodded. "That's my guess. I'll know more later."

George nodded. "Any forensics?" He looked at Lindsey.

"Nothing." She pointed to the tent. "Rain washed everything away." Lindsey grimaced and then pointed up. "Grass was discoloured, though. He was killed here."

## CHAPTER THIRTY-TWO

"Unlike Larisa Raggett."

"Correct. I've ordered a fingertip search of the area."

"Thank you. What else do you have other than a licence?"

"Phone and wallet. No cash in the wallet. The phone requires a passcode."

"Send it to IT ASAP. I want everything from it."

"Thank you both." George inhaled deeply. He didn't want to look at the body but thought he might as well since he was here.

As the DI entered, a forensic photographer was still snapping pictures of the body. It was the same one who had photographed Nick's wife, the one in her forties, with short black hair.

The smell of blood was thick in the air, and he was grateful for his mask, but dizziness overcame him as he walked towards the corpse.

George understood now why they'd erected the tent with the flap at the top of the hill. Watery blood was spreading out from Nick's body and seeping into the grass before flowing downhill.

Nick wore a light beige jacket highlighting the entry wounds, with black jeans and Nike trainers. There was no real need for a formal identification; after all, they'd only seen him recently.

The photographer stepped aside for George, who crouched next to the body for a better view. He immediately shouted, "Lindsey, Dr Ross, can you come here, please?"

Both entered quickly, and Lindsey was the first to ask, "What's up?"

"Is there something in his mouth?" George asked.

Dr Ross squatted beside George and prodded Nick's cheek with a gloved hand. "So there is, son."

Christian ordered the photographer to fetch him some tweezers, and suddenly, the cloying atmosphere got too much for George. "I'll be outside when you're done," he said.

After five or ten minutes, George wasn't sure, Dr Christian Ross left the tent, waving an evidence bag at George. "It's money, son," he said.

"Money? Just like with Gin Creaser."

"Exactly."

"Get it to the lab and tested, please," George said.

Lindsey had followed the pathologist out and beckoned a SOCO over. The young lad took the evidence bag and left the scene immediately.

"Fifty quid, ten fivers," Lindsey explained.

Was that the same as Gin Creaser? Or did she have five twenties? He couldn't remember.

\* \* \*

A lyrical voice roused Jason Scott. It said, "Good morning, handsome."

He felt like utter shite. His mouth was so dry, his throat was killing him, and he was very drowsy. Sweat was literally pouring from his pores.

The young DC tried to open his eyes but immediately had to shut them again.

He tried to swallow his spit in an attempt to moisturise his throat, but he got nothing. He eventually managed to say, "Morning," but it had been a feeble attempt.

Jay's need for water was immeasurable, but he couldn't get up. He was too dizzy and couldn't open his eyes.

"Your phone keeps going off," the lyrical voice said.

"Who?" was all he could manage.

He reached for his phone on the bedside table but knocked a glass of water all over the floor.

Fucking hell!

"Whoops," said the voice. And then she giggled.

Jay then felt a hand snake across his washboard abs. The movement made him feel sick.

The young man squinted with one eye; it was too painful to open both. Light streamed in through the window. As usual, he'd forgotten to draw the curtains.

Once his eye managed to focus, he saw Flora Ogram, fully nude, staring at him. She passed him a bottle of water which he greedily imbibed.

"Better?" she asked.

"Better," he replied, though that single word thumped behind his eyes like a woodpecker was going at his skull.

"I enjoyed our date last night," Flora said, "especially dessert." She raised her brows, then started giggling again.

"Me too," Jay lied. He couldn't remember much, but he knew it'd come back to him as the day progressed. "Who's calling me?"

"Your boss." A little smirk curved towards her eyes.

"What time is it?"

"After ten, I think."

"Oh fuck!" Jay said, forcefully sitting up. "I need to go."

"But it's Sunday." She pouted and buried her face in the pillow.

"No, yesterday was Sunday," Jay said. "And it doesn't matter what day it is. I'm a police detective." DC Scott looked around the room for more water but couldn't find any. So he ambled into the bathroom and stuck his head under the tap.

Lowering his neck sent pain down his spine, and he had to stop for a moment. Then he gulped down more water.

With one eye, Jay looked in the mirror. He looked a right mess. His blond hair was spiking up at all angles, and he looked like he'd seen a ghost.

Time for a quick shower? No, he needed to get to the station.

He thought he only drank coffee last night.

Jay ran a toothbrush over his teeth, gargled mouthwash and sprayed some lynx.

He had only been gone five minutes, but she was up and fully dressed, grinning.

"Is this the life when dating a detective?"

"We're dating?"

"I thought we were," she said. Jay's phone rang again, and she looked over at it. "Looks like you're needed, Detective Scott."

"Will I see you tonight?" he asked, getting dressed in a fresh suit.

"Only if you want to." She buried an embarrassed face into the pillow.

God, she was so cute! "I do."

"Good."

After about five minutes of discussing their date last night, Jay was finally ready and, with his keys in his hand, got up to say bye to Flora.

"Cases going well?" she asked, stepping on her tiptoes to kiss him.

"Yeah, and no." He wondered whether he should ask her about Lesley and the alibi she gave. "You never did tell me how you got home that night from the Falconers Rest."

"I did," she protested. "I called Nick, and he came." She

ran a hand through her blonde curls. "I'm sure he did." She looked down at the floor as if assessing her memory.

They walked down the stairs towards the front door. "He said otherwise, that's all."

"Are you sure? Because he's been quite confused of late. My mum dying has really fucked him up."

"I guess we could ask him again."

"You don't believe me?"

"No, no," he said, holding his palms up. "I never said that; I just wanted some clarification, that's all."

"I can't be in a relationship if there's no trust, Jay," Flora said. Then, she headed towards the door. "I'll see myself out, OK?"

"Wait, Flora, I didn't mean to accuse you."

She shouldered her handbag. "You're a detective; you're probably suspicious of everybody."

He winced. "I'm not suspicious of you."

"Don't worry about me." She licked her lips, then paused. "I'll see you around, I guess."

She left and walked down his front path.

"I want to see you tonight at eight. I'm going to pick you up, and I won't be late!"

Jay didn't see it, but she grinned as she exited through the little black gate. She blew him a kiss and shouted, "Text me!"

Jay nodded and pulled out his phone, wanting to be cute and to text her right then, but saw it was nearly half-ten.

Shit!

He pulled on his shoes, pulled his coat from the newel post and headed outside. The sun was too bright, so he retrieved his sunglasses and plonked them on. Then he locked the door and sprinted down the path, feeling sick and dizzy still.

The DI was going to have his bollocks.

# Chapter Thirty-three

Jay breezed into the incident room for the morning briefing, and George could see he was hoping no one would notice him—some hope.

"You look totally hung-over," Tashan said in a loud whisper. He passed his colleague a mint as Jay sat next to him. He smiled his thanks.

"Good of you to join us, Detective Constable Scott," said George before pointing to a photo of the victim. "Nick Creaser's been murdered, hence why you have a million missed calls and messages on your phone."

"I'm really sorry, boss." Then he turned to each detective in the room. "I'm really sorry, everyone." He felt like utter shite. His mouth was so dry, his throat was killing him, and he was still drowsy. Sweat was literally pouring from his pores. "I don't know how, but I slept through my alarm." He closed his eyes. The light was hurting them. "I think I need to see a doctor," DC Scott explained.

"Your eyes do look big," said Tashan. "Really dilated."

"How did Nick die?" Jay asked. Flora was going to be gutted. He wondered whether she knew.

"If you had answered your phone, you'd have been at the scene with us and already know," said George. He shook his head and then said, "From his initial assessment at the scene, Pathologist Dr Christian Ross suggests the exsanguination is the likely cause of death. A full post-mortem should confirm it. He was stabbed repeatedly."

"Like Gin Creaser's murder?"

"Pretty much the same," said Tashan. "They found cash in Nick's mouth. It's at the lab getting tested."

"How much cash?" Jay asked.

"Does it matter?" asked George. He was angry with the lad. But even so, they had to work together. He took a deep breath. "Fifty quid."

"How much was left in Gin's mouth?"

Tashan said, "Fifty pounds."

"Same killer then?" asked Jay.

"Most likely," said George. "Or a copycat. Dr Ross says he will measure the wounds to see if the same weapon was used. He's rushing the PM for us."

"Anything else?" Jay asked.

"Phone and wallet on him, just like with Gin Creaser," George explained. "Not a burglary."

"Where did they find him?"

"Some green land just off St Georges Road in Middleton. Bloodstains on the ground suggest he was murdered where he was found. The constant rain we've had has most likely compromised the scene. And before you ask, a dog walker found him."

"It's usually the case," said Jay. "Why was he there?"

"No clue at the minute, son," Luke chimed in. "We're looking into known associates. We sent Uniform to the flat but can't find Flora Ogram."

"It's looking like she's our prime suspect," George said.

## CHAPTER THIRTY-THREE

"She can't be," admitted Jay.

"Why not?"

"Nick was murdered last night, right?" asked Jay.

"Or the early hours of this morning, yeah," confirmed George. They didn't have an exact time of death yet.

"Flora was with me last night."

George frowned. "Explain."

"We've been seeing each other."

"You've been dating a witness?" asked Luke.

Jay nodded and looked down at the floor.

"I thought you and PC Nichols were a thing?" Luke asked. He scratched his greying stubble.

"We are... We were..."

"How many times have you been out with Flora Ogram?" George asked. He felt guilty. He'd fancied Mia from the moment he met her, but at least he'd had the sense to ask her out after the case had been closed. And she wasn't a suspect like Flora was. "Do you realise what you've done?"

"No, boss."

"It could affect the entire investigation. What have you told her about the case?"

"Nothing, boss."

"But you haven't investigated her as you should have."

"Don't accuse me of not doing my job, boss," Jay argued.

"You let us listen to the tape, Jay. You didn't ask her about her alibi for Lesley's murder. Instead, you skirted right on over it."

"I made a mistake, boss. That's it."

"I want you to make an official statement, Jay. The super will take it because he's not involved in the investigation. You need to be honest with him about every time you've seen Flora outside of your detective duties."

Jay stood and nodded. "I apologise if I've let you down, boss." He turned to the team. "I'm sorry."

He swayed on his feet and had to hold a chair. "It's not an excuse, but I really don't feel well."

* * *

George was very familiar with the Manor Farm estate. As a PC, he'd been called out to the area weekly because of his local connections. The constant rows of terraced housing had practically been a second home.

DS Luke Mason pulled up outside Manor Farm Gardens, next to an open green that quads and motorbikes had destroyed.

George thought Luke was lucky he'd managed to get parked. Unfortunately, the roads were narrow, and there was a distinct lack of driveways.

All in all, it was a nightmare.

But then, that was why they'd come in a squad car instead of George's Merc.

George and Luke, with Sergeant Greenwood and a PC he didn't recognise, strolled up to the terraced house. The garden, as ever, was a mess, the grass too high to attack with a mower. The front door was wide open, as were the windows in the living room. Rap music blared out.

George shook his head. The neighbours probably had to deal with the Capplemans constantly disturbing the peace.

The DI turned to Sergeant Greenwood, who was holding the big red key and smiled. They'd not need to break in. But his attention was drawn to a man across the road, sitting on a large, blue grit bin. His bare belly hung down to his knees, and he wore shorts. It was March, for Christ's sake!

George turned back, looked at the frayed wooden door, and walked carefully along the path of the property. Then he banged on the open front door.

"Hello?" he shouted. When he got no reply, he knocked again, this time stepping inside the narrow hall and pushing open the living room door. "Hello, police."

A woman sitting on a filthy settee asked, "What the fuck do you want?"

"Turn the music down; I can't hear you," George advised. Luke had followed him in. The two other officers had stayed outside in the hallway.

The woman didn't move, so George strode over to the stereo and pressed the off button. The silence was almost as deafening.

"Hey, you can't do that!"

With Freya Bentley still missing, Jake Cappleman was their prime suspect. "Oh, stop moaning, Mrs Cappleman." George cocked a brow. "We're after Jake. I'm told he's back home?"

Cherry Cappleman had lived on the estate all her life. She'd been brought up alongside two brothers and a sister, all in constant trouble or behind bars.

She'd apparently been a looker back in the day, but even when George had met her when he'd first been on the beat, she looked as she did now. Short and thin. Gaunt. With tar-stained fingers.

Cherry had children other than Jake. Her other two boys were in prison, and her daughter was well-known in Holbeck.

"Back 'ome, officer?" she asked, and George nodded. "Nah, not seen 'im in ages," she muttered, folding her arms across her filthy T-shirt.

"We've had three of four calls this morning alone telling us Jake's here." George shook his head. "We even have pictures."

"Well, they is fucking liars, right."

George decided to play along. "OK, Cherry. When did you last see him?"

"Couple o' weeks ago."

"You mean he's moved out?"

"Yer, shacked up with that skinny cow on the brooms."

"Which skinny cow, and what address on the brooms?"

"The one that thinks she's fuckin' better than me."

George was losing patience. It was too hot inside, and the mixture of nicotine, BO, and alcohol made him nauseous. "Give me his number."

"You think I know 'is number?" She started laughing. "I don't even fuckin' know what day o' week it is!"

"Give me your phone, and I'll have a look."

Cherry sighed and reached for her phone. She scrolled for a moment and then passed it over to George. "Here."

George pulled on a disposable glove, took the phone from her outstretched hand, and noted the number down. But he didn't hand the phone back.

Then a noise came from above.

George and Luke looked up and then looked at Cherry. She said, "Nigella's home."

"Are you sure you're telling us the truth, Cherry? Because if I find out Jake's here, I'm going to arrest you for obstruction."

"Go see for yourself."

George nodded at Luke, who gloved and booted and headed upstairs. The PC George didn't know followed him up, and Sergeant Greenwood entered the living room in Luke's place.

"He's a bit fit," Cherry said, pointing at Greenwood. "You

want to take me out, officer?" she asked.

Greenwood said nothing. He stared at the floor.

Luke returned and shook his head. And that was when they heard a noise coming from the door behind Cherry—the kitchen.

Cherry paled and stood up to try and block the officers.

George dodged her and burst through the door to find Jake tearing out of the back door. The DI, with his DS in tow, raced after him.

Jake was off, sprinting up towards the bit of wasteland leading him towards Town Street.

George legged it after him, wondering what he had to hide. He was obviously guilty of something. But what.

The cold and damp settled in George's throat. He'd not been boxing as regularly, but he was still fit. Then, just before he reached the brick stairs at the edge of the land, George caught up with him. The DI pushed Lanky Jake to the ground and then cuffed him.

"That was really stupid of you, Jake. I only wanted to speak to you. Got a guilty conscience?"

"I haven't done anything," he cried.

"You see because you ran away from me, I'm not going to believe a word you say."

"But I still haven't done anything."

George said nothing more as he caught his breath. Greenwood appeared from the steps, clearly having run around to try and intercept Jake. The PC showed up, barely out of breath. Then Luke arrived. Heaving.

"I'm getting too old for this," Luke said.

The PC and the PS picked Jake up from the floor.

"We'll talk your lies back at the station," the DI said.

"But I'm busy," Jake groaned.

Cherry was on the doorstep when they got back to the squad cars. She shouted at George. "I'm going to put in a complaint about you. He's fuckin' done nowt!"

"Unless you want to be arrested for obstruction," George warned, "I'd keep quiet if I were you."

As Luke pulled away, George glanced at Jake, sat in PC Greenwood's car and shook his head. Jake didn't come across as a serial killer, but then they never did.

\* \* \*

After leaving Jake Cappleman to be booked into custody, George headed upstairs to advise the team.

There was still no word on Freya Bentley. Nor had they received anything back regarding Nick Creaser.

But it seemed Flora Ogram was no longer a suspect. Jay had been with her from 8 pm the previous night, right up to when he woke up at 10 am this morning. And, from the statement he'd given DSU Smith, Flora was still adamant Nick had picked her up the night of Lesley's death. Tashan and Luke had, in their own statements, expressed their concerns over Nick's confusion, and George had seen it first-hand, too.

That meant Jake was now their prime suspect. Their only suspect, really. Unless Freya Bentley was involved.

Once Jake Cappleman was ready to be interviewed, George went downstairs to question him. Jay knew the lad, so he took him into the interview room. He still looked a bit peaky, but Jay said he could handle it.

But before entering, George told Jay their first line of attack would be to find out why he ran. Then he'd challenge Jake about Flora Ogram's comments.

George began the interview after introducing them and reeling off the usual spiel.

"Why did you run, Jake?" Jay asked.

"Police, innit mate?" he said.

"Makes you look guilty, though, Jake," Jay explained.

Lanky Jake shrugged.

"I think you're guilty," George said.

"Well, you can fuck right off." Jake scratched the stubble on his chin. "I'm not guilty of owt. Look around, knob. Do you see a solicitor?"

"Could be a bluff, Jake," George explained.

Jake looked confused, but George didn't see any point in explaining. "Where were you on Thursday evening, Jake?" George asked. "Specifically, between the hours of 5 pm and midnight?"

"Wow, that's a long period of time." Jake paused for a moment. "I was at the pub between seven and midnight. You can ask Baz."

"Baz Cross?" Jay asked, and Jake nodded. The young DC made a note and then turned to his boss. "I know Barry Cross, boss," he said. Then he turned to Jake. "We will ask him, you know."

"Ask away. Lots of people saw me there."

George knew they had the footage from that night and fired off a text to Yolanda, asking her to search through it with a fine-tooth comb.

"We know you were there when Lesley Ibbetson slapped Julia Brown," George explained. "We saw you on the CCTV."

Jake grinned. "There you go."

"Where were you between five and seven, though, Jake?"

George asked.

"With Baz." Jake then hesitated and looked up at the ceiling. "At his house. Ask him."

"Oh, we will." George scratched his nose. He could smell Jake's BO from across the table. "Where were you between midnight and 6 am on Saturday?"

"Home."

"Can anyone vouch for you?"

"Mi mam."

"Is that it?"

Jake nodded.

George sat forward, annoyed at his rapid-fire answers. "Do you know Nick Creaser?" George asked, and Jake nodded. "And Gin Creaser?"

Again, Jake nodded.

"You know Gin Creaser's dead, right?"

"I do. Horrible business." Jake wiped his nose with his hand and, after looking at the silky snail trail, wiped it on his trackie bottoms. George physically shuddered. "Wait, is that why you're asking where I was the night she was murdered?" He shook his head then Jake frowned. "You're seriously not trying to pin Gin Creaser's murder on me?"

"We'll speak to Barry Cross and hope he gives you a solid alibi." Then George said, "I heard you beat Nick Creaser up."

Jake grinned. "From who?"

"That doesn't matter, Jake," said George. "Did you beat him up?"

"He owed me fifty quid. I asked him for it, and he shoved me. Self-defence."

They couldn't exactly speak to Nick, but Flora's testimony contradicted Jake's. Fifty quid was also the exact same amount of money they'd found in Nick's mouth.

Interesting.

But they'd come back to Nick soon.

George asked, "The night Gin Creaser was murdered, what time did you go home?"

"It'll be on the footage, but not long after the slap, actually."

"Did you go straight home?"

"No, I went for a kebab."

"On your own?"

"Yes, I went to the one at the bottom of the ave next to the Chinese." He leaned back with a grin. "Satisfied?"

"Not yet." They'd have to speak with the takeaway and see if they had any CCTV to corroborate Jake's story. But George knew if he was telling the truth, that put him out of the picture for Lesley's murder.

"No, wait, that was last week," Jake added. "Sorry, I went to Caesars."

George frowned. The best way to the district centre from the pub would have Jake walk straight by the murder scene. He thought about Ida Bruce and the man wearing the balaclava. "What were you wearing that night?"

"Fucked if I know. Next question."

"How well do you know Lesley Ibbetson and Julia Brown?" George asked.

"Not very. Next question."

"We were told you threatened Flora Ogram over some money Nick hadn't paid you back in time. Was that true?"

Jake shook his head. "Nah. I just asked her to get Nick to contact me. I confronted Nick, who thumped me, so I hit him back. Self-defence."

"When?"

"When what?"

George sighed. "When did he thump you?"

"Saturday night."

"Where?"

"In Miggy."

"But where specifically?"

"Why does it matter? I don't want to press charges."

George had heard enough. The man had an answer for everything. It was time for them to get real. But first he asked, "Do you know a woman named Freya Bentley?" The DI locked eyes with the scrote.

They didn't even flicker. "Nope. Next question."

"Tell us where you were on Sunday night between 9 pm and midnight."

The change in Jake's posture was so slight that if George didn't have his eyes trained on the lad, he wouldn't have noticed it. His leg also started lightly tapping. He'd been so confident before.

"Home."

"You're sure?"

"Yes."

"Can anybody corroborate?"

"Mi mam had a flare-up, so was in bed by eight. Nigella was out." He shook his head and looked down at the ground.

"So that's a no, then?"

"Take it however the fuck you want." Then Jake looked at Jay. "Are we finished here, mate?"

"No, we're not finished," George explained. "Nick Creaser is dead. Murdered."

Jake shook his head. "And you think I did it?"

"Did you?"

"The prick owed me money. So why would I kill him?"

"Maybe you lost your temper," George said, thinking back to the reports on his desk. "It's certainly not the first time, is it?"

"I'm always calm around money."

"Yet you kicked the shit out of him on Saturday night."

"No, Detective, I defended myself."

"And you have no alibi for Nick's murder?"

"No."

Upstairs, George sat across from Isabella while he relayed the interview. She'd been watching the footage, and he wanted her opinion.

"He did change when you asked him about Sunday night," Wood said. "It was obvious on the camera."

"What does that mean?" he asked.

"Means he's guilty of something on Sunday night."

"Does it mean he murdered Nick Creaser, though?"

Back in his office, George thought about the day's events so far. They were sinking. With Nick's murder, their five suspects had been shrunk down to four. And now their prime suspect, Jake, possibly had alibis for two of the murders.

They needed a break, and they needed it soon.

# Chapter Thirty-four

The New Forest Village Book Club members met at the Corinthians Rugby Club as promised.

"Do the police have any idea what happened to Nick?" Sophie asked, looking at Flora.

"I don't know," Flora replied. "I've just learned about it myself."

"Oh, my sweet, should you really be here?" Sophie asked.

"Probably not, but it's better than being at the station answering questions." She knew they'd want to speak with her. It wasn't lost on her that her two parents and good friend had been murdered.

"At the station?" asked Ellie.

Flora took Ellie in. She looked a mess. Flora knew Ellie had kids, but Ellie looked like proper shit. Putting that to the back of her mind, Flora explained what she'd been thinking, and Aurelia gasped. "Surely you're not a suspect."

"I don't think I am. Plus, if they ask, I have a perfect alibi for last night. I was with a boy." She blushed. "I'm just not ready to speak with them yet." Flora looked around at the book club members. "I just need all of you."

"Are you sure you're OK, Flora?" Ellie asked.

"Yeah, are you?"

"What?"

"Are you OK?"

Ellie wiped a tear from her eye. "That's four people murdered now who we know, Flora. It's getting to me, that's all. What if I'm next?"

"I don't know the fourth; who was it?" Flora asked. "And why would you be next? If anybody's next, it's me."

"You didn't know about Larisa Raggett? They found her near Sharp Lane," Sophie said.

Aurelia gestured as if figuring it out. "I think she left just before you joined, love, though I'm sure she said she was going to come and see Balthazar Crane. She was a big fan, apparently."

"I know her name, actually," Flora admitted. "So Nick's the odd one out?"

Ellie said, "How's he the odd one..." before she clicked. "Not a book club member. Are you sure his murder is linked?"

"I don't see how it's not, but I haven't spoken with anybody." She considered ringing Jay, but he'd pissed her off. Did he really not trust her?

"Shall we go through the tasks, ladies?" Ellie asked. "It's why we're here, after all." The group nodded at her. "Flora, did you and Rebecca look through your house for clues?" Ellie asked.

"We did," Flora explained. "The police also had a look, too. We got nothing. Nothing from her emails, too. I still don't know who she was meeting, but Nick gave me the number." She slid the piece of paper across the table.

Rebecca said, "Is this the number who lured–"

Ellie cut in, "Does anybody recognise the number?" She gave Rebecca a death stare.

Each member checked their mobile contacts and shook their heads in turn.

"Is it a burner, then?" Bea asked.

"Ooh, look at you with the lingo," said Aurelia.

"Must be, Bea," Flora said.

Looking at Florence, Tasha and Bea, Ellie asked, "Did you look at the CCTV footage?"

Florence said, "It's been pretty busy with all the murders and the appeals the police have put out," she said, and then winced. "Sorry, Flora, love."

"I'm OK, really. I just want to get the bastard."

"We didn't recognise anybody in any of the footage, did we, ladies?"

"I saw that Lanky Jake fella in the pub footage," Bea said. "Did you lot not recognise him?"

The three women shook their heads.

"He was at the pub?" Flora asked.

Bea said, "Yeah, and we know he's sold Lesley drugs loads of times. What if it's him?"

"It could be him, actually," Flora said. "He threatened me on Friday. I don't want to go into details, but it looked like Mum and Nick owed him money."

Aurelia patted Flora on the arm. "Oh my God, are you OK, love?"

"Yep, yep."

"Didn't he recognise you from the pub?" Sophia asked.

"I didn't recognise him, to be fair." She moved a finger across an eyelash. "He also attacked Nick on Saturday night. Beat him up and everything. Plus, isn't he Colby's mate?"

"Is that why he had cuts and bruises?" Ellie cut in.

"Yeah, how do you know he was cut and bruised?"

## CHAPTER THIRTY-FOUR

Ellie blushed. "The list."

And then Flora clicked. "So you did look at those people on the list I gave you?" said Flora.

"I did, yes. I spoke with Nick and Gaynor, and..." she paused, placing her hand to her mouth.

"I don't think releasing the names on that list matters now," Flora said.

Ellie nodded. "Fine. I spoke with Nick and Gaynor, and Aurelia spoke with people who were at their wedding."

"What did you say when Aurelia rocked up at your door?" Flora asked.

"What?"

"Did Aurelia not visit you?" Flora asked. She turned to the older woman, who blushed.

"I don't think it's Ellie. Come on now, love," Aurelia said.

"But Sophie said it could be anybody in here," Flora said.

"Why would Ellie want Larisa, Nick, Lesley and Gin dead, love?" Aurelia asked.

"I'm not saying she does," Flora said; I just want to look at this with clarity.

"It's Lanky Jake," Sophie said. "From all my experience watching crime shows, it's that bastard. He has links to all four murders. He's the only one who does."

\* \* \*

George was in the shared office, talking to Isabella about Jay. They'd sent the DC home. He'd started to get all dizzy and disorientated, and to be honest, George was worried about the lad. He'd promised to get checked out at St George's Centre immediately.

The pair were then about to discuss Jake Cappleman, when George's phone rang. He sat on a spare chair by DS Wood's computer and took the call from the pathologist.

"Hi, Dr Ross; what have you for me?"

"I've completed Nick Creaser's post-mortem. Exsanguination, as I said. He was killed with the same knife as his wife. A hunting knife."

"Thank you."

"Anything else?"

"Nick had sex before he died. There was the presence of well-known condom lubrication on his penis."

"So he was cheating on Gin," George said aloud.

"No clue, but I'm calling because I have a predicament, son."

"Go on." He leaned his elbow on the desk. They needed a break and fast.

"Lindsey's SOCOs found a hair inside the roll of money," Dr Ross explained. "The lab's checked it, and the follicle is attached."

"So what's the problem?"

"They can get a DNA profile from it as usual, or they can use a handheld fast-track DNA testing device. Basically, your sample will be mixed with chemicals to produce a genetic profile in ninety minutes that can be compared against crime samples held on a database."

"So we can find out who the DNA belongs to in ninety minutes?"

"Only if they're on the database," Dr Ross warned.

"Why on earth hasn't this been an option before?"

"Because of the cost, son."

George bit the inside of his cheek. "Go on, how much."

"Twenty-three and a half thousand pounds per device, son."

George scratched his head. No wonder they weren't using them to solve murders. "Wow."

"Yes, it's quite expensive, but it could steer your investigation towards a specific suspect, son."

"When do they need to know by?"

"Well, they won't do both for cost reasons, so you need to decide now."

"Shit."

"Shit indeed."

George laughed. He wasn't sure he'd heard the pathologist swear before.

"Have you found anything else before I make my mind up?"

"Nope, and Lindsey has found nothing else, either. Unfortunately, the rain has really made it difficult to get any forensics. But the money was inside Nick's mouth."

"Could it be tainted, then?"

"They're well used to DNA samples being tainted. They have Nick's DNA already, as he was on the system," the pathologist said. George wasn't aware of that. His colleagues had done background checks on Nick and said nothing about a record. "They would simply subtract his profile from what they get, and then that would give them a profile to work with."

The DCI would probably kill him if he said yes, but he wasn't here. DSU Jim Smith was in, though. He really should seek clearance, but lives were on the line. They had a murderer out there who had killed four people.

"Do it, please, Dr Ross."

"You're sure?"

"Yes, I'll take responsibility for this. Thank you, Dr Ross."

"OK, son, I'll call you in a couple of hours."

\* \* \*

After making a hot drink and locking himself in his office, George pulled up his emails. There was one from DS Josh Fry, who was working with the digital forensic unit, regarding a hidden folder on Nick Creaser's phone. Despite Nick saying he had no pin on his phone, there'd been one when they tried to look through it. So George had asked Josh to unlock it. An attached zip file had been sent over.

George clicked on the attachment, and the photos were downloaded. They were of Nick and a woman. Nick had his arms around her in one. In another, he was kissing her cheek. In others, they were snogging or holding hands. Then there were images the woman alone. In some, she was fully naked. In others, Nick and the woman were having sex.

George closed down the email and deleted the images from his laptop. Then he sat back for a moment; his fingers steepled while he thought of the ramifications.

He recognised the woman.

And the woman wasn't Nick's wife.

## Chapter Thirty-five

The DI gathered the team in the incident room.

"Okay, I have a bit of news," George said on entering, a steaming mug in his hands. "The digital forensic unit retrieved a hidden folder on Nick Creaser's phone. Recognise anyone?" He'd un-deleted some of the more modest pictures before plugging his laptop in so it appeared on the whiteboard.

Wood looked and said, "Ellie Addiman," raising her eyebrows afterwards.

"Looks like Nick was cheating on his wife," George told everyone. "Ellie Addiman is the New Forest Village Book Club organiser that many of the victims belonged to. She's single, has two kids, and lives in the New Forest Village. Give me a motive."

Tashan cleared his throat. "Gin was Nick's wife and also pregnant. Maybe she confided in Ellie, who then decided to kill her."

George nodded. "Good. How do Lesley, Larisa and Nick fit in with that?"

"Maybe she killed Nick out of spite? Bentley may not even be involved. And I've no idea about Lesley and Larisa." Tashan paused momentarily, then said, "Lesley was a member of the book club, and Larisa used to be a member. Maybe they pissed

Ellie off? It's not uncommon for killers to think, 'what the hell' and off somebody they don't like. Maybe they're decoy murders?"

George had already thought about that. "Regardless, we'll need to have a word with Ellie Addiman. Do we have her address?"

"Waggon Road," Luke said, pointing to his computer.

"That's right near where Nick was murdered. And the pathologist, Dr Ross, told me Nick had recently had sex," said George.

"You think Ellie had sex with him, followed him, and killed him?" Luke asked.

"We don't have much else, DS Mason. We've ruled Flora Ogram out using Jay's statement. Schmidt has solid alibis. Jake Cappleman has alibis, though they are extremely weak. So unless our killer is Freya Bentley, then it's Ellie Addiman."

"We have zero evidence to implicate Freya Bentley," Wood added. "DC Malik looked through Freya's doorbell camera footage, and she got home around one in the morning. Lesley was already dead by that point."

"Look into links between Ellie and Freya, Luke," George asked.

"On it, boss," Luke said, clacking away.

They were obviously missing something. But what?

"Yolanda, take Tashan out to Waggon Road and scour the area for CCTV. We should be able to trace Nick's route home now we know where he started. We may see his killer, too." George then looked towards Wood. "Can you get Reza to look for any council CCTV in the area, too?"

Wood pulled out her phone and looked as if she were typing a text.

"I've already put a request in for the St Georges Road, boss," Luke advised. "I did it when you were at the crime scene this morning."

"Thanks."

"Am I missing anything?" George asked. He looked around at the team. "No? Good. DS Wood and I are going to Waggon Road, too. We're going to speak to Ellie Addiman and see what she's got to say for herself."

\* \* \*

Jake Cappleman was proper buzzing.

Yes, they'd put him on bail, but they'd released him.

Which was a win in his eyes.

As he moved through the silver bollards, he checked his pockets and frowned when Jake realised he only had one cig and no lighter. He turned, wondering whether to go back inside and ask the desk sergeant whether they could lend him a lighter.

Then he thought better of it. He needed to get back to Miggy quickly. He was supposed to be doing an important job for the boss tonight.

Jake headed up Hoxton Mount, craving a McDonald's but unable to afford one.

The air was cold but fresh. The sky was dark. But that would all change as soon as the clocks went forward at the end of the month.

He cut through Holbeck Park towards Beeston Road, where he could catch the bus into Miggy.

But first, he squeezed through the cycle gate and onto Marley Terrace.

A car pulled from Beeston Road and onto Marley Terrace with full headlights on. It swerved up onto the footpath dangerously close to the back-to-back terraced houses, nearly knocking over a couple of green and black bins.

Jake managed to jump behind an orange car whose tyres had been slashed, whacking his elbows and knees on the kerb.

Lanky Jake attempted to pull himself upright. "What the fu–"

A heavy fist crashed into his face, flattening him. His lip smashed against his front teeth, and blood poured from his mouth.

As he attempted to stand, a second punch caught him on the temple, and he fell back to the floor once again.

Jake had won many fights in his life, many more than he'd lost, but he was struggling. The headlights were blinding him, and the hit to his temple had made him dizzy.

Then a solid stamp to his stomach, and a kick to his bollocks, meant he curled up on his side like a foetus. He turned away from the blinding lights.

The black sky above the park seemed full of twinkling stars, but they were soon replaced by sheer black, each star disappearing one by one as the kicks came thick and fast.

His eyelids drooped.

He tried to focus.

But the last star blinked out, and the blackness took hold of him.

Jake Cappleman closed his eyes, and his awful pain disappeared into unconsciousness.

\* \* \*

## CHAPTER THIRTY-FIVE

DI Beaumont and DS Wood arrived outside Ellie Addiman's house on Waggon Road. They stood together and listened. Traffic buzzed from the main road behind them; a swing in someone's garden squealed in the rising night wind. Normality amid chaos, he thought.

Rain fell steadily as the pair approached the house. No lights blazed, and no one opened the door. There was no car on the drive.

"The front door's open slightly," Wood said.

George sped up and stared. Wood was right; the door was slightly ajar.

"Should we wait for backup?"

"I'm waiting for no one."

The door scraped on the carpet as George pushed it inwards. The interior was lit dimly by the street lights from outside. George shone his torch around, searching for a light switch, but couldn't see one, though an elaborate light fixing hung from the ceiling above.

"Look, there's blood on the carpet," George said.

"I'll call it in."

George put on the gloves and shoe covers he always carried around with him as Wood headed back outside.

As he slowly walked towards the end of the hallway, he continued shining the light up and down, illuminating the area in front of him. The blood was thicker, and George wished he had a mask.

A groan alerted his senses.

George stopped and trained his ears.

He heard the groan again and then heard footsteps from behind him.

Turning slowly, George found Isabella, she too wearing shoe

covers and gloves, heading towards him. "Backup on their way"

"Shh," he interrupted. "Do you hear that?"

"Sounds like somebody groaning." She rushed to the end of the hallway and left through a door.

The hallway illuminated as light streamed in. George followed.

On the floor of the living room lay Ellie Addiman.

"Are you okay, Ellie?" Wood knelt beside the prone figure.

Ellie groaned again and opened her eyes. Then she quickly closed them again as if the light had blinded her.

"She's been stabbed," said George, pointing at her stomach.

Wood whipped out her phone and immediately called for medical backup.

"Who stabbed you, Ellie?" George asked. He couldn't get too close as he didn't want to contaminate the scene.

Instead of words coming from Ellie's mouth, foamy blood appeared instead. She was going to die, and they were going to be back at square one.

Maybe she could write down the name of her attacker. He needed a pen and paper of some sort.

George looked around the room and heard a sound from the hallway.

He patted Wood on the shoulder to tell her that she was to stay with Ellie, then made his way from the living room into a darkened hallway.

He had no idea who or what he was facing, so he decided not to turn on the light. The hair on the back of his neck stood to attention, and his heart picked up pace.

It was so loud; whoever was there was sure to hear it.

The torch beam caught the outline of a woman.

"I'm sorry, I was just checking to see if Ellie was finished." Two girls flanked the woman.

"Get outside, please," said George. But when the woman didn't move, he screamed, "Now!"

# Chapter Thirty-six

Annette Fieldhouse was a retired sixty-six-year-old woman who had lived in Middleton her whole life, though she'd only moved onto Waggon Road recently.

Her husband had passed away, so she'd sold up and used the funds to buy a 'newer, nicer' house.

Because she lived alone, was retired, and had no children, she decided to be the granny of the street. And the Addiman girls loved her like one.

Most days after school, the girls would pop into Annette's house for sweets or a choc-ice in the summer. Some other kids also popped in, but not as much as the Addiman girls, Ella and Emily.

Which was why Annette babysat the girls regularly.

She was there whenever Ellie needed her and was proud that somebody would trust her with her two cherubs.

Annette loved the girls as if they were her own. So, when Ellie had asked if the girls could go to hers straight after school that evening, Annette didn't bat an eye.

She'd even ordered them a McDonald's through Uber.

But when Ellie hadn't returned for her girls, Annette had gotten worried, which was why she'd bumped into Detective Inspector George Beaumont in Ellie's hallway.

## CHAPTER THIRTY-SIX

"I'm sorry for scaring you, Mrs Fieldhouse," George said. He sat opposite Annette in her living room, drinking one of the best coffees he'd had in a while. The girls were upstairs, playing.

"Is Ellie OK?"

"We're not sure." It was looking bleak. Whoever stabbed her had done a proper job on her. There was nowhere nearby to land a helicopter, so they'd blue-lighted her to LGI's Major Trauma Centre. "Are you OK having the girls overnight?"

"Of course, love," Annette said.

"Did Ellie tell you why she wanted you to look after the girls?"

"No, I'm sorry, love. I don't tend to ask. I love seeing them."

Fair enough. "Has Ellie been acting strange recently?"

"A bit, yes."

"Can you explain?" asked Wood.

"She's been a bit down. A bit forgetful. Like she's got a lot on her mind."

"Anybody strange been at the house?"

"Not that I'm aware."

"Nobody at all?"

"I don't spy on my neighbours, Detective."

Wood grinned. "I didn't mean it like that. Does she have a boyfriend?"

"No, she's been single since the kids' dad left." Annette took a sip of her tea. "What an arsehole, excuse my French."

George grinned at this. He was just about to ask another question when a knock on the door interrupted them. Annette got up and went to see who it was. It gave George a chance to look around the room.

Pictures of Emily and Ella were scattered about, making

George smile. He wondered whether his own mum would one day be the same. He hoped so.

His thoughts were interrupted when Annette, flanked by another older lady, entered the living room.

"This is Audrey; she lives over the road."

"Audrey Pearce." She held out her hand.

"How can I help you?" George asked, lightly shaking it.

"Is Ellie OK?"

"I'm sorry, I can't comment. I really need to interview Annette, so if this can wait, I'll speak with you after.

"It can't wait.

"Why not."

"I saw a woman take Ellie's car."

Wood looked up from her notepad. "What woman."

"Young and blonde." Audrey looked at Annette. "It's the visitor I told you about. I saw her running out of Ellie's house, get into the car, and speed away."

"Can you describe the young blonde woman for us?"

"Young and blonde, wearing a short skirt, and if I may, a top far too short and far too tight for March. But each to their own."

George's phone rang, and he excused himself. Wood would get a description of the blonde woman and put out an APB for the vehicle.

"DI Beaumont."

"Boss, I've had a call from Gaynor Eastburn, Gin Creaser's sister," said Luke.

"Go on."

"She's just found out about Nick and is horrified. She's been thinking about the murders whilst she's been in Wales and thinks Flora might be involved."

"Why Flora?"

"Flora held a bit of a grudge against Larisa. Flora hated her, apparently. They went to school together and were always competing for boys and that."

"How does Gaynor know this?"

"Flora keeps a diary. Gaynor saw it in the living room one day and read it. It's filled with poems about wanting to kill Larisa."

"We didn't find one during our OSU search." OSU stood for Operational Support Unit. They are search-trained officers who are nationally accredited by the Police National Search Centre.

"Well, if Flora is our killer, then she probably got rid of it."

"True. But that's not all Gaynor told me."

"Go on," said George.

"Flora and Nick were also seeing each other."

"What?"

"Yep. Well, that's what Gaynor's just told me." Luke paused as if allowing the news to sink in. "She entered the flat in secret a few weeks ago to surprise Gin on her birthday but found Nick and Flora on the sofa. Gaynor was sure they'd been kissing just as she entered the living room. There was the smell of sex in the air. And both Nick and Flora were pretty awkward about the situation. Anyway, boss, Gaynor broached it with Gin, and they argued about it, especially as Gin had just found out she was pregnant with Nick's child."

"Shit."

"Shit indeed."

"So we're looking for Flora."

"I guess so, boss."

"The line went silent.

"I'm worried about Jay. He's not been himself. And he looked really poorly earlier. What if Flora drugged him so she had an alibi?"

"We'd need proof."

"Well, Jay's at A&E as we speak, so they should be able to do blood tests and stuff. If I know anything more, I'll contact you."

"Thanks, Luke. Before you go, can you please get Ellie Addiman's make and reg from the DVLA?"

"George, I think you should come back in here," came Wood's voice from the living room.

With a quicker pace than usual, George entered the living room. "What's up?"

"Tell DI Beaumont exactly what you told me."

Audrey cleared her throat and held out her hand. Wood passed her mobile over. "This is the girl who stole Ellie's car."

George looked down at Wood's phone.

"Thank you, Audrey, and thank you, Annette. We'll be back soon."

The pair of detectives rushed from the house.

\* \* \*

The woman awoke on a chair. Confusion shot through her. How did she fall asleep? She looked around, and nothing made sense. Where was she?

Anguish rippled inside her stomach like the crashing of waves at the beginning of a storm. The more she looked around, the fiercer the waves, and soon bile rose up her throat.

Then, somehow approaching clarity, she recalled what had happened.

## CHAPTER THIRTY-SIX

She'd been drugged and abducted.

# Chapter Thirty-seven

George brayed on the door of Flora Ogram's flat. "Doesn't look like she's here." He looked around at the cars parked up. Luke had given them the reg, make and model of Ellie Addiman's car on the way over. The Green Fiat was nowhere to be seen.

He looked at Isabella and said, "I'll take the two flats to the left; you take the set to the right. We'll meet back here and tackle Flora's neighbour."

After ten minutes and plenty of knocking, detectives returned to Flora's flat and knocked on the neighbour's door.

"What the fuck do you two want?" a voice asked.

George stepped back. The pungent stench of weed made his eyes water. He held up his warrant card, and Wood did the same. George then identified themselves and asked for the man's name.

"It's medicinal, officer," the man named Joe said.

"I don't really care. All I care about is when you last saw Flora Ogram."

"Who?"

"Your neighbour. Young, blonde."

"Oh, I know her. She's fit as fuck, mate."

George folded his arms and raised a brow.

"Soz, mate." Joe pondered upon the question for a moment.

Then he turned and shouted, "Ere, love. Police got some questions for you." Then Joe shrugged and returned to the flat. Or he tried to. George gripped him by the wrist. "When was the last time you saw Flora Ogram?"

"This afternoon. Or late morning. I don't know. She looked like she'd been out on the piss last night." He tried to get away from George, but the DI held tight. "Ow, you're hurting me."

"You'd better not be lying to me."

"I'm not."

George let go of Joe's wrist, and he escaped into the flat. A moment later, a chubby dark-haired girl of about twenty said, "How can I help?"

Her perfume suffocated George. He couldn't keep his eye off the large mole on her face when he asked, "When did you last see Flora Ogram?"

"Tart from next door?"

"Your next-door neighbour, yes."

"Not long ago. I was washing my hands after being on the loo. She pulled up in a car. I wouldn't have noticed, but she left the engine running. She went into her flat and two minutes later came out with a bag."

"When?" George demanded.

"An hour ago. I dunno, do I?"

\* \* \*

Shit.

Why was she here?
And where even was here?
What day was it?
How long had she been here?

Turning her head around again, the woman focused. The walls looked like they had been covered with various pillows and cushions. She figured she was in some sort of padded room. Was it for soundproofing?

The room wasn't huge. Probably the size of her bedroom.

Did that mean she was in someone's house?

Her whole body hurt as she tried to twist her neck to look around some more.

It was definitely someone's house.

But whose? And where?

And why had she been taken?

On the floor was a stained, grey carpet. The walls were adorned with yellow wallpaper. The roof Artex was peeling. Apart from the chair she was sitting on, the place lacked furniture.

The chair was bolted to the ground, and her feet were chained to it. It meant she could stand and move her arms around, but she couldn't walk.

Then a noise caught her attention. It sounded like metal scraping on metal. Then she heard a thud. The door was opening. Was she saved? A surge of hope caused her heart to beat erratically. She held her breath. Or was it her abductor?

The door opened fully.

A figure entered the room. The woman couldn't figure out their gender. Whoever had taken her was a monster.

The monster was dressed head to toe in black: a black top, black bottoms, black boots, and a black balaclava.

A pair of large eyes stared at the woman, unspeaking.

It was a good thing the monster was concealing their identity. It meant there was a possibility of release. Right? There was a possibility she would survive. Right?

## CHAPTER THIRTY-SEVEN

The monster cocked its head to one side and then shook it. Did the monster know what she was thinking?

"Who are you?" she asked. "Why am I here?"

When the monster said nothing, she asked, "Where am I?" Again, the woman was met with silence. "Please! Tell me!"

The monster chucked the woman a bottle of water which she greedily guzzled, at one point swallowing far too much and almost choking herself.

The monster only watched until the woman was finished. Then the beast turned and opened the door.

That's when the woman took her chance and screamed, though only a croak came from her mouth. She stood up and tried to pull the chains from her feet. She stared at her abductor so hard she felt tears burn her eyelids. The monster held her gaze. Its eyes were cold and dark, and she felt like it was looking straight into her soul.

"Somebody will know I've been taken, so let me go!" She breathed deeply. "Let me go, and that'll be the end of it. I promise."

But the monster shook its head and closed the distance. It pulled out a syringe, and the woman felt a sharp scratch.

Darkness enveloped her.

\* \* \*

They rushed back to George's Mercedes, George on the phone with Luke, and Isabella on the phone with Malik.

"I need Gaynor's number, Luke," George said. Whilst the DS was finding it, he explained Flora had been to the flat and how DC Malik was currently trying to track the Fiat via ANPR.

Luke said, "I've got it. I'll text you it."

When George's phone beeped, he hung up on Luke without saying bye, and immediately clicked the number.

"Hello."

"Hi, is that Gaynor?"

"Speaking."

"This is Detective Inspector George Beaumont."

"Hi, Detective."

"Thanks for calling the station earlier; it was very helpful."

"My pleasure."

"We're trying to find Flora. She's not at the flat, and Uniform is outside your house now. Nobody's home. Could she be anywhere else?"

"Only mi mam's home," Gaynor explained. "Mum died of cancer last year, and the house is still up for sale. I had a set of keys, and so did Gin."

"What's the address?"

Ten minutes later, they pulled by the kerb outside the Ogram family home on Sissons Terrace.

Stepping through the open door and onto the cold stone floor, Wood listened to the door creak open and felt George's soft breath on her neck. In different circumstances, she would have welcomed his closeness, the safety of having him by her side. But they needed to find Flora, and fast.

There was blood on the floor that led them upstairs.

"This way. I see a faint light," she whispered once they were on the upstairs landing.

"What's down there?"

"Looks like a bedroom."

Wood edged along the wall towards the room at the end, where a thin slit of light seeped from beneath the door. She wondered what awaited her.

## CHAPTER THIRTY-SEVEN

With one hand on the handle, she took a deep breath and opened the door.

"Fucking hell," George exclaimed.

"Holy shit," Isabella said once she could form the words.

# Chapter Thirty-eight

She was terrified.

Seated in the rear middle seat of the Fiat, the woman watched as the monster flew through the empty streets at breakneck speed, with a succession of crunching gear changes and sudden braking–mounting the kerb at one point and demolishing several traffic cones as they went.

The woman wearing the balaclava had said nothing since roughly bundling her into the vehicle and driving off. Still, she was acutely conscious of her abductor darting glances at her as they drove.

The drugs made it so she couldn't resist or try to escape, so in her opinion, the cuffs were unnecessary. Pink tufts adorned the cuffs, and she tried not to smile. They were obviously from a sex set and could easily be opened, especially with someone of her skill. But the drugs made that impossible.

As they flew down the road, the woman was mystified as to why the masked woman had not killed her immediately. The woman had already told her about her victims, Ginny, Lesley, Larisa, Nick and Ellie.

The woman wearing the balaclava seemed to read her thoughts and laughed suddenly but without humour. "Wondering where we're going, Sister?" she mocked. "Well, you'll have to work that out for yourself, but I'll tell you one thing, it's somewhere very special. You're going to love it! I've got a special punishment reserved for you."

"Sister? I don't have any siblings," the woman said. Then she added, "Please don't do this. I've done nothing wrong."

The Fiat swerved again, clipping the kerb and causing the masked woman to brake heavily. The woman was grateful for the cuffs and seatbelt; otherwise, it would have put her through the windscreen.

"What do you mean you've done nothing?" the masked woman snarled. "Everything I've done is your fault!"

"How?" the woman asked. "Explain it to me."

The woman laughed. "You wanted what has always been mine. You fucking bitch."

The woman still had no clue. "You're frightening me." She paused "What's yours? What have I tried to take?"

"It matters not, Sister, because you're going to pay for all the years of misery you subjected me to."

But then the masked woman emitted an unexpected sob. "All I ever wanted was to meet you, but I was told you didn't want to meet me," she choked. "Do you know how that feels, Sister?"

"I didn't know you existed!"

Ignoring the woman's pleas, the masked woman continued, "I tried for years and years. I sent letters and birthday cards. You know we're twins, right?"

"I know nothing!"

"Lies!" She hammered the steering wheel violently with the palms of both hands, sending the Fiat careering across the road towards the double gates of a large house before managing to wrangle it back on course.

"Where did all the letters go then? And the cards?"

"I don't know! Please, just stop the car, and we can talk about this."

"It's too late," the masked woman shrieked. "You've had years! And I'm fed up with being ignored!"

"Please believe me!"

The driver twisted her neck and stared at the woman for a moment, the eyes behind her balaclava smouldering with hate. "Just enjoy the ride, Sister, because it's the last one you're ever going to have!"

* * *

George called it in. Blood was everywhere, as well as evidence that at least two people had been imprisoned there. He thought about Freya Bentley. Had she been abducted and left in this room? And was this where Larisa Raggett was also held?

A blonde wig was on the floor in the corner and various skirts, tops, and pairs of jeans scattered about the place.

All he had were questions with zero answers.

Reza's just texted me," said Wood. "We've got an ANPR hit on the Fiat. It's heading down the A654 out of Middleton."

"Why would it be heading that way?" George asked.

"Reza's just messaged me about something else," Isabella said. "He's sent an email with an attachment, too."

"What is it?"

After a moment of reading, she held out her phone for George to look. "The warrant DSU Smith procured for me came through," she said. "Or should I say, the Adoptions Section in Southport did. They've sent over the information we needed."

"Go on."

## CHAPTER THIRTY-EIGHT

"Freya Bentley was abandoned by her parents when she was barely a month old," Wood explained. "They left her at Springfield House."

"What's this have to do with anything?"

"Freya's mum is Ginny Ogram, Gin Creaser, and her father is a man named Gary Holt."

"Gin Creaser abandoned Freya Bentley?" That explained the medical records Dr Ross had unearthed.

"Yep. But that's not all. She's Flora Ogram's twin sister."

"What."

"Freya and Flora have the same date of birth."

"So Flora could have abducted Freya and imprisoned her in that room?" George asked.

"Maybe."

"Why, though?"

"Jealousy, maybe?" Wood shrugged. "Everything's coming back to Flora Ogram. It's her, I know it!"

"Holy shit."

"What?" asked Wood.

"I've just realised the children's home is on the A654," George said.

"Go."

"I can't just leave you!" George complained.

"It's better if I stay here and you go. Reza's called for backup, but we're a lot closer. Go."

He nodded as he stepped close and kissed Isabella on the forehead. "I love you."

"We love you more."

\* \* \*

"What have you got for me on Springfield House?" asked George.

Luke said, "Not a lot, boss. I've managed to find a bit about the history on the internet, which I printed off. But it doesn't help us much." George could hear the rustling of paper. "Apparently, the place was originally built in the Georgian era for the Brandling Family. Eventually, the Brandling's fortunes declined, and the estate was sold to the Middleton Estate & Colliery Company in 1862. They rented it out to the local authority for use as an asylum—or a madhouse, as places were called back then. Then during the Second World War, it was closed and turned into a school."

"How does this fit in with Freya Bentley?"

"Hang on, boss." Luke took a deep breath. "The school didn't last long after the war ended, and it became a private orphanage for—and I quote—'challenging juveniles'. They ran the orphanage until the eighties until it was closed due to a series of awful accidents." Luke paused. "I say accidents, boss, but it looks like a couple of the 'juveniles' committed suicide by jumping from the third floor. A staff member was stabbed by one of the kids. Apparently, there'd been rumours of sexual abuse floating about for years, and after the staff member was murdered, all of that came out during the police investigation."

"But if it was closed in the eighties, how was Freya Bentley there?"

"It was re-opened in the late nineties as a children's home, boss. A charity bought it and refurbished it. Then in 2010, after another staff member was killed, more allegations of sexual and physical abuse came out during yet another police investigation. They unearthed a lot during the investigation.

Quite a few kids had committed suicide by the look of it, and the staff had covered it up."

"That's when Freya was there, then."

"Correct."

"Shit."

"She could have been abused, boss."

"Still no excuse to murder anybody."

"But it gives her a bloody perfect motive, boss."

"Who owns the building now, Luke?"

"The charity, still. They've had tons of offers, but they think it's cursed. So they're leaving it to, and I quote, 'to rot'."

"Anything else?"

"I spoke with DSU Smith, who was involved in both investigations."

"What did he tell you?"

"Initially, he pointed out that before the Jimmy Saville business and all the child abuse inquiries that scandal has generated since complaints of sexual abuse by juveniles were unlikely to have been given any priority in terms of policing as they are today."

"That's awful."

"Tell me about it, boss." There was more ruffling of paper. "I'm just looking at the notes I made." Luke then cleared his throat. "DSU Smith said the kids were considered juveniles, too, especially in the eighties, so again, they weren't given much consideration the poor things."

"Smith suspects the alleged abuse was probably cuffed?" asked George.

"Correct, son. He told me he thought the SIO was bent."

"Christ. Did the super say anything else?"

"Yeah, and this is silver tuna if you appreciate the reference.

George was getting impatient. Luke should really have led with this information. "Hurry up, Luke."

"The super told me that before being adopted by the Bentleys, Freya Bentley was one of the children who had been physically, mentally, and sexually abused."

George was getting impatient now, but Luke said, "We finally have a link, boss."

"What link?"

"A link to Larisa Raggett and Lesley Ibbetson."

"Go on."

"It was Lesley Ibbetson's dad and Larisa Raggett's mum who abused poor Freya."

\* \* \*

The sign on one of the open gates read 'Springfield House', but a wooden notice had been attached to the other gate, warning, 'Keep Out. Trespassers Will Be Prosecuted'.

The Georgian property was falling down, rotting from the inside.

"Come on, no dawdling," the woman wearing the balaclava said, prodding her forwards.

The woman stared across the overgrown garden at the rotten three-storey building facing them as she stumbled along ahead of her abductor. She could feel her flesh start to prickle as her gaze took in the boarded windows and the crumbling façade.

"Why don't you just kill me and get this over with?" the woman asked, turning her head and looking at the monster behind her. "And take that balaclava off. Show me who you are!"

## CHAPTER THIRTY-EIGHT

"And ruin the surprise?" the woman asked. "Not a chance."

* * *

"DI Beaumont," he said into the speaker of his Merc.

"Hi, this is Ahmed Allen from Calder Park Forensics," a man explained. "We have the results from the handheld fast-track DNA testing device you ordered, sir."

His heart began to hammer in his chest. "I'm listening."

"We found nothing on the DNA Database—"

"OK, thanks for your time," George cut in.

"Sorry, sir, for interrupting you, but we found a match on a different database."

"Which database, and give me a name!"

# Chapter Thirty-nine

In the gathering dawn, the Georgian building towered over the pair of women.

Her old room was on the third floor, but she avoided looking at it. She also tried not to look at the balcony.

"Are those happy memories coming back, Sister?" the woman wearing the balaclava sneered, prodding the woman in the back.

"I have no sister!"

"Then who am I?" the woman asked. But without awaiting a reply, she then pointed at the battens that once secured the front door. "I've already opened the front door for you."

A short, humourless laugh came from the monster's mouth as she pushed the woman ahead into the foyer, training the torch she had produced on the floor so they could see their way.

The woman froze, and the masked woman had to push her further in.

The main staircase to the upper floor was uncarpeted, though the torch beam in the woman's hand caught the occasional glint of nails with bits of carpet still attached. There were ragged holes in places where the wooden beams had rotted, and some sections of the bannister rails were no longer there.

"Careful, Sister," the woman said, shining the torch past her as she prodded the woman forward with her other hand. "You dying now would spoil all the fun."

Upstairs, open doorways yawned at them, and the captive jumped when a bird flew out of one room, grazing the top of her head.

Still, the woman pushed her prisoner onwards as if knowing exactly where she was going.

As the masked woman pushed and prodded the woman nearer and nearer towards the location of the narrow stone ascending staircase, she thought about her abductor's identity.

But she couldn't think straight. From what she knew, she was an only child. Plus, the drugs were still in her system, making her feel dizzy and disoriented.

Jerking the door open to reveal a flight of narrow stone stairs ascending steeply into the murky darkness, the masked woman gestured for her hostage to enter.

She'd often had nightmares about the staircase, thinking that monsters climbed the steep steps on a night. The steep stone steps looked even more scary now, the shadows distorted by the torch.

The woman wearing the balaclava pushed her prisoner towards the first step, but she shuddered, shrinking back instinctively. But the masked woman pressed against her, panting. "Up you go, Sister!" The torch homed in on the tight, circular staircase.

And then the terrified woman was thrust forward, onto her knees.

The climb took all her strength, but with the prodding and pushing from the masked woman, they eventually met the yawning door at the top of the staircase.

Like the rest of the house, the tiny room beyond was devoid of furnishings of any sort.

There were no wooden boards across the single window, and it was immediately apparent that there was no glass there either. It had been knocked out entirely, and, in the strengthening grey light, jagged shards were clearly visible on the balcony floor.

The masked woman pushed her victim towards the glass and then further out towards the balcony railing.

Rain was coming down from the heavens now.

"What an incredible view," the woman sneered. "Though I know something you probably don't realise. You don't like heights." The woman pushed her victim into the railings and the woman grabbed hold of them.

The wind whistled and buffeted the woman, and she screamed.

"Oh, what an incredible noise!"

Producing a coin from her pocket, the monster leaned past the woman. The beast then grabbed the woman's wrist, forced her palm open, and placed a coin in there. "Toss the coin off!" the demon demanded.

The terrified woman did as she was told.

"Listen!" she ordered.

For a few seconds, there was nothing and then a soft but definite metal jangle from far below.

"It's a long way down, isn't it?" the masked woman said, smirking as she felt her captive shaking fitfully. "Why don't you have a closer look before we go back inside and out of the shit weather."

But the woman shook her head.

And suddenly, the masked woman thrust her sister forward so forcibly that, but for the hand gripping her wrist, the shaking woman would have pitched over the railing and down onto the ground below.

"Whoops!" the monster cackled.

* * *

"The Contamination Elimination Database, sir," Ahmed said.

Some police forces were permitted to take DNA samples from serving police officers and special constables, who were likely to come into contact with, and therefore have the potential to contaminate the physical evidential chain. As such, these officers were asked to provide a DNA sample to generate a DNA profile for inclusion on the Contamination Elimination Database.

"Who does it belong to?" George asked.

"Freya Bentley," said Ahmed.

# Chapter Forty

"What do you think I've got planned for you?" Freya asked, her tone laced with venom.

Flora's dull eyes remained fixed on the floor. She was no longer trembling, and it appeared all her tears had stopped. It seemed as though she had lost interest during the agonising last stages of shock.

Her silence was met with a fake frown.

"Come on, Sister; I've gone to a great deal of trouble. I did everything in my power to set this up. You could at least show some interest."

There was still no response, and Freya sighed. "You're such an ungrateful cow," she went on, "after everything I did for you."

Flora slowly raised her head, a glimmer of life returning to her eyes, and her gaze now fixed squarely on the face of her tormentor. "I'm not afraid to die," came the low, exhausted reply. "I know you're going to kill me, so get on with it."

"Don't fucking lie to me!" Freya screamed. "I can see you shaking. Though maybe you're excited?" She shrugged. "You should be proud of my efforts on your behalf. I struggled to think of a spectacular send-off at first." She tugged a clear-coloured bottle from the pocket of her coat. "I brought the voddy to have a last drink together before you die. I heard it was your favourite."

When there was no response, Freya returned the bottle to her pocket with a manufactured sigh. "Ah well, fuck you. I'll drink it alone. I did get you a present."

She slipped her hand inside her jacket pocket and produced a sealed manilla envelope, which she waved in front of her captive's nose.

"Your confession, Sister—for the police. It will be left for them to read after you have killed yourself. I already have another identity set up for me. I'm thinking of Spain or France. Maybe Italy. I haven't decided yet. Brilliant, isn't it?"

"You'll be caught," Flora whispered. "People like you always are."

There was a high-pitched, distorted giggle as Freya placed the envelope on the floor.

"Maybe I will, maybe I won't, but whichever way it goes, there will be a smile on my face for what I will have done to you."

Flora started to shake a little but retained her composure, meeting her gaze without flinching, and Freya grinned again.

"You look scared now, Sister," Freya said. The psychopath pulled an eight-inch hunting knife from the front seat and grinned maniacally. "This is what I used to kill Mum, and our sibling, I guess. And Nick! What a cheating bastard!"

Flora closed her eyes tightly for a second, her hands clenching and unclenching by her sides. "Just get it over with!"

"I don't want to kill you here, Sister," Freya said. "Take off your shoes."

Flora stayed exactly where she was, a look of defiance on her face.

Freya sighed. "I knew you were going to spoil it, Sister, which was why I brought this big fuck-off knife! You see, knives this big are apparently very persuasive."

"Not when you know you're going to die regardless, Sister," Flora spat.

She still refused to remove her shoes, and Freya sighed again. "You can die in pain, or die quickly, Sister," Freya said. "I was trying to be a good sister, but it's your choice." She put the knife to Flora's throat. "Decide."

Flora shook her head in another act of defiance, and Freya hit her sister with the knife's hilt. It was a mighty blow, and Flora staggered back against a rotting bed frame and fell to the floor.

Then, with hardly any effort, the powerful killer dragged Flora by the collar and down towards a particularly large shard of glass. "I know how detectives think, Sister. You're their prime suspect, and I was abducted from my home. You brought me here to laud your superiority over me. Then I suppose we'd fight, and you'd go crashing through the window! I even watched a video on the internet to see how I could frame the glass."

Flora did nothing as Freya removed her sister's shoes. The woman went to the balcony and threw them away. This meant Freya had her back to Flora, who reached down and picked up one of the larger shards.

"But instead, I'm going to kill you differently." Freya turned back and pointed. "You're going to stand there, and I'm going to push you through onto and over the balcony, OK?" She shrugged. "You may survive the fall, but I doubt it. That's my sisterly gift to you."

Flora doubted it.

So did Freya. She'd known many people who had jumped from that spot, but nobody survived.

"Fine, Sister. But before you kill me, tell me why. Confess!"

Freya nodded. "This was my bedroom – or cell, as I liked to call it – where I was confined most days and forced to sit and memorise texts from the Holy Bible. Abandoned little girls had to atone because their mothers had deserted them."

"I'm so sorry about that," Flora said.

"Sorry because you got the life I should have got?"

"Yes."

"Why did you ignore me all those years?"

"Mum must have kept your letters and cards from me, Freya. I had no idea."

"Lies!"

"It's the truth." Flora began to cry now. "Let me go. I'm innocent."

"No you're not. And neither were Nick, Lesley, Larisa and Ellie!"

"What did they do to you?"

"Lesley and Larisa's parents abused me when I was here! I bet you didn't know that!"

"I didn't and I'm so sorry."

"I had to pay for the sins of my mother, so I figured Larisa and Lesley had to pay for theirs."

"Why Ellie?"

"Because she was fucking Nick!"

"What?"

"And so were you!"

Flora said nothing.

"Did you think you were special?" Freya laughed. "Only Ellie was special. He didn't even love Ginny. In fact, he fucking hated her!"

"You're lying. Why would he stay with her?"

"For you and your tight pussy, I imagine!"

"No!"

"Yes!"

"Did you know Mum was pregnant?"

"I did."

With the shard of glass hidden behind her back, Flora took a deep breath and stood up. "Thanks for telling me that. Shall I face you as you push me to my death?" she asked her twin sister.

"Yes, I want to fucking look you in the eyes as I kill you!"

Freya removed her balaclava and Flora thought it really was like looking in a mirror. Whilst Freya had dyed her dark curls, Flora's were their natural colour.

"You're so beautiful," Flora said.

"Fuck you," Freya said, closing the distance. "Look at me so I can watch you die and finally get my revenge!"

"I'd like the same." Flora pulled her arm from behind her back and stepped forward, slicing the shard of glass vertically against Freya's gorgeous face, slicing through her left eye, and parting the cheek as neatly as a surgeon's scalpel.

With blood streaming between the fingers of the hand that she had instinctively cupped over her eye, Freya's screams became a mixture of demonic fury and pure agony.

Flora, still clutching the bloodstained piece of glass, assessed the situation. There was only one way in and out of the room, and Freya had staggered back, blocking it, that hunting knife poised and waiting in her hand.

Flora could go no further. And at that moment, she knew that she was dead.

## CHAPTER FORTY

\* \* \*

Within seconds of hearing the shouts, George rushed through the front door and up the stairs. He knew there had to be a second staircase or a ladder in some place on the floor above, as he needed to figure out how to get to the balcony.

Almost immediately after reaching the landing, he noticed the open door with stone stairs leading to the third storey. He was about out of energy at that point. Senses in overload. Fire in his lungs. His hammering heart was contending with a high-pitched voice screaming obscenities from somewhere above his head. He managed to drag himself up the stairs and climb out the window onto the balcony using the last of his power, but he suddenly stopped.

Freya must have heard George climbing through the window since she was standing there waiting for him with her left eye damaged and blood spurting from a horrible face gash. While George was denied the chance to fully assess the situation, he was only dimly aware that Flora was pressed against the wall at the far end of the balcony to his right. Then he was fixated on the murderer, who was advancing on him while holding a hunting knife and yelling obscenities.

In that split second, George didn't even have time to go for the CS gas spray in his pocket, even though all police training books would have given a textbook solution for this kind of incident. So instead, he was forced to direct all of his attention to the knife and the madwoman's homicidal intent as she drew near.

Because of his boxing experience, George avoided the initial rush by lurching to the side and as the knife sliced through his trench coat with no injury. Freya recovered quickly from her temporary loss of balance, despite the horrific facial injury. Unfortunately, before George could seize the opportunity to use the CS spray, the killer had turned to face the DI again. This time, George did not fare as well. He was able to evade the blade's lunge, but in doing so, he lost track of how close he had gotten to the balcony's edge.

The next instant, his dress shoes had slipped on the greasy surface, and, after a second's desperate effort to regain his balance, he pitched backwards, over the balcony railing and into the air, plunging towards the ground far below.

\* \* \*

From a few yards away, Flora could see that the fight had ended and that her would-be saviour would soon fall to his death on the ground below. However, fate was not yet through with George Beaumont.

His flailing arms struck and instinctively managed to grip the stone edge even as he fell over the railing. He eventually found himself hanging from it, both hands' fingers tightly clasped, his feet treading air.

George had miraculously avoided what should have been certain death, but as he dangled precariously over the edge, it appeared as though his reprieve from death would only be temporary. Because, out of nowhere, Freya's face appeared over the top of the railing, her ugly wound still oozing blood.

"Well, well, well, Detective Inspector Beaumont, you're a bit fucked now, aren't you?" the psychopath cackled.

George felt the blood from the killer's wound dripping onto him. The next moment the disfigured face was very close as Freya leaned over the wall, her knife gently stroking the backs

## CHAPTER FORTY

of George's fingers.

George tried to get his elbow up from the edge to give himself some traction, but Freya lightly kicked his forearm, and the DI slipped back, now in a worse position than ever. He was sure his fingers would give way, and he'd fall to his death.

In a panic, his feet scrabbled against the upstairs window frame, futilely searching for a hold of some sort, but there was nothing.

And then the knife was sliced across the back of his left hand, the razor-sharp blade drawing a thin line of red that ran down his arm.

"Sharp, eh?" she crowed, enjoying the moment despite her own pain. "I bought it for my mum and sister. I used it on Nick too, but I suppose I could use it on you."

The knife sliced upwards and was thrust into George's knuckle, pressing down very slowly and scraping the bone. At the same moment, his fingers started to shake from the exertion.

Freya released another of her distorted laughs. "You should have left this well alone, Detective." She licked her lips and raised the knife for George to see. "Let's see how well you hold on with seven fingers, shall we?"

George gritted his teeth, waiting for the agonising pain as his fingers were severed, but the pain never happened.

Freya was no longer in George's face and no longer raising the knife. Instead, there was a loud commotion on the roof above. As George looked up, Freya's face again appeared over the edge. This time, however, the look on her face was different. For one surreal second, it felt as if Freya was lunging at George.

But then, the bloodied face of Freya, showing a mix of

terror and anguish, hurtled past George, her arms flailing and clawing at the air, a shrill scream emanating from her gaping mouth.

The DI quickly turned his neck, wincing at the pain and trying his best to hold on. But he was fighting against the rain, and his strength was diminishing. Still, he watched as the psychopath crashed to the ground and heard the splintering thud.

When he caught sight of the blue lights speeding up the driveway, he was still fixated on the gruesome scene with a sort of horrifying, mesmerising fascination. He heard the recognisable voice shouting his name from above him simultaneously.

"Come on, George, give me your hand."

A cold look that George had never seen before appeared on Isabella's face as she leaned over the edge of the balcony towards him with one arm extended. George couldn't move from the edge of the balcony, and for a few seconds, he stared up at Isabella in shock.

"You need to give me your hand now, George," she said in a much sharper tone. "Otherwise, you'll fall! Our baby needs you!"

As she spoke, George's fingers started to slip one by one until they finally parted company with the edge.

"George!" Isabella yelled. But he was already falling.

## Chapter Forty-one

Following her arrest for manslaughter, Flora Ogram was cleared of all charges. DS Mason was in charge of the investigation.

Flora's statement, as well as fingerprint analysis carried out on the envelope, exonerated her from all of Freya's crimes. In addition, the letter inside the envelope explained why and how Freya killed her victims.

CCTV evidence proved Freya Bentley abducted Flora Ogram, stole her clothes and wore a wig to gain access to Ellie Addiman's home.

Ellie Addiman survived her ordeal and is currently in hospital. Unfortunately, she may never walk again. She was stabbed a total of eighteen times across her body, with one of the wounds severing her spinal cord.

CCTV footage taken from the bars and pubs in Morley proved Freya Bentley had spiked DC Jason Scott's drinks with scopolamine. Jay remains in the hospital but will be discharged soon.

Jake Cappleman recovered from his injuries quickly. A combination of CCTV and doorbell footage proved it was Freya Bentley who assaulted him.

# Epilogue

George Beaumont awoke.

After falling from the balcony back at the old children's home, everybody thought George was dead. But somehow, he'd managed to cling to a window ledge on the second floor before falling and hitting his head on the ground.

The DI had been lucky. Very lucky. An air ambulance was dispatched immediately and landed in the grounds of the abandoned home.

Medics were already on the scene, fighting to save George. He was bleeding from his nose and right ear. The medic had advised George had a GCS score of 8.

George had initially started fighting the medics and had exhibited unusually aggressive behaviour. Isabella had watched, unable to do anything. She hadn't a clue what a GCS score was until later.

The Glasgow Coma Scale provided a practical method for assessing impairment of consciousness level in response to defined stimuli.

They'd diagnosed George with a bleed on the brain, and pressure had been building inside his skull. They'd told Wood back at LGI's Major Trauma Centre that this was the reason for George's aggressiveness.

They gave him a general anaesthetic at the scene. Then, the doctor decided to put George into an induced coma through a procedure called an RSI. Later they told Isabella the procedure was usually done in the hospital, but because of George's injuries, he had more chance of survival if they did it at the scene.

What they didn't tell her was they needed to do it by the book. It had to go flawlessly.

DI Beaumont looked around the room. His head was banging, and his body hurt, yet he felt numb, too.

Why was he in the hospital? And why were people looking at him?

"Can you hear me?" a woman asked.

He looked up to find a nurse hovering above him suddenly.

"You had a nasty fall, love. You were put in an induced coma for four days but didn't wake up," she explained. "After eight days, we pulled you out. Can you talk?"

George tried, but his throat was too dry. The nurse gave him a sip of water.

Immediately after landing, they instantly started to operate on him. George's mum had arrived, and they explained he could have died if not for how quickly the surgeon got on with his job.

The surgeon had to cut his skull open, and at first, they weren't sure the operation had succeeded.

On the fourth day, when George should have awoken, he was moving his arms. But that was it.

His family and friends stood by him, hour by hour, day by day.

Some of them even prayed.

"Do you know your name?"

George looked around the room at the five people who stood there. He blinked rapidly, not believing what he was seeing.

Finally, after a moment, he managed to say, "George."

"That's brilliant, love," the nurse said. "You had a bleed on the brain, as well as two skull fractures, a punctured lung, a broken collar bone, broken ribs and a fractured wrist."

He didn't take his eyes off the man he recognised. Eventually, he managed to speak. "You got old, Luke."

"Old?" DS Mason asked. "What do you mean? I was bloody worried about you, George, but I haven't aged that much in a week, have I?"

George blinked rapidly again. Two young lads, one wearing a hospital gown, looked towards him expectantly. A black woman with short hair wiped a tear from her eye.

And then there was a beautiful woman with cascading brunette curls. She was holding her stomach, with tears falling freely down her face.

Eventually, he managed to say, "There you are, Isabella."

# Afterword

Dear reader,

This is the eighth book in the George Beaumont series, and I am hugely indebted to so many people for supporting me on this writing journey.

I'm so grateful to you for sharing your precious time with George, Isabella and the team. I thank you for your support and reviews.

It would be fantastic if you could post a review on Amazon or Goodreads. It would mean so much to me. And thank you for the reviews received so far. You can also connect with me on my Facebook author page or my website.

I decided to head back to Middleton for practically the entirety of this novel because I miss the place. I've recently moved to Rothwell, and writing about Miggy has given me a chance to head back home so I can research.

As I mentioned at the start of the book, Springfield House is entirely fictional, but the Brandling family, who I pretended once owned the Georgian house, are not.

The history of Middleton, and Leeds in general, is fascinating. I'd recommend Leodis.net, which is a photographic archive of Leeds.

This novel really would never have happened without the people or groups below.

I wish to thank Mandy Wilkinson for her input on this novel.

I appreciate you.

The writing community is very supportive of me and my work. Thank you to the UK Crime Book Club Facebook group for that.

And a big thank you to the real New Forest Village Book Club for inviting me to speak last year, for being so supportive, and for allowing me to use their name.

And finally, to my wife, Lisa. I've recently been diagnosed with a severe illness; without her, this book wouldn't have been finished.

Lee

# Also by Lee Brook

The Detective George Beaumont West Yorkshire Crime Thriller series in order:

*The Miss Murderer*

*The Bone Saw Ripper*

*The Blonde Delilah*

*The Cross Flatts Snatcher*

*The Middleton Woods Stalker*

*The Naughty List*

*The Footballer and the Wife*

*The New Forest Village Book Club*

*Pre-order The Killer in the Family*

More titles coming soon.